WEIGHT OF ASHES

ROOK WINTERS

For my kids, who are awesome

Chapter 1: Court

COURT ADJUSTED THE position of his fingers on his mag gun. Something was in the trees ahead.

Probably a deer. Too quiet for a moose, he thought. Moose would've been a nice treat.

They'd eaten a lot of deer and feral dog lately. They'd be heroes if they brought back a moose.

Beside him, he heard a hint of a wheeze in Walker's breathing. His hay fever was bad this year. Court found it ironic that the kid was allergic to the outdoors given that his people had lived off these lands hundreds of years ago, before the expulsions, before grav tech, before electricity, before anyone had even built cities here.

Court raised the gun and looked over the sight lines at the spot where experience told him the deer would come into view. He saw its head for a fraction of a second. A doe with her ears forward but not facing Court. Something else had her attention. Before he had time to react, the animal bolted.

"What spooked it?" Walker asked.

They heard the answer a moment later. An inorganic sound, something out of place so far from civilization. It was coming from the old road.

"Let's check. But stay out of sight."

They moved faster than they would while stalking prey. Their noise didn't matter compared to the mechanical whining and the sound of fallen branches snapping as something sped along what was once a highway for gas-powered vehicles.

"There." Walker pointed to a two-wheeled machine bouncing over the remains of asphalt mangled by decades of frost heaves.

"That's a motorcycle," Court said. The driver was old like Marsh and the other council members but this man's white beard and hair were neatly trimmed. A smaller passenger sat behind the driver, dressed in black, including a helmet.

"Should we flag them down? They're lost for sure."

"Don't be foolish. We don't want anything to do with city people."

Then Court heard a hum that wasn't from the motorcycle. He grabbed Walker by the shirt and pulled him deeper into the thicket for better cover. It was a sound Court had heard twice before. The first time was with his father on their way home from trading venison for seeds. The second time was a week later when explosives fell on their village. His parents...

Court squeezed his eyes tight. This wasn't the time.

"What's that other sound?"

Court scowled at the younger teen. "It's a gravity control flyer. Shut up and don't move."

The ground under the tangle of bushes was damp. Moisture soaked through the elbows of Court's shirt. It wasn't great cover, and he hoped that whoever was in the grav flyer only cared about the people on the old motorcycle.

The bike had to be at least fifty years old. It couldn't outrun a grav flyer, especially not driving over a neglected highway that was more footpath than road.

Walker flinched at the sound of a thunderous crack. They couldn't see clearly through the trees but they saw enough. A section of road was sucked into a black dot then spit back out as dust in all directions, leaving a hole the size of a bear in the ground. The leaves around Court and Walker danced as the air reacted to the disruption.

There was no way the old man could avoid the hole but he tried, leaning to his left and jerking the handles. They hit the edge at an angle, launching the passenger from the back. The motorcycle flipped and the man screamed as it crushed his leg.

Walker started to get up and Court clamped his hand on the boy's arm. "Don't move."

The flyer settled a few inches from the ground, hovering over the old asphalt and weeds. It was quiet for something that literally floated in the air. This one looked big enough to hold a half-dozen men but was no louder than a croaking toad. Court could hear the ground crunch under the weight of a Qyntarak as it stepped off.

The sketches and pixelated photos of Qyntarak that Court had seen didn't prepare him for how huge and inhuman they were in real life. This one was twice the size of the man it was bearing down upon. Its four spindly legs supported a long body that curved up and then hung down at the end, like a branch bearing too much fruit. It wore body armor and cradled what Court guessed was a weapon in its two shortest arms, the ones that looked most like human arms with finger-like parts. Its other arm equivalents, two long ones with pointed ends and two shorter ones with blunt pincers, were fanned out like tree branches made of snakes.

He'd once heard Qyntarak compared to giant centipedes crossed with spiders crossed with horses, but that comparison was inadequate because it didn't capture how alien they looked. Court knew that underneath that body armor, there was nothing resembling a face.

"Dr. Donovan," the monster said, its voice synthetic and unnatural through the speakers of its body armor, "you left the compound without authorization. Guilt of desertion is upon you."

The man, Donovan, wiped blood from his mouth and said something in a language Court didn't recognize.

"The governor has a message for you."

A long moment passed in silence then a different but equally synthetic voice said, "Donovan, friend of many years, the disappointment you have created in me is great. Your actions are foolish gestures. This failure brings shame to me. It was selfish of you."

Donovan uttered something else in the unknown language. Then in English he said, "You are the fool. The human spirit cannot be contained. Oligarchies never last. Empires always fall."

"Your time has expired. Others will resume your work and you will be forgotten. You have accomplished nothing but to bring cold to my mandibles. Goodbye."

The alien moved forward. "Traitor."

Another crack, this time quieter.

The Qyntarak returned to its flyer and it shot upward with a deep hum.

Walker began to move again but Court kept his grip on him and shook his head no. They waited until the hum was gone and the chirping of birds resumed. Cautiously, they moved to the road. The old man was lying on his back with a hole in his chest almost as large as his head. What was left of his torso was covered in gray powder. Blood oozed and mixed with it, creating a sludge in the cavity.

Walker steadied himself against a tree and vomited.

"You alright?"

"I'm fine."

"Where's the other one?"

After a brief search, they found the body, stiff and unmoving, among the trees at the edge of the road.

"It's a girl," Walker said. "Or a woman, I guess."

She wore a dull black bodysuit with no visible seams or fasteners. Her helmet was solid with no visor or eyeholes. Court pressed his fingers against her neck and then her wrist.

"The suit's cold. I can't feel a pulse through it, and I don't see how to remove it."

"We can cut it open with my hunting knife."

"No, not out here. We need to get them closer to the village and find Marsh. He'll know what to do."

Court was weeks away from his twentieth birthday, almost a year since he became a full adult in the village, and even though the fourteen-year-old Walker thought the older teen knew everything, Court was well aware of how much he didn't know. Like what to do with two dead bodies.

"We'll push them on the motorcycle," he said.

They followed the road for nearly a kilometer to where a dry creek bed reached the road. It was slow moving with the bodies draped over the bike. Blood trickled from the dead man and Court worried that it might attract coywolves or a bear. He didn't say anything to Walker. If the kid was worried, he wasn't showing it.

With considerable effort, they pushed the bike far enough up the creek to be out of sight of the road. The road wasn't frequently traveled but that didn't mean it was wise for Court to linger there with the bodies while Walker fetched Marsh.

It would take the better part of an hour for Walker to return. Court sat on the ground and rested against a maple tree with his mag gun in his lap. It was a beautiful day. Late summer or early fall, depending on one's point of view. A day too beautiful for death and dying.

Eventually, Court heard the crunch-crunch-tap of Marsh with his walking stick and stood to meet the village council leader.

"Where are they?" Marsh said, forgoing the normal pleasantries of conversation that he'd drilled into Court for years.

"There."

Marsh stopped several feet away and brought his free hand to his chest. "Clint." He knelt and put his hand on the man's face. "I don't understand."

"You know him?"

"Knew him, yes. A long time ago. Clint Donovan. He was a researcher. Became a collaborator to avoid exile."

Walker asked, "What about the woman?"

"Impossible to say with that helmet."

"We couldn't find any obvious way to take it off," Court said. "I didn't dare take a knife to the suit."

Marsh felt around the woman's wrist and elbow. "Wise choice. It might be booby trapped." He studied the suit and helmet for another minute. "Try pressing Clint's hand against the front of the helmet."

Walker looked like he might be sick again as they rolled the body and lined up the dead man's hand over the helmet and pressed it down. The helmet clicked and air hissed as a seam appeared. The woman's hand twitched and Walker yelped. Her arm knocked him off balance as her hands flew to the helmet. She pushed it open, two curved panels sliding to the sides as if on invisible tracks.

Chapter 2: Court

THE WOMAN IN black rolled and sprung to her feet. Marsh and Court stepped back while Walker slipped in the pine needles and dirt, struggling to create some distance. Her eyes didn't stop moving as she took in her surroundings. When she saw Clint Donovan on the ground with a hole in his chest, she dropped to her knees and cradled his head in her hands. "No, no, no..." Her words trailed off into sobs.

"You're safe now," Court said.

Marsh put a hand on his shoulder. "Let her be for now. And don't promise what you don't know to be true. She may not be safe at all."

When the intensity of her crying softened, Marsh knelt beside the woman. "I knew him a long time ago. He was a friend. I'd like to take him to our village before animals come around, if that's alright with you. It's not far."

The woman didn't speak but nodded as she set the dead

man's head back on the dirt. Her face was wet from tears, and she wiped mucus from her nose. Marsh pulled a square of fabric from a pocket and offered it to her.

"What's your name?" he asked, but she didn't acknowledge the question.

While she cleaned her face, Court and Walker placed Donovan's body back on the motorcycle and resumed the arduous task of pushing it up the creek bed.

They emerged from the forest into the clearing that surrounded their village, an area where nothing was allowed to grow and the children were forbidden to play. A no man's land between humanity and the wilderness.

"Walker, get Vaidehi and help her move Clint to the hospital. I need to gather the council. Court, why don't you take our visitor to sit with Pica by the fire?" Marsh gestured with his head to a ring of benches hewn from tree trunks where an old woman was tending a pot over a campfire. Marsh leaned in and whispered, "Keep a close eye on her. We don't know what we're dealing with."

Walker returned with the doctor and they moved Donovan's body to a simple stretcher of moose hide stitched around two poles. The woman in black made a noise that wasn't quite a word when they took away the body.

"It's alright," Court said. "They're taking him to the hospital. We can wait over here."

He led her to the campfire circle where the old woman bowed her head to greet them but said nothing, as if motorcycles and women dressed in black bodysuits materialized from the woods every day.

The woman used her index finger to draw an invisible pattern on the left forearm of her suit, and the material went slack so that it hung off her like a child wearing a parent's clothes. With a slight movement, the suit fell to the ground. Underneath, she wore a sleeveless shirt and pants that looked cleaner than Court's clothes ever had. Her skin was pale. When she removed the helmet, her hair was equally pale, a yellow so light that it was nearly white.

"Those are lovely braids. I haven't seen hair that blonde in a very long time." Pica moved as if to touch the woman's hair and the pale woman jumped back. Pica looked confused and a little insulted.

"She's had a rough day. Do you have any needle tea? That might relax her."

Pica nodded and rummaged through the satchel hanging over her shoulder.

The pale woman laid the suit on the bench farthest from the fire and swiped her finger along the sleeve. It beeped and steam began to rise from it. Court felt the heat coming from it.

"What's it doing?"

When it had become obvious that the woman wasn't going to answer him, he turned to watch Pica preparing the tea.

When it was ready, the woman accepted her cup and sat. As she sipped, her tears fell in fat drops. Pica resumed her cooking, oblivious to the grief of the younger woman.

When Marsh returned from the village council's cabin, he beckoned Court away from the fire.

"The girl is in shock. Whoever she is, she obviously cared about Clint. We may need to give her some time. Grief doesn't like to be rushed, but I suppose you understand that better than most."

Court pursed his lips and rolled a small stone under the

toe of his boot. He gave a small nod without looking up.

"Now then, judging by her appearance, where do you suppose she comes from?"

"A city?"

"Perhaps. But she has no signs of markings, no tattoos, no brands. And her hair is long. Uncommon in the cities."

"If she isn't from the city, then where? She's too clean to be from a squatter town."

"Clint was a researcher. She could be from one of the state-sponsored facilities. There's a rumor of one at the old tidal power station. That's not so far from here. Regardless, the council will have no shortage of questions for her when she's ready to talk. You can listen in if you want to. You found her and likely saved her life. I think you've earned the right to hear her story directly from her."

"Thank you. I'm curious about her suit. It's strange. It was stone cold before. Now it's giving off heat."

Marsh went to the bench holding the suit and held out his hand. "Incredible."

"Why is it doing that?"

"If I had to guess, I'd say it's a heat capture suit. We were working on the concept years ago when I left, although our prototypes were a lot bulkier. The suit traps the body heat of the wearer so you can control how much thermal energy is given off. The Qyntarak don't see light the way we do. They see temperature. They have a kind of thermal equivalent to our nonverbal body language."

"What's that mean? Thermal equivalent?"

"Parts of their bodies change temperature when they communicate. It helps them express emphasis and emotion. To them, humans always seem to be shouting because our bodies are naturally warmer. The suits were supposed to give us some control over that."

"I knew you worked on advanced technology, but I never imagined it was this kind of thing." He brushed his fingers over the suit.

Court still had his hand out when he heard a twig snap behind him. He turned to see the woman charging him. He put a hand up to defend himself but she was too fast. She grabbed his wrist and used her momentum to pull him off balance. She swept his leg out from under him and he crashed to the ground. The thin layer of evergreen needles did nothing to soften the blow and it knocked the air out of him. While he gasped to refill his lungs, she planted herself between the men and the suit.

Marsh looked amused but his tone was stern. "Young lady, I am a tolerant man but I will only ask you once to refrain from attacking my people."

"Don't touch the suit." Her voice was intense. Court had expected it to be soft after the way she had sobbed.

"You could've just asked," Court said as he scrambled back to his feet.

"It's not a request. Don't touch the suit."

"She's right, Court. It's not our place to handle her property without permission. Why don't we sit and talk instead?"

Court clenched his teeth. Marsh was head of the council. He didn't need to be deferential to this girl or woman or whatever she was. Without the telltale signs of a life lived outside, Court couldn't decide how old she was.

Old enough to take me down, he thought. *Once.*

Marsh steadied himself with both hands on his walking

stick as he sat on the nearest bench. Court didn't know exactly how old Marsh was either, but he was at least seventy and his advancing age was becoming more apparent. Eventually, the village would lose him and it would be devastating. Court forced the thought from his mind.

The woman looked at her suit then gave a wary look to Court before sitting down between it and him.

"Where did you take Dr. Donovan?"

Marsh pointed to a building with the remains of a red cross on weathered white walls. It was the only building not made from interlocking logs. "That's our modest hospital. Our doctor is cleaning up his body so we can give him a respectable burial."

"Burial? You bury people? In the ground?"

"I'm sorry. That was insensitive of me. You're no doubt used to the practices of state facilities. Our customs out here will be a bit foreign to you."

"How do they bury people in state facilities?" Court asked.

Marsh waved his hand dismissively. "Let's leave that for later. We haven't done proper introductions yet. You know Court and Pica already. My name is Marsh. And you are?"

"Dr. Donovan called me Elle."

"Elle. French for she. That's a lovely name."

"It's not my name. It's what he called me."

"That's what a name is," Court scoffed. "It's what people call you."

Is she dumb or did she just knock her head too hard falling off that motorcycle?

Elle didn't respond. She didn't even look at him.

"Is it alright if we call you Elle as well?"

"That's fine."

"I'm not sure if you took this in earlier but I knew Clint—Dr. Donovan—a long, long time ago. We used to work together."

Court chewed on his lip, trying to be patient. This Elle woman wasn't quick to volunteer anything and Marsh wasn't getting to the critical information. It was driving him crazy.

He blurted out, "What were you doing on that old motorcycle way out here?"

Marsh frowned at him. Elle ignored him again, a pattern he was finding frustrating.

"Clint was a friend," Marsh continued. "I didn't honestly expect to see him again. I would like to know what he was doing way out here."

"He said we needed to find the rabbit and the tour guide."

Marsh's eyes widened. He drew in a breath to speak but a voice interrupted him. From the steps of the hospital, Vaidehi yelled, "Marsh, you'd better come look at this."

Chapter 3: Marsh

"FOUND IT SCANNING the body before we wrapped him up. Almost missed it. He had metal pins in his ankle and after I removed them, there was still a faint reading. I assumed it was a fragment that we overlooked but it was in the wrong place. Found this embedded in the bone."

Vaidehi tapped her finger on the display screen where a red circle highlighted an anomaly.

"What is it?" Marsh asked.

"Hoping you can tell me. It's like nothing I've seen in a body before. Not natural and not serving any obvious medical purpose."

"What did the expert system say?"

"Unidentifiable. Very low probability matches on a couple things. But we haven't had a database update in over a year. If this is new tech, the expert system won't know anything about it."

"What were the low probability matches?"

Vaidehi swiped her finger across the display screen. "Fragment of electronics from a childhood accident that the bone grew around or a tracking chip. Neither seems likely in this case. There's no signal or radiation coming off him so not a tracking chip unless it's broken. Looks to me like he had a notch of bone removed and surgically implanted whatever that is. It was undetectable with the pins in the ankle right next to it, like he meant to keep it hidden."

"How long do you suppose it's been in there?"

"Hard to be sure. There's a hint of what could be a rash from tissue growth accelerant where you'd go in to implant something in this spot but there's no way to be sure."

"Let's remove it and take a closer look."

"That's the thing. Looks to be fused to the bone. Can't guarantee that I can get it out without damaging it. Don't have the equipment for that."

"Let me try talking with Elle. If this is important, she might know something."

Outside, a couple dozen villagers had gathered to stare at Elle and Court. They stepped back a few paces at the sight of Marsh but didn't disperse. Marsh kept his voice low as he described the doctor's discovery.

"He was limping the other day, and he said if anything happened to him, the rabbit needed to look at his ankle. He didn't say why."

"That's got to be connected," Court said. "Right? He must have implanted something before you left."

"Jumping to conclusions is a good way to get hurt." Marsh scratched at his cheek through his beard. "You said that you had to find the rabbit and the tour guide."

"Yes."

"Well, I'm pretty sure I know what the rabbit means at least. It's almost time for the emergency council meeting. Please come with me."

Marsh was several strides toward the council's cabin when he realized Elle wasn't following. She was glancing between her suit and the cluster of onlookers that had grown by several more people.

"You don't have to worry about our people. No one wants trouble. But bring the suit with you if you're concerned about it."

The council members wore grave expressions when Elle and Court entered. Marsh took the empty spot at the head of the rectangular table that dominated the room. Two council members sat on either side. "Have a seat, please." He motioned at the guest bench that ran along the wall. The room was small—the bench was close enough for conversation but still far enough away for visitors to know unambiguously that they were not at the table, physically or metaphorically.

Court sat at Marsh's invitation, but Elle didn't so he stood back up awkwardly.

"Or stand if you like. Doesn't matter." Marsh grinned and Court's cheeks flushed red.

Colleen, the council member to Marsh's immediate right, asked, "Ready?"

Marsh nodded, and Colleen tapped on her tablet. The cabin door swung shut of its own volition, causing Elle to jump.

"Sorry," Marsh said, "I should have warned you. We hold our meetings in private. A bit of old timer paranoia."

"Cloaking activated," Colleen said.

"Thank you, everyone, for dropping your work to make time for this emergency session. I'll try to keep it brief. I know some of you need to get back to finishing up the corn harvest. I call this meeting to order. Let the record show that all five council members are present and are joined by village member Court and the visitor Elle."

Marsh asked Court to recount the events of the day. Council members interrupted a few times to ask clarifying questions. When he got to the doctor's discovery, Marsh took over.

"Whatever's embedded in the bone, we don't have the tools required to extract it safely. I want to cut out the surrounding bone and take it to Alma. I have contacts there who should be able to tell us what it is."

Elle winced at the mention of cutting out the bone.

A small, bald council member reacted first. "That sounds like a significant risk. And an unnecessary one. Taking some unknown tech from the body of a scientist killed by a Qyntarak and walking into Alma with it? Half that town is collaborators and the other half is criminals. We should dump the body deep in the woods and let the coywolves drag it away."

Elle squeezed her hand into a fist.

Colleen said, "Paul's right. It's a tremendous risk. What could possibly justify that?"

"Clint Donovan and I were students together. We worked together. And we were friends. When I left to come here, we vowed that if either of us were ever in inescapable danger, we would be there for each other. It's no coincidence that he showed up on the old road. He was looking for me."

"How do you know that?"

"Because he told Elle that they needed to find the rabbit and the tour guide. Like most of you, I'm old enough to be from a time and place when people had family names. My family name is Lapin. That means rabbit in French."

Chapter 4: Marsh

Vaidehi handed Marsh a wire necklace threaded through tooth and bone fragments.

"Best I could do under the circumstances. This one is the fragment with our mystery object in it." She touched a piece of bone between a chunk of antler and a bear claw.

"You're convinced that people will believe we wear things like this?"

"They think we're unhinged savages. They'd believe it if you walked into town wearing a bear mask with a coywolf fur around your shoulders."

"So you'd walk into town with me wearing this if I asked?"

"In a heartbeat."

They both knew Marsh couldn't call that bluff. The village had at least a dozen people old enough for the trip but young enough for the ruse of an old man and his grandchild bringing pelts to town for trading. Not only was Vaidehi too old to be convincing, she was the most educated person in the village after Marsh. They'd need her while he was away.

"I think I'll wear it under my shirt, just to be safe."

"I'll try not to be insulted."

She pushed him out the door with a warning. "Take care of Walker. That boy shows a lot of potential."

"I know. That's why I'm taking him. You watch out for Elle. Maybe keep a tranquilizer in your pocket as a precaution. I'm still not sure what to make of her."

Chapter 5: Court

ELLE SLAPPED ANOTHER blood-engorged insect, leaving a smear of red on her forearm.

"What are these things?"

"Mosquitoes," Court said. "I told you to wear long sleeves."

"They're awful."

"This is nothing. I've seen them so thick you couldn't breathe without sucking one in."

"How can you stand to live like this?"

"It's the way things are. You just deal with it. And wear long sleeves when you go out. There's a spray that keeps them from biting but it's not easy to get and it makes hunting harder because the animals can smell you coming. There's some kind of system at the village that Marsh rigged up a long time ago to keep them away so at least we only have to deal with them when we go out. That was before I was born.

It must've been awful here back then."

"Have you lived here your whole life?"

Court weighed possible replies in his head, unsure of how forthcoming he wanted to be. Elle had opened up a little bit in the three days that Marsh and Walker had been away, but she'd shared almost nothing about the life she'd left behind. He was no more interested in exposing his emotional wounds to a stranger than she was.

Have I lived here my whole life? Not exactly...

What he said was, "Pretty much."

"Well, don't take this the wrong way but I think the animals can smell you coming even without that special spray."

"Hey, now, we can't all be fancy city girls."

"I'm not a city girl."

"No? Then where are you from?"

She turned her head away and let her hands run through the leaves of a cluster of small trees as she passed them.

"You shouldn't do that. Good way to pick up a tick."

"A tick?"

"A type of bug. Some of them carry disease. You don't want Lyme disease, trust me."

"It's so different out here. You worry about things I've never heard of."

"Different from what? You've got a pretty good view of my life but I don't know anything about yours. You're not a city girl, so what are you?"

"Something between a patient and a prisoner."

Court was trying to think of what to say next to get her to share more when they found a brown rabbit trapped in a snare.

Elle went to her knees and reached out to touch its fur. The animal's grasp on life was tenuous.

"The poor thing." She turned to look at Court, her eyes wide. "Can you save it?"

"Save it? That's dinner." He let his pack fall from his shoulders and pulled a knife from his belt. "I snared it on purpose."

"How can you eat such an innocent little animal? It's just trying to survive out here."

"No different than the rest of us."

She didn't move out of his way.

He frowned and waited for several long seconds but she stayed on the ground with the rabbit.

"It's suffering. It's cruel to leave it like that. If you make some room, I'll put it out of its misery."

Elle nodded and gave him space. She looked away as he worked. The neck crunched as he broke it. He was fast tying the rabbit to the outside of his pack and resetting the snare.

"Done," he said and continued walking.

He heard her slapping at mosquitoes behind him as she followed at a distance. The silence felt different than the quiet times when he walked through the woods with Walker. Even the birds seemed to have grown silent. It made him feel heavy.

By the time Court checked the final snare—all empty save for the one rabbit—the silence had grown too uncomfortable for him. "I should have warned you what checking the snares meant."

"Yes, you should have."

"But you know that all the meat you eat comes from animals, right?"

"We didn't eat meat where I lived."

The idea of surviving without meat made no sense to him. They couldn't survive the long winters without hunting.

"What did you eat then?"

"Food."

"Food?" He stopped and turned to face her. "Meat is food."

"Meat is not food."

"You're not making any sense."

"Meat is meat. Food is food. They are different. They don't look the same. They definitely don't taste the same."

"Lots of food looks and tastes different. We had corn and apples yesterday. Corn is different from rabbit which is different from apples."

"No, food is always the same. Those things aren't food."

"You don't know what you're talking about." He pulled his pack to one side and fished a piece of dehydrated fruit from a pocket. "Here. Dried apple. Food."

"That isn't food."

He pulled a chunk off with his teeth. "It's something you eat so it's food." Fragments of apple sprayed out as he spoke through a mouthful of pulp.

"No."

"Well, whatever you call it, here." He handed a piece of dried apple to her and reseated the pack on his shoulders.

After they'd walked for a few minutes, Elle said, "It's good. The apple. It's better than food."

He rolled his eyes but she was behind him and didn't see.

They continued that way, walking single file, for the rest of the return trip. The air was comfortable for walking although the warmth of the afternoon was starting to yield to the cool of the coming evening.

"Salut," Court shouted and waved to the person keeping watch from a platform suspended twenty feet up between the trunks of three trees. There was rarely any need for a watch but it was part of the routine of the village. Court had scared off a pair of coywolves a couple months earlier but the wildlife usually stayed away. It was more important to keep track of who left the village and make sure they returned before dark. They'd lost an amorous couple when Court was younger. Teenagers a few years older than him who'd snuck off for some privacy. From what they found, it looked like a rutting moose had attacked the boy and the girl had hit her head on a rock trying to run away. Court had found the girl's body. He hadn't thought of that in a long time. He shook his head, trying to push the memory away.

After the blood was drained, he skinned and deboned the rabbit. He mixed the chopped meat with potatoes, carrots, and onions in a pot hanging over a snapping campfire. With Marsh and Walker away, Court's common table would have only Pica and Elle tonight. The modest stew would be more than enough.

The stew was thick and fragrant when Colleen wandered over and inhaled over the pot as Court stirred. "Smells good. I'd add more thyme."

"I'd prefer to add garlic."

She leaned in conspiratorially. "Between you and me, I asked Marsh to barter for new garlic bulbs if he can find them in Alma. If I can get a new crop started, I'll trade you a dozen cloves for a night's watch in the winter."

"I'll take that deal anytime."

"You'll change your tune when your bones are as old as

mine. How is the girl?"

Court looked at Elle, who was watching a pair of young boys practice printing the alphabet in the dirt with a stick.

"Strange. She was upset about killing a rabbit to eat. And she was going on and on about the things we eat not being food."

"Interesting." Colleen tapped a finger against her chin. "Could be she's used to only eating government rations."

"You mean that gray stuff Vaidehi brought when she moved here?"

"Yes. Tastes awful but keeps people alive."

"If that's what she's used to, she should kiss my boots for giving her apples and stew."

Colleen laughed at him. "She doesn't seem like the boot kissing type."

He grinned back at her. "True. Any word on Marsh and Walker?"

"Nothing, but that's how we want it. If we hear from them, it means something's gone wrong."

Chapter 6: Walker

"CAN WE TAKE a short break?"

Walker didn't understand how the much older Marsh could keep going for hours without stopping. Their pace was leisurely but shouldn't someone his age need to rest? Or take a piss?

Well, he's not carrying a pack loaded with fur and animal parts.

Marsh looked at the sky. "We're almost to Chignecto and the sun's getting low. Another hour at most. We'll find a place to sleep there for the night. We should push through."

"I at least need a second to piss."

"Go ahead." Marsh waved his hand toward the edge of the narrow trail. Walker let his pack slide from his shoulder and stepped a few feet into the trees. Despite spending a significant amount of his life walking through the woods with other people, he still liked a bit of privacy when he relieved himself.

The mosquitoes weren't concerned with his sense of modesty and he had to do some maneuvering to keep them away. He splashed his pant leg in the process. "Nack," he said in frustration.

"You alright over there?"

Walker felt his ears burn with embarrassment. "Fine," he called back. "Just the nacking 'squitoes."

"Mind your language."

"What? I can't say 'squitoes anymore?"

"That's not what I meant and you full well know that."

Walker returned to the trail and pulled up his pack, rotating his body so Marsh wouldn't see the wet spots on his pant legs.

"Loads of people say nacking. What's the big deal?"

"You need to mind your context. Not everyone is as easy living as those in our village. Mark my words, we will run into those who will be offended by impolite talk of any kind and we don't want to attract attention to ourselves. You must stay quiet and be invisible. That means no talking about the village. No mention of the Qyntarak. And no coarse language. We're close enough now that we could run into someone at any time."

"Fine, I get it. I'll watch what I say."

"Good." The old man started walking again. "And you pissed on your pants. Try to stop doing that as well. We'll smell bad enough when we reach Chignecto."

Walker's entire face flushed red, he could feel it, and he was thankful that Marsh was walking ahead of him.

They arrived at the outskirts of Chignecto an hour later. Walker knew that Marsh had visited countless times over the decades, but it was his first time. He was dumbstruck by the spectacle of merchants selling roasted meats on sticks, clothes, antique trinkets, and scrap salvaged from the old machines of pre-Qyntarak society.

Marsh tugged on his arm. "Come along. We aren't here for the bazaar."

"I had no idea it would be like this. Look at all the people. It's like a village festival."

Marsh squeezed the boy's arm and narrowed his eyes.

"Sorry," Walker whispered.

"Mind your context."

They pushed through a crowd of forty or fifty people milling around a dozen makeshift stalls. Walker tried to take in each face as it passed but was quick to avert his eyes when someone looked back. Beyond the bazaar, Chignecto teemed with humanity. Shelters of various states of permanence were packed tight along the road. Marsh pressed on, the click of his walking stick drawing the stares of a cluster of old women resting in the partial shade of a threadbare canopy.

After several minutes of walking deeper into the settlement, Marsh stopped in front of a small metal building surrounded by weeds as high as Walker's waist.

"Watch this," Marsh said. He took one step forward and a dog—or maybe a coywolf, Walker couldn't be sure—lunged from the grass barking.

Walker jumped back. Spittle flew from the beast's dark snout. Marsh laughed and stood his ground.

Through the barking, Walker heard the jingle of metal and realized as he grabbed Marsh's sleeve that it was a chain. The dog stopped a foot short of Marsh, straining at the tether and snarling.

From inside the building, a woman's voice yelled out, "Elon's fire, what the blazes is going on out there? If you kids are teasing that dog again, I'll loose his chain, I promise you that." The flimsy metal door flew open and a bull of a woman stormed out. Her wide shoulders filled the doorway. Her white hair, cut short, glowed against her dark skin. The menace in her eyes faded when they took in the sight of Marsh laughing at the dog. "Marsh Lapin, you old coot. Leave poor Jean alone."

"She started it."

"The two of you are fit for each other. Jean, to rest."

The dog looked at the woman, let out a whimper, and slunk back into the grassy weeds with a snort.

"How are you, Moriya?"

"As good as you'd expect. Come on in." She disappeared into the building and Walker followed Marsh inside. Every available space was filled with scraps and fragments of old technology like what they'd seen for sale in the bazaar.

"I see you haven't cleaned up the trailer any since last time I was here."

"If you'd told me you were coming..."

"You'd have locked the doors and pulled the shades."

"You might be right, but it's good to see you." Moriya slapped Marsh on the shoulder and pulled him into a hug.

"This is Walker."

"Salut," Walker said.

"Oh, don't use that greeting around here," Moriya said. "You'll stand out like a one-armed porter. But welcome to Chignecto." She stuck out her meaty hands, palms up, and Walker touched his palms to hers. It wasn't a greeting they used in the village but Marsh had taught him about it on their walk.

"This is his first time in Chignecto. We're headed to Alma."

"Trouble?"

"I don't know yet."

"We're getting too old for that kind of uncertainty."

"Speak for yourself, old lady."

"Watch your tongue, gray beard, or I'll send you back out to see Jean."

Walker had never heard Marsh speak with someone this way. Moriya must have recognized the confusion on his face.

"Marsh and I are old friends. No need for alarm there, pup."

Walker attempted an understanding smile but doubted he was fooling anyone.

"I was hoping we could spend the night here and barter for fresh clothes and a wash before going into town. We brought pelts and dried venison."

"Aye, a sure thing. I'll go borrow a storage bin and we can clear a space for you in here."

"Thank you."

"Someday I'm going to come visit you to return the favor."

"You've been saying that for twenty years. I've stopped holding my breath."

"Fair enough," Moriya said as she slipped out the door.

"Who is she?"

"Moriya's an old friend from a previous life. And, more importantly, she's someone we can trust. You can take your pack off here and relax."

Walker set the pack down, being careful to avoid disturbing the stacks of unfamiliar metal and plastic components. "Why do we need to buy clothes?"

"To blend in. Alma's hardly a fashion center but—well, you'll understand when we get there. Our old clothes would stand out." Marsh eased himself into a cracked leather chair, the only piece of exposed furniture in the place, and let out a long groan. "I'm going to rest for a bit. When Moriya gets back, help her with moving things."

Walker agreed and sat on the floor. Marsh started snoring in less than a minute.

The old man didn't stir when Moriya opened the door. She pointed to one of the piles near Walker. "Pass those things out to me."

They filled three bins that Moriya sealed shut and chained to the outside of the trailer. "Most the folks in Chignecto would sacrifice their left nut for you, but you still want to lock up your stuff." She sat on a bin and patted the empty space next to her. "Have a seat, pup, and we can get acquainted while the old guy naps. How old are you?"

"Fourteen."

"Blazes that's young. I have socks older than you. Who are your parents? Anyone I might know?"

"They were Claimers. They got pregnant without permission and were sent away on an expulsion ship a few weeks after I was born."

"That's awful. I'm sorry."

"It's fine. I don't remember them at all. I don't even know what they looked like. Harry and Sugar were their names. Or are there names, I guess, if they're still out there somewhere." He pointed to the sky. "The village is the only family I've known."

"You listen to me carefully, Walker. It is not fine. Never

forget your parents' names. The Qyntarak have taken so much from us. We need to cling to everything we can, to the things that make us human." She slapped him on the knee. "Let's go wake the old man up and get some grub into the both of you. You must be famished."

Moriya took them to a cookhouse, a building with large chimneys belching smoke and big windows with the tattered remains of bug screens visible around the edges. She asked for three helpings of an egg-and-potato dish. The girl at the wood-burning stove had her head wrapped in a sweat-soaked piece of cloth. She muttered something incomprehensible when Moriya said, "Put it on my tab, hon."

Walker looked at the food on its thin metal square. "Is this a tab?"

Marsh and Moriya burst into a fit of laughter that drew the attention of everyone around them. With tears running down his face, Marsh said, "No, that's a plate." That made Moriya laugh even harder and Marsh had to set down his plate so he didn't spill his food. His whole body convulsed while he steadied himself with his walking stick.

"Come on then. Sit over here before tears start rolling down my legs," Moriya said through the tail end of a series of belly laughs.

They sat with their food at a wooden table with built-in benches.

"What was so funny?" Walker asked once his curiosity had outgrown his embarrassment from being the subject of a joke he didn't understand.

"A tab is like a running bill. They keep track of how much I owe for the food I get here and I pay it off with money, supplies, or services."

"Saying to put something on your tab is an old expression to tell someone that you'll pay later," Marsh added.

"You bought this food? You use money here?"

"Yes, sometimes. I also barter my time."

"Moriya is quite skilled at salvaging and repairing old tech."

"Among other things," she said with a wink.

"I was expecting money in Alma but I thought here would be more like the village."

"It may have been once upon a time," Moriya said, "but those days are long gone. Chignecto is more and more just an outskirt of Alma. A place for the poor and the disagreeable to settle down without sacrificing all of their dignity."

"Which are you?" Walker blurted out the question and immediately regretted it.

"Walker," Marsh snapped in a low voice.

Moriya smirked. "It's alright. I don't mind an honest inquiry. I'm the latter by birth and the former by choice. I have what I need and I've got nobody telling me how to live. I can earn a bit of copper if I want and go into Alma for some sweets or some medicine, but I don't have to. I'm free to stay right here and live my life without anyone bothering me."

Walker listened with saucer-wide eyes as Moriya described a type of freedom so different from the life of responsibilities and order that he knew.

"And no one to look out for you when the sleet flies sideways."

"Listen to you with the old person expressions. Ah, I've missed you, Marsh. You should come visit more often."

The older pair stared at each other and Walker felt inexplicably out of place.

"I always mean to," Marsh eventually replied.

"Well, let's get you sojourners off to the shower house before the light leaves us completely. You smell like a pair of salmon leaped to the shore and rotted in the sunshine. I'm not sleeping with that in my trailer all night. I'll see if I can get town clothes for you from someone back here. You don't want anything from the bazaar. Nothing but cheats and swindlers out there taking advantage of the idiots visiting from Alma looking for a quick thrill out in the slums."

Chapter 7: Walker

IN THE MORNING, Walker was served his first ever cup of coffee. They didn't have coffee in the village but Marsh spoke of it with a fond nostalgia that inspired him to sample it. His nose curled at the taste and Marsh gladly finished both cups before they bid farewell to Moriya with a promise to stop again on their return trip the next day. Moriya said she would give their "disgraceful vagabond rags" to the neighbor's kid to be washed and mended.

They passed through the empty bazaar while the morning air was still cool and damp. Marsh asked, "Has anyone shown you pictures of what our cities used to be like?"

"No. I've heard that they were full of people, like the bazaar was yesterday."

"That wasn't even a large crowd. Chignecto is a squatter slum. Alma is a proper town, and it's a speck compared to the cities. If you could have seen the cities before... Toronto, New York, Chicago. They were grand in their time. Millions of people. Staggering numbers of humanity living out their lives."

"What are they like now?"

"It's been a long time since I've visited a real city but I've heard stories. Lots of people still there but they feel sparse because so many were forced off planet. I suspect it would be depressing for me to visit now."

"I'd like to visit a city someday."

"How come?"

"It sounds like a good reminder of how much was taken from us. Of what humans could be again."

"It seems you have more of your parents' Reclamation spirit in you than I realized." Marsh laid his free hand on Walker's shoulder, an awkward position for walking. "You're still young, and there's a lot you need to learn about the world. But far be it from me to dictate your destiny to you. If you decide you want more than village life in the future, I will help prepare you. For now, let's try to get through your first visit to Alma without losing our chests. Do not utter another word of anything even smelling of Reclamation talk until we are back home."

Walker bobbed his head in understanding. The reference to the hole in Donovan's chest was a blunt reminder of the risks.

They continued downhill for an hour. They had traded their pelts and meat for copper and silver coins that they could use in town. The rough metal disks jingled as Marsh's new satchel bounced against his hip. Walker was thankful to be free of the large pack and even more thankful that he wouldn't have to lug it back up such an interminable hill.

They passed another bazaar that was cleaner and more

orderly than what they'd seen in Chignecto. "This all used to be government-owned land. Human government, I mean. If you can believe it, people used to pay to come sleep here in tents on the ground instead of their beds at home."

"Why?"

"Recreation, I suppose."

"That's bizarre."

"Perhaps. When the Qyntarak started to purge the cities, people fled to places like this to hide. They believed that places of low population wouldn't be worth the Qyntarak's bother. Several hundred people living off the land aren't much of a threat."

"Why wouldn't the Qyntarak just vaporize the place?"

"It's not their way. There's a lot we don't understand about them even after half a century, but they don't appear to simply kill for convenience."

"Ho, travelers. Care for some chicken to speed you on your way?" The source of the voice was a wiry man hunched over a grill.

"Ho, friend. We are well fed and content."

"All the best to you then. Safe travels."

When they were well out of earshot, Walker asked, "Is that really how people talk down here?"

"Some, yes. We're very close to Alma now so best to keep your questions to yourself the rest of the day."

They descended the final hill into town, and Walker's eyes grew wide at the sight of buildings of the sort he had only ever heard about, the size of four or five cabins at least. They walked past the ruin of an even larger building, three levels high judging from its rows of broken windows.

"Look at that."

"Would you please refrain from looking like a baby doe?"

"I can't help it. I've never seen a building like that before."

Marsh chuckled at him. "If I'm not mistaken, that was once a hotel. It's a miracle how much is still standing after so many years."

Walker pointed to an assortment of clothing hung over the remains of a wooden railing, presumably laundry being dried in the sun. "There are people living there."

"Oh, no doubt. Desperation will drive people to lay their mat anywhere that keeps the rain off. Some year, the weight of snow will crush that old building and the desperate people living in it."

Melancholy hung in the air between them as they passed the former hotel with its walls washed gray by the sea breeze. Marsh nodded politely to a few passersby. Walker kept his head down and didn't dare make eye contact with anyone.

"I've seen pictures from here from a hundred and fifty years ago," Marsh told him. "It looked almost exactly the same. Wooden houses along the street. Wooden fishing boats in the water. It's remarkable, when you consider it. This place managed to survive rising sea levels, the arrival of the Qyntarak, the receding sea level, the mass displacement of humanity. Of course, back then—"

Marsh stopped talking when he realized that Walker was no longer at his side. He turned to see the young man staring through a grimy window.

"What is that?"

"What did I say about looking like a baby doe?"

"I'm sorry, but I've never seen anything like—"

"It's called a movie, or at least that's what we used to call them. Like the videos we record with our tablets sometimes."

"But it's not like that at all. I mean, just look at that. It's like a whole other world."

"Yes, that's a good way to say it. I haven't seen a movie in… well, it's been a very long time."

"How come you've never told us that things like this existed?"

Marsh's voice was barely a whisper. "Let's discuss this later, Walker. There's much you'll learn and see as your education advances. No one has been keeping movies a secret from you, we just don't have the resources for them in the village so they're not part of our day-to-day conversations. Now, please, you need to discipline yourself or you'll put us both at risk."

Walker kept his eyes on the screen through the dirty glass for several heartbeats before dropping his gaze and turning away.

"Our destination is just ahead on the left. The Squid and Whale, a miserable place for the insufferably unscrupulous to kill off brain cells. And also the best place to find Polk."

Chapter 8: Elle

ELLE HAD OPTED out of a repeat trip to check snares with
Court, so she had some time to herself. She sat on her bunk
staring at the suit. It looked so out of place sitting in a log
cabin in the middle of the wilderness. The village felt like a
safe place, but how safe was she? She didn't know the story
behind the suit. There could be a tracking device in it. Would
someone from the center show up looking for it? For her?

Who could she trust if that happened? She didn't know
these people. Was Marsh actually a friend of Dr. Donovan?
Was he the rabbit? Those first few hours were a blur. She
didn't trust her own memories of them. Was Marsh telling
her what she wanted to hear? Telling her that this place was
safe and that, yes, of course this is where Dr. Donovan was
bringing her all along? But he knew Dr. Donovan's name was
Clint. Or had she given that information away? Or did the
Qyntarak say it and Court heard and told Marsh?

Court seemed genuinely naive; he was capable in his

familiar environment but ignorant of the wider world.

She would know if they weren't being truthful with her, wouldn't she? Wouldn't she see something in their faces? The village didn't feel like a place built on deceit but wasn't that the way of dishonest people? You never knew for sure.

"Dr. Donovan, why?" she whispered, almost sighing the words.

Unbidden, her mind replayed the sight of his missing chest. She pressed her palms into her eyes. "Stop stop stop."

It didn't stop. She kept seeing it over and over.

Air wouldn't come into her lungs. She tried to inhale and gasped desperately with no relief. It felt like she was drowning.

She flung herself out the door into the fresh air and braced herself against the cabin wall. Her heart threatened to come through her ribs with each beat.

L37, control your breathing.

She focused on the memory of Master Zheng.

Control my breathing, right.

She forced a long exhale then a ragged inhale.

Again.

Again.

Eventually, her heart rate slowed. She put her palms on her sides, arms akimbo, and walked a small circle in front of the cabin.

I have to stop staring at that suit, it's making me crazy.

She went to the white cabin where she found Vaidehi organizing a cabinet.

"Afternoon, Elle."

"Hi. I was wondering, do you have a waterproof container that I can have? A pouch or something would be great. I want to wrap up my suit, to be safe. I don't know how sensitive it is and I hate to keep it just laying out."

Vaidehi pulled on her lower lip as she thought. "Well, I suppose you don't need anything that's medical grade sterile, so..." She flipped up the lid of a blue container and pulled out a semi-transparent bag. "This could work. Had a splash pad in it."

"What's a splash pad?"

"For wrapping injuries. Technically, it's a wound-sealing antiseptic mesh wrap with embedded growth accelerant. Way easier than stitching up skin and less likely to get infected, which is pretty important out here since antibiotics are hard to come by. Used this one to patch up Evangeline. Sliced her leg open trying to get a chicken back into its pen. Her foot slipped off a grip and tore a gash down most of her thigh. Would leave a nasty scar without the growth accelerant. Her kid let the chicken out to play, if you can believe that. Anyway, not sure why we call them splash pads, but that's what everyone called them back in med school."

"You went to medical school? You're not from here?"

"Blazes, no. Went to John Hopkins. Got stationed up here as an itinerant medic for some of the state facilities."

"So, why are you here then? This isn't a state facility."

"Love."

"What?"

"Met a guy while I was traveling. He thought I should leave my job and live the simple life. You know, pick up work for cash or barter. Deliver babies, set bones, that kind of stuff. Anyway, that worked for a while then the weaselly bastard cheated on me, so I left. A friend introduced me to Moriya who introduced me to Marsh who invited me here and been living the free life ever since."

"Wait, who's Moriya? Someone in the village?"

"No, an old friend of Marsh's. More than a friend, if you want my opinion, but Marsh'll never admit to anything. Lives down in the Chignecto settlement. Kind of a kooky old bat but she's got connections. Here, take this tape. If you put your suit in and squeeze out the air, you can seal it with the tape and that'll keep the water and dirt out."

"Thank you."

"Hey, no worries. Listen, I know it can be hard adjusting to life here. Thought about leaving a bunch of times myself the first couple of years, trust me. But these are good folks."

"It's definitely different here."

"That it is. If you ever want to just sit and talk it out, let me know. We can get into my stash of corn whiskey. It'll burn your insides but it does the trick now and then."

"I've never had whiskey before. We weren't allowed to have alcohol. Dr. Donovan and the others said there was too much risk that it would interfere with the study results."

"Study results? And I thought I had stories to tell. Well, when you're ready, I can introduce you to your first ever whiskey then. Good news is that anything you drink in the future will almost certainly be an improvement."

Elle gave her a genuine smile. Vaidehi seemed decent. Maybe even someone Elle might consider opening up to.

"Thank you again for the bag and the tape."

After the hospital, Elle borrowed a shovel from the village gardens and went back to her cabin. By rolling up the suit and stuffing it into the helmet's cavity, she was able to squeeze everything into the bag and seal it shut with the tape.

Elle didn't know how long she would leave it hidden, only that she needed it away from herself and there was no one to trust with it. She carried the suit and shovel across the clearing and into the woods, following a trail away from the village until she found a pile of rocks as big as a cabin.

According to Court, the pile was there long before the village, from a farmer clearing rocks from his fields hundreds of years earlier. It was a tradition in the village to have the teenagers carry rocks from the land they farmed now to the old rock pile. Court said it was to build strength and endurance. Elle suspected it was a way to keep teenagers busy and tired so they stayed out of trouble. She also suspected that Court was too naive to have figured that out.

She cleared away some rocks from the edge and began digging. It was hard work, harder than it looked in the old movies she'd watched with Dr. Donovan. Her hands burned, and she was soaked with sweat by the time she had a big enough hole. She lined it with thin, broad rocks to create a crude floor and walls before she laid the suit in.

A blister tore open on her hand while filling in the hole, which was now a bulge of dirt rising above the ground. She covered the small mound with rocks and stepped back to inspect her work. Other than footprints in the dirt, there was no evidence.

The task had been more work than she'd expected but she felt refreshed as she returned to the village, like a thousand pounds had been lifted from her shoulders. The open sore from the burst blister stung as she walked. She thought again of Master Zheng and observed the pain instead of feeling it. Tomorrow, she'd go see Vaidehi about it. For now, she would observe.

Chapter 9: Marsh

MARSH TAPPED A copper coin on the bar top to get the bartender's attention. Nine other patrons sat scattered throughout The Squid and Whale. A quartet of men with sinewy arms played a game with little wooden tiles at a table crowded with empty glasses. There was a man and woman, her not much older than Walker and him much older, pawing at each other in a corner. Two men that Walker guessed to be late twenties chewed wordlessly on sandwiches. And one man sat slumped over with his face on the weathered bar, a half full bottle of something yellow an inch from his unmoving fingers.

The bartender, a gaunt woman who looked ancient to Walker but moved behind the bar with ease, eyed the coin first and then its owner.

"We don't serve kids in here. I ain't lookin' for trouble from no one. The religious nuts'll ruin me if I do."

Marsh waved his thumb at the other customers. "They

don't care about the rest of the folks you're serving?"

"People can do whatever they like when you're grown but corruptin' the youth gets em into a lather."

"Then we can be on our way. I came in looking for a friend but I see he's not to be found here."

The bartender eyed the copper coin again. "Who's that you're looking for?"

"A man named Polk."

The woman's laugh sounded like someone had dropped a handful of stones on the bar. "You must be confused. Polk ain't got friends."

"I suppose that's true. I have business with him."

She eyed Marsh again and waggled her finger. "Yes. You've been here before. Your beard's longer and grayer, I almost didn't recognize you."

"Is he around?"

"Leave that copper and I'll pour you a drink while I send for him."

"For a copper, I'll want a proper beer and a cup of clean water."

The bartender clucked but pulled out two glass mugs, both heavily scratched. She pumped a plunger on a metal canister and used a hose to fill one mug with amber beer until the foam threatened to spill over the lip. The other she filled with water from a jug.

"Give me a minute. My son will go fetch Polk."

She slipped out through a frayed curtain tacked over a doorway. When she was out of sight, Marsh reached over the bar and topped up his mug with the hose.

"A whole copper coin and she doesn't bother to pour a full pint. Unbelievable." He pushed the water in front of Walker.

"Drink. Good water's hard to find here."

The bartender was back in seconds. "My boy's off to find him."

Walker had finished the water and Marsh's mug was nearing empty when the slap of the screen door slamming shut behind them grabbed the attention of all but the customer sleeping on the bar.

A stout man entered; he was oddly proportioned, like his legs were too long for the rest of his body. The whites of his eyes seemed to glow. Those eyes troubled Walker. They were small and radiated disdain.

"I told you to water down his hooch." He tilted his head toward to the unconscious bar guest.

"I did but he can tell. I watered it down more as he drank but he doesn't stop. I been pouring a long time. Ain't never seen anyone get sober by being tricked."

The man snarled at the bartender and she moved away to check on her other customers.

He turned to Marsh. "I hear you have business to discuss."

"I do. Something requiring a more private venue."

Polk nodded to the curtain behind the bar and led them through.

"I don't forget faces. You're from one of the little villages. March, I think."

"Close. Marsh."

"How's that water purifier working for you?"

"Humming along nicely. Three years and counting."

"Good, good. Always happy to see a satisfied customer. What can I find for you this time?"

"Not looking to acquire anything. A friend gave me a piece

of tech that I can't make work."

"Why not ask them for help then?"

"Because he died."

"He died or you killed him?"

"I didn't kill him. He was a friend."

"In my line of work, those aren't mutually exclusive." Polk laughed at himself. "I suppose that's why folks like you live far away from us."

Marsh smiled at the comment but Walker could tell it was forced.

"So where is this tech?"

The bone fragments clinked as Marsh pulled the necklace out from under his shirt. "Embedded in a piece of bone."

Polk stuttered a little when he replied, "A piece of bone?"

"Yes, we think it might be a data chip of some sort but we don't know how to access it. Is there a problem?"

"No problem. Not exactly a water purifier this time though, is it?"

"Not exactly."

"And you have payment? Real coin?"

"Yes."

"Let's go take a look then. Follow me."

Through an old door, they descended stairs that groaned with each step and Walker feared one would give way before he made it to the bottom. In a dark corner, Polk picked up a metal rod with curved ends. Walker sucked in a breath and felt his chest tighten as fight-or-flight instincts kicked in. He bent his knees, memories of lessons with Court buzzing through his mind. But Polk turned his back to them and slid the rod between the dusty glass jugs on a shelf of a wooden cabinet. With a twist of his wrist, something clicked and Polk pulled on the rod, leaning back to use his weight for assistance. Sounds of wood scraping on stone accompanied the shifting of the shelf.

"Old moonshine room. The main reason I bought the tavern in the first place."

"Fascinating," Marsh said.

Walker followed the older men into the room, which seemed to be made entirely of metal and glass like the tablets used by the village council members.

Marsh removed his wire necklace and gave it to Polk. "This one." He tapped the chunk of bone from Clint Donovan's leg. Polk winced as he took it and placed the fragment between a pair of metal panels.

An image appeared on a wall-mounted tablet. Polk manipulated the image, stretching and sliding while he examined the magnified 3D image.

"Looks like an Aldebaran data vault to me."

"Aldebaran..." Marsh repeated.

"Yeah, biggest company there is for hybrid human-Qyntarak tech. Was your friend associating with Qyntarak?"

"It seems likely."

"A collaborator?"

Marsh shifted his weight and adjusted his grip on his walking stick. His body language seemed to answer Polk's inquiry.

"Let me try pinging it."

"What's that mean?" Walker asked.

"Basic challenge-response type protocol signals. We'll see if it responds to any of the standard stuff. If I'm right and it's Aldebaran, we should get something back."

While they waited on Polk, Walker studied the room. It

was not, in fact, all metal and glass even though that was the dominant impression. Their chairs were white leather. In addition to metal and glass, Walker saw wood and the material that villagers called plastic but that Marsh insisted was called restin—an organic polymer, whatever that was.

"I've got something," Polk said.

Chapter 10: Elle

"JUST LINE UP the two sights and squeeze the button." Court let go of the mag gun and Elle held it in front of her eye. She drew in a slow breath and squeezed.

The gun whirred and snapped. The projectile, a wooden arrow not much longer than her index finger, shattered against a slab of shale behind the apple she was aiming for. Dr. Donovan had let her train with a lot of weapons, high and low tech, but she'd never shot something like this.

"A good first try," Court said.

Give me an hour and I'll outshoot you with your own weapon, she thought.

Aloud, she said, "Let me try again."

She pressed another arrow through the gun's reloading slot. Wooden arrows were a clever choice given how easily villagers could make new ammo in the forest.

"It uses magnets to launch the arrow. Marsh designed it himself."

"Magnets? But wood isn't magnetic."

"Yeah, I'm not good with all the engineering and inventing stuff. Marsh can explain it when he's back."

She aimed and fired again. The arrow brushed the left side of the apple and it wobbled on the tree stump.

"Nice shot."

"Again."

Elle reloaded and fired, clipping the upper right curve of her target. Her next shot struck a little left of center, sending the apple flying off the stump. She fired once more, this time at a rotting apple on the ground, and it exploded into a pulpy mass of brown mush.

She held out her hand for another arrow.

"That's all I brought. I was just giving you a feel for it. I didn't expect you to take to it like that."

Elle did like the weapon. It was quiet and surprisingly accurate. Sure, it was primitive with a limited range and wouldn't take down anything serious, but she respected the ingenuity. For the first time, she could imagine Dr. Donovan and Marsh Lapin being friends.

Chapter 11: Walker

"IT'S DEFINITELY ALDEBARAN tech," Polk said. "An encrypted personal data vault. Very short range signal, so hard to detect if you don't know it's there. It uses a standard handshake but requires a decryption key."

"Can we brute force it?" Marsh asked.

"Just a moment. Let me check the specifications." Polk tapped and swiped on one of his many displays. "No, it says here that it makes you wait longer between every failed attempt, maxing out at one attempt per day. Huh, it says that you can request unencrypted metadata. That's unusual. Let me try that."

Walker understood the individual words they were saying but was missing the meaning of the conversation. Too self-conscious of his ignorance to say anything, he tried to look like he was following along but Marsh wasn't fooled. He said to Walker, "We can't read what's on the data chip unless we can figure out the combination of letters and numbers to unlock it. And if we guess wrong too many times, we have to wait twenty-four hours between guesses."

Walker nodded to acknowledge that he understood.

"Well, now, this is interesting. Unencrypted metadata isn't part of any standard protocols but this could be a clue to the key." Polk tapped on the screen and Marsh leaned in to read it.

"C-H-E-R-I-C-I-T-R-U-S." Marsh ran his fingers through his beard as he considered the word. "Che-ricit-rus. Che-ric-itus. Che-ri-citrus. Oh, it's cheri citrus. Of course. I wonder... How long does the decryption key have to be?"

"It depends. A lot of human encryption technology is long past obsolete but a personal device like this would use a human-friendly key, something a human could type or speak."

"Like the words to a song?"

"Yes, it could be something like that. The length of the key would depend on how paranoid the person is and how good their memory is."

"Are you saying that cheri citrus makes sense to you?" Walker asked.

"It took me a moment but I think it's a reference to an old joke Clint and I had with a friend of ours when we were in school. A woman named Sofia. She desperately wanted to work in space. She had her heart set on low gravity research. We used to tease her about leaving us behind. We made up our own words to the song Oh My Darling Clementine. Cheri citrus has got to be a reference to that. It's the only thing that makes sense."

"It's worth a try if you're confident. You don't want to make a bunch of wild guesses."

"How much of the song would it need?"

"How much is there?"

"Not a lot, although remembering it after fifty years will be the trick. Oh my darling, oh my darling, oh my darling, Clementine..." Marsh spoke the words but was clearly struggling. "This is embarrassing but I might need to sing it."

Polk's wide eyes matched the bemusement that Walker felt as Marsh started to sing.

"Oh my darling, oh my darling
Oh my darling, Clementine
You are lost and gone forever
Dreadful thought, dear Clementine

On a spaceship, on a spaceship
Searching for her Nobel Prize
It's biology's defender
Our dear classmate, Clementine

Oh my darling, oh my darling
Oh my darling, Clementine
You are lost and gone forever
Dreadful thought, dear Clementine

Growing peas in zero Gs
And Einstein messing with the time
All her research will expire
If the stars do not align"

"Well, that is a first. I've helped a lot of folks with a lot of problems over the years but no one's ever sung to me before.

I recognize the tune. There have been some lewder versions of it in my tavern."

"Did it work?" Walker asked.

"We'll need to type the lyrics in first. The clue is in uppercase with no spaces and no punctuation so I'm guessing that's how we type it in. Can you repeat the words slowly?"

Marsh half spoke and half sang the ditty a second time.

"Here goes nothing." Polk tapped several times on a screen. Nothing moved. No lights flashed. There was no audible signal of success or failure.

"What's it doing?" Walker asked.

"It didn't work. It's possible the vault is damaged but just as likely that it simply doesn't acknowledge a failed attempt."

"That's inconvenient," Marsh said.

"To us maybe but think about how you'd feel with a chip embedded in your bone. You don't want it being chatty with malicious devices. Someone sits down beside you on a transport and locks you out of your own data vault by silently bombarding it with bad decryption keys?"

"But what about the metadata? If the device responds to metadata pings, doesn't that defeat the purpose of not responding?"

"Like I said, that part's not standard. I can only tell you what I'm seeing and what the specifications say."

"How do you even have the specifications for something like this?" Walker asked. This world was foreign to him but he understood enough to find it suspicious that Polk had so much conveniently at his disposal.

Marsh elbowed him roughly, and he had to suppress a grunt.

"Listen, kid, I can see your grandpa hasn't clued you in to what you're involved with here but I'm giving you one warning. I make things happen that otherwise don't happen easily. Have you studied any chemistry?"

"A bit."

"You know what a catalyst is?"

"Yes."

"That's what I am. And my work affords me some privileges and access. And like a catalyst, I'm a constant while the things around me react and change. That requires discretion. My means and my sources are private and will stay that way. And once you walk out my door, you were never here. Do you understand that?"

Polk's tone was soft and his words were mild. The threat was in those tiny eyes that projected menace with the subtlest narrowing of the lids.

Walker gave a single bow of his head. The air suddenly felt thicker, and the walls seemed to draw closer. Walker wanted out of the room.

"I got the words wrong," Marsh blurted. "We didn't sing dreadful thought, dear Clementine. We used to say going to miss you, Clementine."

Polk tapped the new words into a tablet and waited.

"Ah, here we go."

Chapter 12: Kane

"The governor called for me," Kane said to the human receptionist. She was pretty, although far too young for him. Not that it mattered. His arrangement with the Qyntarak didn't leave room for relationships.

"You can suit up and I'll check with the boss."

"How's the mood?"

"I don't know. You're the first human today."

"Sour split. Just my luck."

"The governor ate not long ago so it should be in gentle spirits."

A door to his left was marked with the silhouette of a human. Inside, a variety of ambassadorial suits hung sterilized and ready for use. He found one labeled LARGE and pulled it on. These suits used to be tight in the chest and loose in the belly on him. He noticed today that it felt a little snug everywhere.

He swiped the panel on the left forearm of the suit and it

dinged after completing a self-diagnostic test. Kane set its emotion-to-temperature conversion sensitivity to its lowest setting and pressed his palm on a wall panel where a virtual READY button pulsed green.

Alien sounds came through a speaker which his suit translated for him. Inside his helmet, a synthetic voice said, "Kane, you will wait for many seconds. You may sit if you desire."

Modern translation systems had a large catalogue of generic synthesized human voices so that humans could differentiate between individual Qyntarak in group conversations. The computer would normally decide on the appropriate voice to use for each speaker, but the Qyntarak elite were assigned dedicated voices in all translation systems by law.

Kantarka-Ta was the governor's second-in-command and gatekeeper to the most powerful being on Earth so it had a dedicated voice. And when that voice said to wait, you waited. As far as human affairs went, Kantarka-Ta was in charge. All humans reported to it, excluding Kane and his small team.

He stayed standing for a long time. One could never know when they were watching, evaluating, judging. He didn't want to enter the meeting tired, though, so when the first wave of fatigue hit, Kane sat. Eventually, he let his helmet tip back and rest against the wall.

He was starting to doze off when Kantarka-Ta's voice returned. "Kane, your entrance is permitted now."

A new virtual button began pulsing on the wall panel: OPEN. He shook his head in an attempt to clear the fog of sleep that had started to encroach and entered the governor's meeting hall.

"Governor Torkanuux, it is an honor to once again be in your presence."

Humans were not physically capable of emulating the Qyntarak gesture of respectful greeting so Kane knelt on one knee, something diplomats had agreed upon a couple decades earlier after the balance of global power had clearly shifted to the Qyntarak. Kane didn't care for it himself but he had few reasons to complain. Compared to most humans, his life was very good. Kneeling occasionally was a small price to pay for that.

"The Akarrak assembly vote will happen in eighteen days. Failure of yours to reveal more evidence of human interference creates in us large quantity of doubt that your group has any usefulness left."

"Honorable one of many, with the death of Clint Donovan we have closed the door to any possible interference. He didn't have a following, only a relationship with two voting members of the Akarrak."

Kane's heart throbbed in his chest. The suit, which was capable of translating his human physiological responses into temperatures that the Qyntarak could comprehend, was muting his reactions. He didn't see any value in letting the Qyntarak ruler know how panicked he felt.

There was almost no light in Torkanuux's chamber. With the assistance of his helmet, Kane was able to see the creature as it shifted forward and curled its upper body, a move meant to communicate authority and dominance. Kane didn't have any instinctual response to the inhuman movement but he'd spent enough time around Qyntarak that he reacted anyway. He took a step back, which would be barely perceivable to the alien but it was enough to signal his deference.

"Donovan was a friend. A friendship unequalled between our species. Friendship to be forever unequalled with the vote successful in eighteen days. Such alliances between Qyntarak and human will no longer be expedient. My staff report that their statistical models predict discontent with the acceptance of the new laws. Violence from humans is predicted. Passive resistance from human rights advocates among Qyntarak is predicted. Prosperity must be safeguarded."

"Honorable one of many, the Reclamationists are fragmented and scattered. We have no evidence of coordinated activities that would make a meaningful statement, let alone precipitate widespread unrest."

The Qyntarak twisted its upper body, which meant confusion. Kane realized his message was getting garbled in translation.

"The Reclamationists—the traitors—are few and not well organized. They are not able to disrupt prosperity."

The Qyntarak wiggled its frond-like antennae in understanding. "For fifteen days, your group is to act on data from my staff and investigate all risks from their predictive systems."

Kane hated when the translator said staff, as if anyone, human or Qyntarak, had a choice about their work.

"Kantarka-Ta will instruct you on the relationships for work assignment."

"Thank you, Governor, honorable one of many." Kane knelt and retreated from the room. He was taking a few calming breaths in the changing closet when another door opened and he was pulled in. The feeling was like falling but he moved horizontally. He ripped off his helmet just in time for his vomit to splatter on the floor.

"Kane." The first time Kane heard the gurgling hiss of Qyntarak speech, he thought it sounded like a cat coughing up a hairball. With more exposure over the years, he now heard the nuance and subtle variety in timbre between speakers. But even with all his experience, the sound of a Qyntarak barking out English was grating. To hear it a few feet away coming from Kantarka-Ta's vocal slot while bile still sat on Kane's tongue was unsettling. "St-stable miniaturized directional gravity control fr-from our fr-friends at Aldeb-a-aran." The words came out in stutters as it strained to produce each syllable. The training and practice required for a Qyntarak to achieve the level of physical control needed to speak English went deep into obsessive territory.

"You could have just asked to see me."

"Wh-wh-where is the amusement in s-such?"

"You mean where's the fun in that?"

Kantarka-Ta tilted backward and lowered its fronds. The Qyntarak gesture for mild irritation.

"Inso-so-solent h-human."

"Insolent? Remember, I don't work for you."

"Not y-yet. I heard Torkanuux. Y-y-y-your time is drawing to an end. S-soon you w-will work f-for me."

"Then it's off to the gulags, is it?"

The Qyntarak twisted in confusion.

"Never mind," Kane said. "Did you actually want something or were you just seeing if your new toy would make me throw up?"

"Th-that w-was an unexpected bonus." It waggled its frond antennae in circles. Humor. Delight. Joy.

What an asshole.

"Then you'll excuse me." Kane turned to leave but Kantarka-Ta reactivated the gravity device for a fraction of a second, pulling him back just far enough for his foot to slip in the puddle of his own vomit and he fell to the floor. He was back on his feet at once.

Stay in control, Kane. Stay. In. Control.

Kantarka-Ta was small for a Qyntarak. Kane figured just over 400 pounds and seven feet when its upper body was folded over, the normal standing position for an adult Qyntarak. Unfortunately for Kane, it was still twice his mass and incredibly fast. He was at the alien's mercy when its clutching appendages grabbed him. One took hold of his right arm, the other his neck. Kane winced at both the pain and the unnatural feeling of the alien's leathery scales over braids of its muscle and fat equivalents.

Its long stabbing appendages poked at Kane's torso, a move that the Qyntarak knew to be intimidating to humans. It was not wrong about that.

"You are th-th-the most arrogant human I know. When the governor is done w-with you, you w-will learn your place. The fa-fascination with humans that Torkanuux carries w-will pass and yo-yo-your kind will f-f-f-fade."

Glaring at a Qyntarak was pointless since they couldn't see it but Kane did so anyway.

"Will that be all?"

The blunt pincer around his neck tightened and he wheezed. The antennae waggled in circles again. "You come to me pe-personally for work for yo-your crew. And to review progress."

Kantarka-Ta released its grip and Kane's hand went to his neck involuntarily, the instinctive self-defense reflex taking precedence over his ego's desire to appear strong.

The alien croaked a command in its own language and the door reopened.

Once through the doorway, Kane said, "Your Fs are getting sloppy and you still slur S sounds, which is weird given that you don't have a tongue." The closing door obstructed his view of the alien swaying with rage.

"Thank goodness killing me would be bad for business," he muttered at the closed door.

Chapter 13: Marsh

THE VIDEO OF Clint Donovan looked like a rush job. His face wasn't centered in the frame and distracting shadows danced when his head and hands moved.

"Marsh, I'm recording this as a backup in case something happens before I can explain everything in person. It's time, old friend."

Clint changed to a different language and Polk paused the playback several seconds in.

"What the hell is he talking?"

"French. And a bit of Latin."

"What kind of unholy hensuckle are you two mixed up in that you're talking in dead languages?"

"French isn't a dead language."

"It is here, but that's beside the point. I need to know what he's saying."

"Why?"

"Why? Because I need to know what I'm mixed up with.

An old man and a kid from the woods show up with a data vault in a piece of bone with a video of some guy in a science uniform talking in French and nacking Latin? This ain't some water purifier falling off the back of a transport. If you guys are Claimers, you better tell me right now and then get out of my town while you still can."

"We're not Reclamationists. Yes, he was a state-licensed scientist. So was I until I chose a different path. We spoke French when we were young and we learned Latin in school because that's the language of scientific naming. It's just our way. Nothing sinister or treacherous there."

"He said in case something happens and that it's time. Doesn't sound like a trip down memory lane to me."

"If you'll play the rest of the video, I'll let you know."

"I play, you translate. In real time."

"Fine."

Polk started the video from the beginning and Marsh translated.

"It's time, old friend. I hope things have gone well for you and that your people are keeping alive some of the old ways. Our work here has proceeded as you predicted it would years ago. No doubt you've heard rumors. Temperature translation suits, gravity control equipment modified for human operators, and lots of genetic engineering. We've raised children with tolerance for extreme gravity variations and even high g-force acceleration. One kid could carry on a conversation at 14g.

"We've also had success with introducing thermal vision. One group of subjects had hybrid vision, able to see colors and temperatures. From a scientific point of view, it has been incredible.

"But I've been uncomfortable with the way patients have been managed for a long time. Like animals instead of people. With the help of allies in the Qyntarak leadership, I was able to get new policies implemented so that patients could at least live with the families of the human researchers instead of in glorified cages. I was raising a girl myself. Elle, a clever and resourceful young woman. If all goes according to plan, you will have met her already. Although, if you're watching this, we're on plan B.

"Elle's become like my own daughter. If something has happened to me, please look after her.

"All those years ago, we agreed on a few things when the two of us decided to go separate ways."

Marsh said two but that was not an accurate translation. On the video, Clint had said trois. Three, not two. It was a calculated risk—it didn't seem like Polk knew any French and Marsh didn't trust him enough to talk about Nora.

Polk didn't notice the brief deception, and Marsh continued to translate without faltering.

"We agreed to focus on the big picture and the long game. That we would do our small part to protect humanity, to contribute in some way to the long-term survival of our people even if we were no longer the dominant species. We agreed that if our personal situations ever demanded it, we would be available for each other. Most importantly, we agreed that we would not sit idly if the situation ever became so dire that it demanded action.

"Well, my friend, the situation has become dire. My contacts in the leadership leaked to me that a new law is coming. Humans are being reclassified. We will effectively become livestock on our own planet."

Polk stopped the playback again. "I told you if you were Claimers to get out. This maniac sounds like a Claimer propagandist to me."

Marsh felt lightheaded. "And I already told you we're not Claimers. I don't believe Clint was either. He's not a radical or an activist. But if what he's saying is true…"

"I want you out. Pay your bill and leave."

"We're not paying until we see the whole thing."

"Listen, old man…" Polk gripped Marsh's shirt sleeve. Walker, who had been watching silently, grabbed Polk's wrist and twisted it. The man was a couple decades older but the boy was strong from a life of manual labor. Polk lost his grip on Marsh and swore at Walker. "You two are a pain in the ass. Get out."

"Let's all just settle down," Marsh said. "Polk, you and I have a decent history. You're a business man. This video is just the rambling of an old man who's dead now anyway. Let it play and get paid. No one will ever know we were here."

Polk's eyes rolled upward as he considered the situation. Whether persuaded by the silver or the unexpected strength of Walker's grip or an urge to hear the rest of the video, Polk resumed the playback without further comment.

Marsh listened then said, "It's time for Elle and me to follow your lead. We are abandoning the research lab to live off the land where we can still enjoy some freedom. If something happens to me, I pray that you will welcome Elle into your community. She is smart and has a strong work ethic. I hope you never have to hear this message. I am looking forward to seeing you face to face soon."

"That's it?" Polk said. "No offense to your friend but that was a little underwhelming."

Marsh shrugged.

"Now you leave and I don't want to see you again. Next time you need to acquire something for your little commune, go elsewhere, understand?"

"As you say." Marsh dropped three rough silver coins and seven copper ones into Polk's outstretched hand.

Polk frowned at the sum. "That's not enough."

"That's all we have."

Polk clamped his hand shut. "Then you'd better go and don't bother coming back to Alma at all. No one's going to deal with you once I spread word that you can't pay your fees. I hope hearing from your dead pal was worth it."

Marsh clasped Walker's shoulder. "Let's go."

They left the tavern and then the town.

Once they were well beyond the last building, it was Walker who broke the silence. "That doesn't seem like it was worth it."

"No, I suppose it would seem that way if my translation had been accurate. Clint didn't ask us to welcome Elle into our community."

Chapter 14: Court

THREE CLANGS OF the bell.

Bear in the village.

Court swung his feet to the ground from the bunk he'd been napping on.

"Elle?"

No reply.

Where is she?

The fog from sleep was still heavy as he pulled on his boots.

Apple picking, she went harvesting with some villagers.

He grabbed a pot and a wooden spoon on his way outside. A bear would leave on its own if given the chance. It didn't want to be around humans any more than the humans wanted it in their village. Court just had to follow protocol— make sure none of the children were roaming in the wrong spot and bang a pot to encourage the animal to move northward through the cabins. He'd done it at least a dozen times over the years.

A mother and daughter were returning to the cabin next to Court's, the little girl almost running to keep up with her mom.

"Where is it?" Court asked.

The girl pointed. "Dat way. By da hospidal."

Court winked at her. "Thanks."

He walked quickly but with caution. Sneaking up on a scared bear was a good way to get an extended visit to the "hospidal." He heard a couple bangs on a pot then someone hollered, "Stop."

Court quickened his pace and found a less-than-ideal scenario. Several villagers were out with pots and pans. The bear was slapping its paws on the ground and snorting at Brighton. Court could hear the clacking of the bear's molars as it opened and closed its mouth. It was agitated and scared. Brighton was only eight but he knew protocol. This shouldn't be happening.

Standing between two cabins in the middle of the bear's escape route was Elle, a basket of apples locked in the death grip of her white-knuckled hands.

Court waved his hand at her, motioning for her to back up. She nodded in understanding.

He kept his voice soft and calm. "Brighton, back away. Slowly."

The boy took a step back and the bear lunged forward. It would be a bluff meant to reinforce Brighton's retreat. The boy yelped and triple stepped backward. Then an apple struck the bear in the side of the head. It grunted and its ears folded back as it turned. Another apple hit the bear's neck and it started to charge. Court didn't think this one would be a bluff and he sprinted after it, not considering what would happen when he tackled a black bear with only a pot and spoon in hand. A third apple hit the bear on the nose and it let out a high-pitched barking sound as its charge faltered.

"Get out of the way," Court shouted at Elle.

She had an apple ready to throw in her hand but she jumped to the side, almost slamming into the wall of a cabin, and Court screamed while smacking the spoon against his pot. With a clear path in front of it, the bear didn't stop.

Others joined in and they chased the unwelcome guest with their din as it ran across the clearing beyond the village and crashed through a stand of birch saplings.

Court returned to Elle who was staring at the apples trampled by the bear.

"What in the nacking hell is wrong with you?"

"You told me to throw apples at it."

"Are you insane? I told you to back away."

"You went like this." She waved her arm in a throwing motion.

"I was telling you to back up."

"That's clearly a signal for throwing."

Court pointed to Brighton who was being led away by his mother, the front of his pants soaked through. "The bear was bluffing. That's what they do. You start throwing things at it and it becomes unpredictable. Brighton could've been seriously hurt. Or worse."

One of the parents, Andrus, jammed a finger into Court's chest. "This is your fault. Marsh left you in charge of watching the girl. Have you taught her any of the protocols?"

Andrus poked Court again and he grabbed the man's finger. Court had fast reflexes and a low tolerance for accusations. He wasn't going to take this from Andrus. The guy had a lot of bluster for someone who let the garlic crop die.

"Bear visits are rare. It wasn't a high priority." He squeezed the finger and Andrus squirmed.

"Let go of me." Andrus pushed Court and he let go of the finger. "Mind your place, boy."

Court clenched his jaw involuntarily. He heard the faint voice of Marsh in his mind, a memory from a lesson long ago.

Control yourself first so you can control your surroundings.

Easy for Marsh to say when everyone respected and deferred to him. Court didn't realize he'd squeezed his hand into a fist until he felt Elle wrap her hands around it.

"I'm sorry," she said. "I didn't know. And Court's right, there have been other things to focus on, like pulling my own weight around here."

"Do better next time." Andrus spun in place and marched off toward the gardens.

Court looked down at Elle's hands on his. She let go and he felt a little disappointed.

"Next time you do better with your hand signals." After an awkward moment of silence, they both laughed. Genuine laughter that melted the tension. It felt good. He hadn't heard her laugh before. He liked it.

"Court."

He turned to see Colleen waving at him.

"Can you go relieve Paulo from watch and tell him to come see me? You can take Elle with you. Wouldn't hurt for her to learn about keeping watch."

"Of course," he said.

Getting to the watch platform required climbing stairs so steep they were almost a ladder. When they were near the top, Court called up, "Hey, Paulo, Colleen wants to see you. She asked me to relieve you."

"About the bear, I suppose."

Court chuckled. "Hard to imagine it's about anything else. What happened?"

"I don't know. It came barreling in like the forest was burning down, and it was really moving. I didn't even have time to grab a noisemaker."

Elle pulled herself up onto the platform after Court. "A noisemaker?"

Paulo flipped open a container and pointed at a miniature mag gun.

"Another Marsh invention," Court said. "Fires a special arrow that makes a loud noise when it hits something."

Paulo pointed at the ground. "If something wanders into the clearing and doesn't leave when you yell at it, you fire one of them at the ground between the animal and the village. Scares the spit out of them most of the time and they take off back the way they came."

"And scares the teeth off the little kids in the village," Court added.

"Alright," Paulo said, "I best be getting over to see Colleen."

When Paulo was gone, Elle asked, "How often do bears come into the village?"

"Not very often. Young ones'll wander into the clearing every year until they learn about the noisemakers. It's pretty rare to get one right in the village. Once every year or two.

Strange for this time of year. Usually, it's in the spring when they're hungry after waking up from hibernation."

Elle stared off into the trees. "So something out there must have scared it."

Chapter 15: Kane

KANTARKA-TA UNCURLED its upper body to expose its feeding slit. It was as long as Kane's forearm. A thick, opaque mucus hung in strands between a dozen mandibles as they pushed open the slit. Kantarka-Ta leaned forward onto its pile of chilled meat. Kane guessed it was gorilla based on the smell but he was no expert.

Kantarka-Ta wasn't the only Qyntarak to develop a taste for primate but he had an extreme proclivity for it. When the new laws come into effect, it wouldn't be out of the question for human meat to appear on its plate, and Kane suspected it wouldn't be the first time for Kantarka-Ta.

When is it too much?

The question was haunting him more frequently these days. One of his informants had said they were selling out their species. The next day, he took his own life.

No, we're just trying to survive like everyone else.

Kane had access that let him occasionally influence

decisions that impacted humans. That was more than he'd be able to do if he was blacklisted and unable to work. And changes were going to come regardless. He might as well be comfortable while they did. That was more than most people could hope for.

Kantarka-Ta finished pushing meat through the slit with its mandibles then retracted them so the slit could close. Kantarka-Ta folded over its upper body, returning to the natural standing position of a Qyntarak.

Kane was careful to hold his place and keep his expression neutral. Kantarka-Ta was skilled at reading human body language, a rare talent among Qyntarak. It was unnecessary for it to invite Kane in during its feeding time. It wanted him to be intimidated. He refused to be.

"Kane," it hissed, "how rude of me to not of-f-fer you any."

Kane tapped the helmet of his suit. "Translator's on. No need to make me suffer listening to your English."

Kantarka-Ta leaned back in irritation and Kane suppressed a smile. Perhaps he'd gotten too comfortable taking shots at this particular Qyntarak. Even though they both reported to the governor, they were not equals. He didn't want to end up on its feeding tray at some point.

"Genuine suffering in reality I wish on you, ape."

"Ape? That's over the line—"

"Shut your talking hole." The translation didn't convey the intensity of the message. Through the helmet's thermal overlay, Kane saw the hot spots at the base of the Qyntarak's antennae. It was not in a good mood. "We have business."

Kane dropped his chin and took a step back, a human variation of a Qyntarak yielding the floor. His instincts were telling him to defuse the interaction rather than escalate it.

"Your team has the requirement to investigate a report from the minor city of Alma."

"Alma? That's near where Donovan was taken down."

"Accurate. Donovan is part of the subject of the investigation. Two human males went to Alma with a data vault two days before today. It stored a recording of Clint Donovan. Clint Donovan talked about the improved laws and a subject from the research organization. A local security team searched the area where Clint Donovan was terminated but the body and transport are not there any longer. You are required to go in the company of your staff and sanitize."

"Two days ago? Why are we just hearing of this now?"

"It took time for the intelligence to ascend the layers of management. A local freelancer sold the information because the two human males did not pay adequate prices for services."

"Do we have a copy of the recording?"

"No."

"And what about the research subject?"

"Clint Donovan was the guardian for a human female patient. The location of that patient is unknown."

"Was she reported missing?"

"No. Not until staff were questioned."

"So people were covering for Donovan."

"Data is insufficient to create that conclusion."

"Did he take her with him?"

"The security staff who tracked Clint Donovan said no."

"So you have a dead scientist, a missing patient, a video leaking sensitive information, and at least three people who know about it. And you thought my organization wouldn't be needed anymore. Someone's got to clean up your messes."

Kantarka-Ta flung its food tray across the room, spraying Kane's ambassadorial suit with the remnants of blood mixed with alien mucus. "Do the job you are required to do."

He looked down at his suit.

Gross.

At least someone else would have to clean that mess.

"Anything else?"

"Yes. The two humans who carried the recording. The older human is called Marsh Lapin."

"Should that name mean something to me?"

"Marsh Lapin was my staff."

Chapter 16: Court

Court thought Marsh looked exhausted. The trip to Alma and back had been hard on the old man.

In a break from protocol, Court and Elle were seated at the council table with the council members. They had only invited Elle, but she'd insisted on having Court with her, so the council had brought in a pair of campfire stools for them. Marsh was recounting the details of his journey with Walker.

"His instructions at the end were a little cryptic. He asked if I would have our friend give Elle a tour and ask her how the suit compares to old A2 jackets. To be honest, I don't know what it means except the part about a friend giving a tour."

"The tour guide?" Elle said.

"I didn't understand the reference at first but when Clint said 'the three of us' in the recording, I knew he meant Nora. We worked on a research project together. She was an anthropologist and used to make extra money doing tours of the city, showing visitors the historic sites. The tour guide is Nora. That's the friend Clint wants me to take Elle to see."

"But why?" Court asked.

"That I don't know. Elle, what did he tell you about her?"

"He didn't tell me anything. We left in a hurry. He came rushing in and said it wasn't safe anymore and we had to leave. That we had to go find the rabbit and the tour guide. The old motorcycle was waiting outside, I don't know where he got it. He sealed me in the suit and we left. We didn't stop until—"

Her voice caught. Court had an unexpected urge to comfort her, to hold her hand or wrap his arm around her, but he resisted the impulse. It wouldn't be appropriate in a gathering with the council, he knew that, and he suspected he'd receive a sharp elbow to the ribs from Elle if he did.

Paul, the bald councilperson, asked, "What are you proposing we do?"

"Clint was my friend, and this was his dying request of me. I need to honor that. But my first obligation is to the ongoing stability of the village. So this is my proposal: I would like a six month leave of absence and the blessing of the council to go with Elle to find Nora Barrett."

Colleen broke the heavy silence. "Marsh, you can't be serious. You're still recovering from your trip to Alma. And do you even know where to start looking for someone you knew forty years ago?"

"It's been a while since I checked in on her but I know she was a professor at the old University of Toronto until it was closed."

"That was a dozen years ago, at least," Paul said. "She could be anywhere now. And not to be indelicate, but she might not even be alive still."

Marsh did not relent. "I understand there are uncertainties, but doing nothing is a bigger risk to the village than not trying. I don't mean to be insensitive, Elle, but you are a fugitive from a state-sponsored research center. At some point, they'll come looking for you."

"No, I understand. Dr. Donovan was the only family I had. If getting to this Nora Barrett was important enough to give up everything we knew, I want to go."

"Marsh, you're chair of the council," Colleen said. "It's not as simple as just taking some time off."

"Ah, but it is. The protocols clearly cover this type of scenario. As vice chair, you'll become acting chair and the council will elect an interim member during my leave."

"Yes, but—"

"And I nominate Court as interim council member in my absence."

"What?" Court and Paul blurted out in unison.

"He apprenticed with me so he knows how I see things. He'll be able to represent my point of view well enough. And he doesn't have a family to care for so he has the time for council business."

"He doesn't have a family because he's barely of age," Paul said.

"But he is of age. That's all that matters for serving on the council."

Colleen held up a finger to halt Paul's response. "Court, Elle, I think you two should wait outside for this discussion."

The two of them waited near the council's cabin long enough for Court to note the shadows of trees slowly drifting across the wall. When the door swung open, Paul walked past them without saying a word. Councilpersons Anica and Jess spoke to each other with hushed voices. Only Marsh and Colleen stopped.

"The council voted you in as interim member during Marsh's absence. As acting chair, I will coordinate your orientation activities. We might be a small village but there's plenty you will need to familiarize yourself with. We'll start the day after tomorrow. I need some time to prepare and do my own knowledge transfer with Marsh before he leaves. Any questions?"

"Only a hundred or so. I wasn't prepared for this."

"I can appreciate that but I mean any immediately pressing questions."

"No, I don't think so."

"Alright, then clear your calendar and buckle up."

"I don't know what that means."

"It's an old figure of speech. It means to get ready, you're going to be busy."

"Oh."

Colleen turned to Marsh. "Can we talk in private?"

"Of course. Just give me a few minutes. I'll meet you back here. Court, walk with me."

The two men walked the perimeter of the village, something they used to do together every few days when Court was apprenticing with Marsh.

"I feel it's only fair to warn you that the vote was not unanimous."

"Paul?"

"And Anica. They share concerns about your age. They think I'm playing favorites."

"So a three to two vote. Not a very welcoming start."

"Give them a few weeks to adjust. Work hard and be pleasant. Soon enough, the demands of daily tasks will outweigh their concerns and you'll simply be part of the team."

"What if that doesn't happen?"

"It will, I'm confident. Besides, it will be a tremendous learning opportunity for you either way. Consider it an advanced apprenticeship, a little bonus lesson from me."

"I'm worried about you going away by yourself."

"I'll hardly be alone. The whole point is to take Elle."

"I mean without someone who knows how to survive in the woods. You should be taking someone else with you, like you did for your trip to Alma."

"That's part of why I wanted to speak with you. I'm not willing to put anyone from the village at risk. I might have completely misinterpreted Clint's message. Or Nora might, in fact, be long dead as Paul suggests. And I think Elle is more of a survivor than you give her credit for. But she is lacking in some basic training. I'd like for you to spend the day tomorrow teaching her as much as you can. Show her what's safe to eat. Make sure she can build a fire. Teach her how to hunt with a mag gun. Show her how to dress and roast what she kills. Rabbit as well as dog or coywolf if you can."

"That'll be a full day. I'd better go tell Elle to be ready for an early start tomorrow."

Chapter 17: Court

COURT AND ELLE spent the morning collecting edible plants and talking about the unpleasant effects of eating the ones they weren't collecting. Near midday, they chanced upon a rabbit sitting in a clearing. Court handed the mag gun to Elle. She hesitated, her face twisted in disgust. She finally brought the gun up and fired, the arrow lodging in the upper hind leg. The rabbit tried to limp away; Court was on it in an instant.

Elle gave a tiny wail as the animal twitched in his hands.

"This time you'll need to watch. First thing you do, break the neck." Court grabbed the neck and snapped the head back with his other hand. Elle flinched as if the movement had hurt her. She watched in silence while he showed her how to skin and clean it.

"I really don't want to do that myself."

"You'll change your mind when you're out here half-starved and living off sour high bush cranberries."

She was more at ease with fire building, which she took to as naturally as she had the mag gun. They sat on the ground and ate a hearty lunch of roasted rabbit, bittercress, peppergrass, and thistle.

"It's not potatoes and corn but it'll keep you alive," Court said as he licked food from his fingers. "What did you think?"

"I didn't mind the thistle root."

"That's good because it's easy to find. I have to say that was a successful morning. I thought it would take longer. Only other thing Marsh asked me to show you was how to dress a dog or coywolf."

"Why would I need to know that?"

"Feral dogs are easy targets and still common enough the closer you get to where people used to live. We'll have to walk an hour or two to find one but I know where a few packs have claimed some territory."

"But why would I need to dress one?"

He raised his eyebrows, trying to understand her question. "Wait, do you think—" He started to chuckle. "Did you think I meant put clothes on a dog?" His chuckle grew into a full belly laugh. She threw a rabbit bone at him and he rolled to one side so that it sailed past him.

"Stop it."

"I mean, sure, maybe that could help you and Marsh survive your trip. I'm not sure how but it might."

She threw a pine cone that bounced off his temple.

"Ow."

"You deserved that."

"Dressing is what we call prepping the animal after the kill."

"I know that."

"Sure, now that I've told you."

She threw another pine cone at him but her small grin told him it was in fun.

Court felt light as he packed the uncooked half of the rabbit and Elle buried the smoldering remains of their fire.

"You will need to be careful with scavengers like dogs and coywolves too close to humans. If they're eating the gar—" He stopped abruptly. "Do you hear that?"

"The humming?"

"That sounds like a grav flyer, like the one that... No. The village. We have to get back. Now."

He didn't wait for her response. He snatched the mag gun and ammo pouch and ran. Branches snapped and whiplashed as he crashed through them at a full sprint.

The hum grew louder then softer as the flyer overhead outpaced him.

Marsh said they would come looking someday. It's too soon.

More humming. Another flyer passed overhead. Then a third.

No!

The undigested meal shook inside him. His lungs screamed for a break. He kept running. Only the village mattered. His legs burned but he didn't slow down. Ahead, he saw the forest brightening where the trees gave way to the clearing around the village.

He spotted a rabbit snare as his foot was about to go into its loop. Court jumped to one side to avoid it and pushed off the trunk of a tree to correct for the sudden change in direction. He lost just enough speed for Elle to catch up and tackle him.

"Get off me." He struggled to get back up, but she kept her full weight on his back.

"What are doing? You can't run in there with a toy gun. They'll shoot you before you get across the clearing."

"You don't know that. You don't know what's going on. I need to be there."

"I do know that. I watched them do it already. So did you."

He turned on his side enough to get his arm free. He grabbed her hair and pulled. She rolled off, moving fast enough to prevent him from ripping a handful from her scalp.

"Court, stop. I don't want to lose you like this. Please." He hesitated on his hands and knees. "They will kill you if you just charge in there."

"What am I supposed to do? Hide out here and hope they leave after a friendly chat?"

"Let's just look first. Quietly. Alright?"

He nodded and hated himself for it. Even if she was right.

Chapter 18: Court

THEY MOVED ALONG the perimeter of the village, staying a dozen trees deep in the woods, until they found a vantage point through a gap in the forest near the southwest trail. The grav flyers floated just above the clearing. Court counted fourteen armed men in body armor. Men, not Qyntarak. He estimated thirty villagers were huddled together, standing back sixty or seventy feet, watching.

He whispered, "Is it normal for humans to use grav flyers?"

"I've never seen it before, at least not at the research center. The Qyntarak always fly them."

One of the outsiders led Marsh into the clearing, yanking on the old man's free arm while he tried to keep pace with his walking stick. Court tensed.

Another man disembarked from a flyer. He wasn't wearing full armor, just some type of protection over his torso.

"Marsh Lapin, yes?"

"Who are you?"

"I am, I hope, the bearer of good news. My friends call me Kane and I do hope we'll be friends at the end of this."

"Parking three of these alien monstrosities in our yard is a poor first impression."

"It's a long walk here and I'm afraid that my schedule didn't allow for such a rustic journey." Kane laughed at his own comment.

Marsh didn't. "And what brings you so far out of your way?"

"Some nasty business unfortunately. I represent the affairs of Governor Torkanuux. There was a defector from a research facility recently. A man named Clint Donovan. I believe you and he are acquainted."

"We were, a very long time ago."

"Dr. Donovan, it seems, carried off some of our intellectual property when he left. We have reason to believe he brought it here and left it in your possession. I've come to collect it. As consideration for your help, the governor's office is prepared to supply you with a full restock of your medical field clinic and commit to buying your trade goods at a twenty percent premium for the next two years. I am led to believe that your community, although isolated, does trade food and pelts in order to buy the things you cannot make or grow."

"That's generous but I'm afraid I don't know what you're looking for."

Kane put his hands on Marsh's shoulders. "You disappoint me, Marsh. Our scanners already found the antique motorcycle he rode here. How can we be friends if we're not honest with each other?"

"We found Clint and his motorcycle on an old road. He was dead already, so we buried him."

"What about the data vault?"

"What data vault?" Marsh's voice sounded convincing but his eyes betrayed him.

Kane didn't miss the involuntarily movement, the eyes glancing down, confirming that a precious item was still safe. He patted Marsh's pockets then his sides and chest. He yanked the necklace from under the old man's shirt. "A bit macabre wearing this, isn't it?" Kane shoved the assortment of bone and antler fragments into a pocket on his leg. "What about the girl?"

"What girl?"

"Honestly, Mr. Lapin—"

"Doctor. It's Dr. Lapin."

"Of course, my mistake. I am trying to be civil here. It's not your fault that Donovan defected or that he kidnapped a girl in the process. We just want our property back and to reward you for your help. Let's not play games."

"Believe me, none of this seems like a game to me. There's no girl here."

"Tsk tsk tsk. You know, a hazard of my job is that it's easy to lose hope in humanity when you are lied to day after day after day. You get to be good, though, at telling when someone is lying to you. And when you can't tell, you just assume. If she's here, my team will find her. If she's gone, we will track her. You've only hurt your community by being pig-headed. And for nothing."

Kane waved his hand and his small army raised their weapons. "Let's make it quick, gentlemen, I have a meeting to get back for."

Court started moving when the first shot rang out. A blue jay flashed across his line of sight as it fled from the noise. He raised the mag gun and looked past the sight marks as he moved forward. The reports of more shots echoed around him. He saw bodies falling. Paulo went down. Anica was staring down at him when bullets tore through her and she rolled forward, her shoulders following the direction her head had been looking, and she crumpled on top of Paulo.

The screams and cries only lasted for few seconds after the gunfire stopped. It was over so fast.

"How could you?" Marsh croaked. He lunged at Kane who stepped to one side then kicked Marsh's knee, sending him to the ground with a howl.

"You had your chance. Places like this are allowed to exist as long as they aren't inconvenient. A flea on a dog, out of sight, out of mind until you become a nuisance." Kane unhooked a baton from his side. It was long enough that he only had to bend slightly to jab it into Marsh's chest. Marsh convulsed then fell still. Kane pressed the baton into him again with no reaction.

Court collapsed to his knees on the path a few paces from the clearing. The trees around him seemed to spin and sway. He wanted to scream but couldn't.

What could he do? His little mag gun arrows wouldn't pierce their armor. He'd be dead in seconds. Then they'd take Elle. Or kill her.

There are still a lot of people in their cabins or hiding somewhere. I'm a council member now. I need to survive this. I owe it to them, I owe it to Marsh.

The thought was still coalescing in his mind when the

men spread out in a light jog. Explosions followed within moments. The village had twenty-seven cabins for living quarters, the hospital, the council cabin, and three communal buildings. Smoke billowed from all of them in less than a minute.

Then more gunfire. And more screams.

"You're too exposed," Elle said. She tugged at his shirt sleeve but it wasn't enough to move him. "Court, come on, they're going to see you." She pulled harder. He didn't resist and toppled to the ground. "Court, hide, please," she pleaded.

She kicked him and he grasped what she was saying. He crawled behind a tree a few feet off the trail.

"They're killing everybody. What are we supposed to do?"

"We stay alive," she said. "For now, we just stay alive."

Chapter 19: Kane

"Did you see that old woman with the fur shawl? What a zoid."

"At least their buildings lit up fast so we could get out of there. I was worried I'd get dysentery if we stayed out there too long."

"You get that from eating stuff. Were you planning to cook dinner with them?"

"Jones, Wilkes, shut it," Kane barked over the comm. Some of these guys were monsters. The humanity had been trained out of them to the point that they cared less about human lives than Kantarka-Ta did.

Wilkes asked, "What's the problem, boss?"

"Show a bit of decency. They lost their lives because of bad circumstances, not because they lived like that. Don't dishonor the dead."

Kane couldn't see their faces behind him in the grav flyer to know whether they were showing remorse or rolling their eyes. Did it even matter? At least the comm was quiet.

I hope some of these sons of bitches have nightmares too.

After a few minutes of quiet, the men slipped into chatter about home life and plans for the weekend. Kane took some small comfort in knowing they still had that much humanity in them.

The other two flyers had flown straight back to New Boston. Kane's flyer had to detour to Toronto so he could personally deliver the data vault to a quantum computing lab that would crack whatever encryption its data was hiding behind. The extra ninety minutes of travel time was inconvenient but worth it to gain favor with Torkanuux. With Kantarka-Ta on the prowl for more power, Kane couldn't afford any mishaps. He would place the data vault in the hand of the lab's director, recording the entire exchange. If something went wrong after that, it wouldn't be Kane left holding the short straw.

Chapter 20: Elle

THE GRAV FLYERS had been gone for at least fifteen minutes and Court was catatonic. They needed to make a plan while they still had plenty of daylight.

"Court, we have to check if anyone is still alive." Elle shook his shoulders, but he didn't respond. "I'm going to look."

He didn't move even when she slid the mag gun out of his hands. The gun wasn't much protection, but she felt better having it as she approached the fallen bodies.

"Can anyone hear me? Does anyone need help?"

There was no moaning, no small movements. Nothing. It was hard to look at them. It was a grotesque slaughter, and she knew there were more dead in the buildings.

Maybe it's better that Court didn't come. This was his family.

The charred ruins of the cabins stood like grotesque monuments. Those monsters had let them burn while they methodically slaughtered each individual. When they had finished, they'd stopped the fires, but Elle didn't understand how. These people, whoever they were, had access to technologies that humans weren't supposed to have. If they wanted her, it was only a matter of time. At least they had left, which meant they didn't know she was here. But how long would that last?

She moved from cabin to cabin, stopping to throw up several times from the sights and smells until she was coughing up nothing but drops of clear liquid.

"Hello?" she shouted. "Anyone? Please? Someone."

She kept shouting until her throat hurt.

The last place she checked was the hospital. Vaidehi was sprawled on the steps, her torso torn to shreds.

Why are they using alien tech but shooting people with guns?

It didn't make sense but it also didn't matter. Elle closed Vaidehi's eyes and sat beside her. She clutched the doctor's blood-caked hand in her own. It felt unnatural but she didn't let go.

So much death.

She sobbed like she had on her first day here. Long after her eyes had stopped spilling tears, her body continued to heave.

She wasn't sure how long she sat there, but the sun was casting long shadows when she heard Court.

"They're all gone," he said. His eyes were puffy and the dirt on his face was streaked with lines.

"I know."

"Marsh... they didn't shoot him. I thought, maybe..."

"They used a Scorpion on him. It's a neuroelectrical

immobilizer. At full strength, it's just as lethal as a gun. They didn't spare anyone, not even the kids."

Fresh tears traced new lines down his cheeks, painting his grief on his face. It was beyond anything a person should know, and she had no idea what to say to that.

Neither of them moved for several minutes, until the sounds of rustling and soft thuds made their heads snap to attention. Elle gripped the mag gun and they followed the sound.

Did I miss someone?

She was sure she had checked everywhere. Her heart sank at what she saw. A dog was dragging one of the children toward the trees. It growled as they approached.

"Leave him alone," she hollered. The dog didn't stop and she raised the mag gun. Court pushed it back down.

"Nothing else dies today." He charged and shouted at the animal. It let go of the boy's leg but looked like it would stand its ground. Only at the last second did it turn and run.

"I thought there weren't dogs around here."

"That was a coywolf. It doesn't deserve to die for trying to eat. But it'll be back and probably with its pack. We need to do something. I don't want the animals to pick their bodies apart. That seems disrespectful."

Elle looked down at the dead boy. She didn't know his name, but she'd seen him playing in the village. There were so many of them, so many bodies. They buried their dead here. Elle remembered how long she'd needed to dig a hole large enough for just her helmet and suit.

"We can't bury them fast enough."

Court looked at the blackened remains of his home. "Let's move them into the meeting hall. Then we'll..." He choked on his words, and it took several breaths for him to find his composure. "Then we'll burn them there, together."

The stretcher from the hospital was still intact, so they used it to carry the deceased, starting with those lying out in the open. As they loaded each body onto the stretcher, Court would say the person's name. For some, he shared a story or a memory while they carried them. Elle felt fresh pangs of anguish with each one.

When they came to Walker's body, Court dropped to his knees and held the boy in his arms. He rocked back and forth cradling him.

"We should've taken him with us today. He'd still be alive if we'd just..."

Elle knelt beside Court and put a hand on his shoulder.

"This isn't your fault, Court."

"But if we'd only—"

"No, there was nothing we could have done. It's what we do now that matters, and we need to keep working. We're running out of light."

When the sun fell below the trees, they built several fires to keep the animals away and provide extra light while they worked. As the night drew on, the bodies grew rigid and harder to move. A few hadn't made it out of the cabins and were burned beyond recognition. Court made guesses about their identities but it was difficult in the dim moonlight.

By the time they were moving the last body, the sun was back in the sky, chasing away the damp chill.

Elle counted the bodies and then Court did the same.

"192. That's everyone. We're the only ones who survived."

They covered the bodies in straw, branches, and kindling from the village's firewood.

Elle's hair and clothes were drenched in sweat, and her arms were beginning to give out, but Court wasn't slowing down. He continued carrying more firewood.

"I need to rest," she said.

He dropped the wood from his arms and fell to the ground on the spot as if he had been waiting for her to give him permission to stop.

"Yeah, let's rest."

She lay down on the ground near him. The warmth of the rising sun almost felt comforting on her face.

I'll just close my eyes for a few minutes...

A soft prodding on her arm woke her. She had to squint against the sun when she tried opening her eyes. It wasn't high in the sky so she couldn't have been sleeping long.

Why is Court waking me up so soon?

She pushed away whatever he was poking her with. It was warm and humid. And it sniffed. She opened her eyes all the way and screamed. A coywolf showed its teeth as it snarled. Her mind raced trying to come up with a viable defense when she was flat on her back. It lunged and she swung her arm. Her fist bounced against the side of its head but without room for a full swing she hadn't connected with enough force to do any damage. Her arm burned as it slid against the tip of a fang.

The beast was on top of her instantly. She kicked and flailed to keep it from getting to her neck. It sunk its teeth into her forearm and she screamed louder. She smelled its foul breath as it snorted and growled. The coywolf shook its head, and she feared it would tear her arm off.

Then the animal lost its grip and flew off her with a yelp. Silhouetted by the sun, Court stood over her with pieces of firewood in his hands. He threw one at the coywolf's ribs then jumped between her and the animal, moving the other piece of wood from his left hand to his right. The coywolf growled and leaped. Court swung the piece of hardwood into the side of its snout. Something cracked as the wood made contact and the beast barreled into him with a whimper.

In the chaos of the collision, Court wrapped one arm around the coywolf's neck and another under its front legs. After several seconds of struggle, he locked his legs around its body and squeezed.

Elle ran for the mag gun. Her arm stung like it was on fire.

By the time she returned with the gun, the coywolf's resistance was little more than twitching. Court's face was tight with rage. It scared her. When the animal stopped moving, he relaxed his legs but kept squeezing the neck. Court made a guttural sound that turned into heaving sobs and a fresh flood of tears.

When he rolled the limp body away from himself, he took the mag gun and fired an arrow between two ribs.

"These things are scavengers," he said. "They'll keep coming as long as they smell death. We need to light the fire and get ourselves cleaned off. And find something for your arm."

"Vaidehi said there was corn whiskey somewhere. If it's still here, we can use it as an accelerant for the fire and a disinfectant my arm."

He pointed toward the hospital. "She kept hers stashed away. She sometimes gave it to patients for minor things to take the edge off when she didn't want to waste real painkillers. Maybe it survived the fire."

They moved cautiously through the remains of the village.

Elle feared another attack from behind every corner. Her arm throbbed with each step.

The inside of the hospital was in better shape than most of the village, its structure and contents clearly more fire resistant than the wooden cabins. There was damage from the explosives but the building itself had not caught fire and its metal cabinets showed promise for holding undamaged supplies.

"Here," Court said. It was a cabinet in the back of the building. "I think it's in here but it's locked."

Elle scanned the room in search of a key that would fit the old-fashioned mechanical lock. She didn't find one, but she found a tank marked OXYGEN. "We can use that. Thank goodness it didn't explode in here."

She didn't realize Court had left the room until he came back in with a metal shaft that he jammed into the cabinet and leaned into until the small lock gave way and the cabinet popped open. Inside was a glass jug holding at least ten liters of whiskey.

Court opened the jug and poured some on Elle's arm. She groaned through gritted teeth.

"I think that hurts worse than the actual bite did."

Court pried open more cabinets until he found first aid supplies. He wrapped Elle's arm in a splash pad and she dry swallowed several pills. He tried to convince her to take a few minutes to recuperate, but she insisted they get the fire started as soon as possible. She didn't want any more coywolf encounters.

They took the oxygen tank and whiskey to the meeting hall. Being careful not to step on anyone, Court waded through the straw and branches spreading the alcohol. Elle passed the oxygen tank to him and told him to leave it in the middle of the room with the valve open. It hissed ominously as he hurried out.

She lit a makeshift torch from the embers of a campfire and tossed it in. Flames rushed along the trails of corn whiskey, igniting the straw.

The fire moved swiftly, and they hurried away from the building. When the oxygen tank exploded, the meeting hall became a temporary inferno.

As it roared, the smell drove them further and further away until they had backed up across the clearing to the edge of the woods. They leaned against trees and watched the tops of the flames dance. Even in the midday light, the fire burned brightly.

"We should take the extra medical supplies with us," Elle said. "If there's anything small and valuable, we can sell it for food or supplies."

"What are you talking about? Carry it with us where?"

"To Toronto. That's our best place to start looking for Nora Barrett."

"Are you nacking insane? We can't go to Toronto. There's only us left. The chickens that haven't escaped need to be fed. The harvest needs to be finished. Vegetables and fruit need to be preserved for the winter. I need to rebuild my cabin. There's—"

"Court, the village is gone. It's pointless to stay here."

"It's not pointless. This is my home. We're not going to Toronto. End of discussion."

"Something bigger than us is happening, can't you see that? They're killing people because they're scared of what they know. I can't ignore that, not now. With or without you,

I'm going."

"Good luck lasting two days on your own." He stood and brushed evergreen needles from his pants. "I'm going to dress the coywolf."

Chapter 21: Britt

"Britt? Britt, you in here?"

She heard Bear calling her, but she hadn't composed herself yet so she didn't answer. She drew in several slow breaths. Obviously, he knew she was in here. He'd watched her go into the storage room. She wiped her eyes and willed them to stay dry.

"I'll be right there."

"The containers need to go out or we'll miss our window."

`"I said I'll be right there." She wasn't one to snap at her crew. She'd apologize to Bear later. He was right, of course. This shipment needed to go out. The *Willow Wisp* wouldn't be in range for another pickup for months. She had to pull herself together.

Britt checked her reflection in the screen of her tablet. Her eyes were red but that would pass. She touched her cheek, remembering how her makeup used to smudge on the rare occasions that something made her tear up. She didn't miss makeup but what she wouldn't give to get back her life when the things that made her sad were small concerns.

Britt pulled her shoulders back, filled her lungs, and pushed open the storage room door. Her small crew was waiting in the loading bay.

"What are you all lollygagging around for? I thought we had a shipment to get out."

Her boots clanged on the old metal stairs as she descended with Bear to the train platform. He hadn't been exaggerating, she'd cut it dangerously close. The grav train arrived in the time between her foot leaving the last step and touching the concrete floor.

The train's rate of deceleration would flatten a human or even a Qyntarak. That was good. That meant the train was all cargo, no passengers, exactly as their intel said.

She waved to Novak, and he motioned for her to hurry. She walked as quickly as she could, which wasn't very quick anymore.

"You're cutting it kind of close."

"We'll see how fast you are at my age." She handed him her tablet. "Here's our addition to the manifest."

Novak tapped his wrist computer against the screen. Both devices flashed green.

"Eight crates. Confirmed. Let's look it over."

Britt waved her finger in a circle over her head and Bear stomped back up the stairs. Overhead, five-foot-long crates slid off tracks and into the column of artificial microgravity that the train was generating above an empty compartment. Drones bumped and pushed the descending crates into position as they dropped at an unnaturally slow rate. Green lights popped on when the magnetic clamps inside the train took hold of the crates.

After all eight were in place, Novak opened the crates. Vacuum-sealed tea and coffee. Luxury items.

"Visual inspection complete," he said as he swiped a finger across his wrist computer. "Digitally signing the manifest changes."

"Keep your disgusting hands off me," a woman shouted from a nearby corridor.

Novak hurried toward the source of the voice and Britt followed. A woman dressed in little more than rags was waving her arms at the lone security guard. He looked hopelessly at Novak as they approached.

"What's the problem?" Novak asked.

"I'm not quite sure," the guard said.

"Oh, we've got a long list of problems here," the woman said. "Not the least of which is this asshole trying to grope me."

"I did not," the guard said to the woman. Then he repeated to Novak, "I didn't. She showed up out of nowhere and started raving like this."

"Raving! Oh, I see, I'm not some emotionally repressed man so obviously I'm a raving madwoman." She swung the bag she was carrying, missing the guard but losing her grip on it and sending it flying. The contents clattered out onto the concrete floor.

"Ma'am," Novak said, "this is a restricted area. You're not allowed to be here. We'll help you collect your things and then we need to escort you out."

Novak and the guard turned their backs to the open train compartment. Britt risked a quick look over her shoulder. From the loading bay above, Wilm jumped into the train's microgravity, hauling another five-foot-long crate. Chemical propellant thrusters in his suit helped speed his descent. He was in the train and gone from sight in less than four seconds. She grimaced at the thought of his rough landing. Impact-absorbing lining in a jumpsuit only did so much.

She began counting the seconds. *One... two... three... four...*

Wilm needed seventy-five seconds to override the magnetic locks, swap out the crate, reactivate the locks, and get back upstairs with the original crate.

"Ma'am, how did you get into this area?" the security guard asked.

"Don't you ma'am me. You can't cop a feel one minute then treat someone like an unwanted rodent the next and then make it up with a polite word or two. It doesn't work that way."

"Ma'am, miss, lady. Look, I'm sorry, whatever you think I did..."

The guard was flustered, which made Britt smile. The woman was showing the guard and Novak the door through which she'd entered.

Sixty... sixty-one... sixty-two...

Britt looked back again. Wilm and a crate were on their way back up to the loading bay.

Seventy... Seventy-one...

They were clear.

The woman in rags was gone and Novak was chastising the security guard.

"Great, the train is late now. Let's get this show on the road." Novak tapped on his wrist computer. The train compartment sealed itself shut, and the train glided away with a hum that belied its incredible mass and breakneck speed.

"What an unusual young woman," Britt said.

"I apologize for the commotion," Novak said as he glowered at the security guard.

With Novak's digital inspection seal on the train compartment, there was no risk of their crates being opened again before launch. Britt breathed a sigh of relief as she climbed the stairs.

Once back inside the safety of their cargo facility, she beamed at her small crew. "Excellent work, everyone. Bear, what was our official time?"

"Seventy-four seconds from jump to cargo doors closed. One second better than target."

The rag lady came in via the public entrance from the street.

"And Ainsley, what a performance." Britt pressed her hands over her heart. "You missed your calling in the theater, my dear."

"I thought that guard was going to piss himself when I accused him of touching me."

"An inspired improvisation. Bravo."

"Wouldn't it be easier to just buy off the guard?" Wilm asked. He was new to the crew. This was his first job.

"You'd think so," Bear said, "but the guards rotate out too frequently. Besides, the sneaky switcheroo is the fun part."

Wilm rubbed his shoulder. "Easy for you to say. You aren't the one slamming into the train."

Bear's massive chest and shoulders bounced as he laughed. "I did my time and I've got the bad knees to prove it. I can predict a storm better than the weather service."

"Plus it's far too expensive to buy Bear-sized jumpsuits." Britt patted his bulging chest and noticed a subtle shift in Wilm's body language. Did he have feelings for the big man? Britt made a mental note to keep an eye out for that. Romantic relationships were a no-go in her crew, not that she worried about Bear. His battered heart was already spoken for.

"Everyone into their street clothes," Bear said. "Leave one at a time. Britt and I will lock up."

Once Wilm and Ainsley had left, Bear looked at her with pursed lips. She knew what was coming.

"So, do you want to talk about it?"

"About what?"

"About whatever had you so upset earlier. We almost missed the train after two months of planning. It had to be something serious to distract you like that."

"You already know that I won't tell you."

He shrugged. "Fair enough. Thought I'd ask in case you needed to talk."

"Let's go." She put on her three-quarter brim hat. The style was in fashion and convenient for obscuring one's face from overhead cameras and nosy neighbors, even if it looked ridiculous. "I'm fine."

As fine as I can be after hearing that an old friend was killed.

Chapter 22: Elle

"Food is ready."

It was the first thing Court had said to her since she declared that she was going in search of Nora Barrett. The meal was a feast. Grilled coywolf, roasted potatoes, corn, carrots, spinach, beets, and turnips. All these things were new to her in the last week. All these foods. It had taken some convincing for her to accept the villagers' use of the word food to describe the meats and vegetables but she had acquiesced.

Elle ate greedily, realizing how hungry she had grown in the last twenty-four hours.

"That was good. Thank you."

"I figured we might as well eat it. What the animals don't get is going to rot anyway."

"Can't you dry it, like the apples?"

"Not if I'm not here."

"What do you mean?"

"I've been thinking about what you said, about something bigger happening and people dying because of it. Marsh spent decades here. If he was willing to leave, it's got to be serious. If these new laws are real and somehow there's a way to do something, then you should go and I should make sure you don't starve to death on the way."

"After all this, there's not much risk of starving. I could walk for days without eating again."

He smiled at that. It was a small smile, like his face wasn't ready to concede to anything positive yet, but it was something. It gave her hope that he wouldn't drown in the darkness. Watching him grieve was hard. They'd both lost everything they knew.

"Do you still want... I mean, is it alright for me to come with you?"

"Yes, definitely. I think it's best."

"Then it's settled. We'll do what you said and salvage what we can to sell. Hopefully, we can find enough supplies for the trip. There's an old storage cellar under the council's cabin. If it survived the fire, I think there are things from the outside world down there. It could be helpful."

"Then we should get started before the light's gone. We'll leave in the morning."

"Not yet. I have dessert."

"Dessert?"

He came back with two green balls.

"Watermelon," he said.

He sliced the fruit. The flavor exploded in Elle's mouth. It was unlike anything she'd ever eaten.

"This is amazing."

"I know, right? Watermelon's my favorite. We don't grow

much of it because it has a long season and it's a bit finicky about temperatures."

"I would grow only watermelon."

They both laughed at that. The watermelon left sticky residue on their hands and faces so Court fetched them a wash basin. Elle let her hands linger in the water. Even something as rustic as the simple bowl was a luxury they wouldn't have on the journey ahead.

Court said, "So we head for Toronto then? Since that's the last place Marsh knew that Nora Barrett was?"

"It's the best plan we have."

"How far is it?"

"I'm not sure."

"Roughly?"

"I don't know. It's west. Sort of west. West and a bit south, I think. I saw it on a map once. It's not close."

"You don't know how to get there or how far it is?"

"It's not like I've been planning this. I'm still trying to figure it out."

Elle's frustration was evident in her voice and she could see the irritation on his face.

He's still processing his loss. Try to be sensitive, Elle.

"Obviously," she said, "we can't just go wandering off in an arbitrary direction. What about Alma, where Marsh and Walker went? Could we find someone there to point us in the right direction?"

"Moriya. We should go see Moriya."

"Marsh's old friend? Vaidehi told me about her. You think she'll help?"

"She'll do it for Marsh. I've only met her a couple times but I know where she lives."

It took them most of an hour to dig out the entrance to the council cabin's cellar. The floor hatch had partially collapsed under debris, which saved them the trouble of breaking the lock, but it was arduous work clearing out the opening so they could squeeze in. An antique lantern hung from a hook. After a minute of experimentation, they realized that turning its crank handle powered the light.

"This place has been around since the first few years of the village. Hard to say what we'll find."

"This box says Marsh on it."

She slid the bin closer to Court but he only stared at it.

"Would you rather if I opened it?"

"Yeah, that would be better."

Elle flipped the clamping mechanisms that held the lid in place. Clouds of dust made it clear that the bin hadn't been open in years. The seal around the lid groaned as she pulled it off. She looked up at Court to gauge his reaction but he was looking away.

The bin didn't hold much: clothing items, a gold disk on a chain, and a small wood box containing a few papers.

"He would have been seventy-one next month, if this thing marked 'Birth Certificate' is right."

Court looked down. Elle understood how he was feeling, or at least she believed she could imagine how he was feeling. She was digging through the belongings of his mentor and friend, looking for anything of value, like a scavenger.

She flipped through a little blue booklet with the word PASSPORT stamped in gold lettering on the front.

"What's a passport?" she asked.

"No idea."

"It has his picture in it. Maybe you should keep it."

She passed the booklet to him and he rubbed his fingers on the pages delicately. His lips quivered and Elle feared she'd lose him again to his grief but he sucked in a deep breath.

"He looks so young."

They searched the rest of the cellar, finding relics from the former lives of some of the older villagers but little of obvious value until they came to a pouch. Inside, Elle found coins.

"Money," she said. "I wonder if it's still good."

Court knelt beside her to look more closely.

"Silver and copper, yeah, we can use that, at least in Chignecto where Moriya lives."

"Is this a lot?"

"I'm not sure. Marsh always handled the money when we went."

"Then we'll take it and find out."

They left the cellar with a metal-framed backpack, a few pieces of formal-looking clothing that Court thought they could barter in Chignecto, and the passport with Marsh's photo.

In the hospital, they made of pile of everything that didn't appear damaged. They found splash pads, painkillers, a small bottle labeled antibiotics, and Vaidehi's tablet. Court packed everything into the backpack then they collected all the dried food they could find in the village. The fires had destroyed so much that they only found enough for a few days at the most.

"We'll have to hunt along the way."

Elle nodded. She didn't like it but she knew they'd have to

eat.

The sky was still bright but the sun was below the trees by the time they finished packing. They used a pair of harvesting bags to hold more food, some water, a pair of blankets, the pouch of money, and Marsh's passport.

"I don't want to sleep in the village," Court said.

"The woods?"

"If you don't mind."

"No, that will be fine. We still need to do one more thing first."

The sky was a gloomy gray when they finished digging up Elle's suit and helmet. To her surprise, Court hadn't insisted on an explanation for why she'd buried it. He'd accepted that she'd done it and that they had to retrieve it for their trip. According to Marsh, it was the reason for their trip.

They slept under a tarp at the edge of the woods. Their blankets reeked of smoke, not the pleasant smell of a campfire but the harsh smell from entire buildings burning. Sleep came easily for Court but the smoke made Elle think of the villagers. They'd done nothing to deserve their horrific demise. She squeezed her fists and then her eyes, pressing out the tears that had been building up. The night air was cool when she felt her exhaustion dragging her to sleep but that was when Court started muttering. His words were nonsensical but the emotions were clear: terror and desperation.

She rolled to her side, an unforgiving root digging into her arm. She found one of Master Zheng's meditations in the recesses of her mind and murmured the mantra to herself. When sleep did take her, she dreamed fitfully.

A rustling woke her. The sun was up but the air was still

cool. She felt damp and realized this would be her new reality for an unknown number of mornings. An acute feeling of loss and a sad longing for Dr. Donovan washed over her. Her stomach clenched at the thought but there was another rustling that pulled her thoughts back to the more immediate concern of safety. She was embarrassed to realize the rustling was just a squirrel over head in the tree. She rolled over to see if it had woken Court as well.

He wasn't there.

Chapter 23: Elle

ELLE THREW OFF the blanket and got up to her knees. She was in the same spot as the night before. The backpack was still beside her, but one of the harvesting bags was gone. The mag gun was hidden under the other. She moved it aside and took the gun.

Turning in a circle, she looked for Court or any sign of a threat. The morning air was still, and she heard only the chirping of birds.

A branch snapped behind her and she whirled around, holding the mag gun up and ready to fire at whatever was there.

"Morning," Court said.

"You're lucky I didn't shoot you."

"Why would you shoot me?"

"Because you were gone, and I didn't know what happened to you."

"You'd shoot me for that?"

"No, I mean you're lucky I didn't think you were—never mind, just tell me next time if you're going somewhere."

"You were asleep. You want me to wake you up to tell you I'm off for a piss and to get apples for breakfast?"

He lifted the flap of the harvesting bag and showed off a half-dozen apples.

"Just let me know next time, alright?"

"Alright," he said.

They ate apples, packed up their modest camp, and stood staring at the blackened cabins for several long minutes. Court seemed to struggle with leaving.

Elle asked if he wanted to say a few parting words.

"No, it's just hard to leave. Whatever we find out there, I know that I might never make it back here."

She wanted to reassure him but Master Zheng's voice echoed in her mind. *The weak cling to fantasies. The strong face reality.*

"If it's important enough, you'll come back."

"You won't be forgotten," he finally said across the clearing and turned to face the forest. "I'm ready. If we keep a good pace, we can be there in two and a half days."

That day and the next were long and they only spoke sporadically. Elle stared at the ground in front of her, watching her feet move past each other over and over. No individual step was difficult but the sum total was monotonous and exhausting. She slept deeply and without dreams the first night. In the morning, Court had to wake her, telling her they were wasting daylight.

The second night, the air was cold and they built a small fire.

"We're no more than two hours from Chignecto in the

morning."

"What kind of place is Chignecto?"

"Like the village, I guess, but bigger and with less order. There's no council of leaders. It's just a whole bunch of people trying to make their way."

"It sounds like anarchy."

"What's that?"

"When there's no government, no authority."

"It's sort of like that."

"Anarchy is dangerous."

"Why do you say that?"

"Because people will just do what's best for themselves when there are no rules or consequences."

"I don't know about that. Don't you believe in people being kind to each other?"

"Sure, people will be kind to each other until it's inconvenient or bad for them."

"That's not a very positive opinion of humanity."

"I haven't had a lot of reason to keep a positive opinion of most people."

"With that cheerful thought, I'm going to sleep."

He lay back and pulled his blanket over his shoulder. Elle stared into the embers, hoping they wouldn't have many more nights outdoors. She didn't like the damp chill. She didn't like the uncomfortable ground. She especially didn't like the constant noise that made her jumpy. If not for the exhaustion of the long day's walk, sleep would have been impossible.

She closed her eyes and listened to the breeze whispering through the trees. Tomorrow, she was walking into the unknown again. She smiled a little when she thought of how proud Dr. Donovan and Master Zheng would be of her. In a small way, that soothed the heartache. She remembered her last promotion ceremony with Master Zheng and how Dr. Donovan had beamed, his boyish smile stretching across his face. And when she had scored top of her cohort in the launch drills... And the first time she had interpreted actual Qyntarak vocal communications...

Her thoughts morphed into fantastical dreams as sleep took her. She saw Dr. Donovan and Marsh picking apples outside the village, Court riding a motorcycle through a city, Vaidehi flying like a bird in a rainstorm. Then a grav flyer was chasing Vaidehi. It shot her down with arrows that exploded into puffs of gray powder. She crashed into the apple tree that Dr. Donovan was picking from and it burst into flames. The fire crackled and snapped.

Elle's eyes shot open. Her heart was racing and her breathing was shallow. She heard snapping.

I thought that was in my dream...

A large brown animal was nudging a harvesting bag with its muzzle. Elle caught a gasp in her throat before it could escape. The animal had four long gangly legs and a spindly tail that whipped side to side. It wasn't a deer, Court had shown her one of those, and it obviously wasn't a bear. Her best guess was a moose.

When the big animal had given up on the bag, it looked at Elle. With its two symmetrical eyes staring at her, she felt inexplicably at peace. She had more in common with this forest creature than the Qyntarak. It belonged to her planet. The moose kept gazing and Elle held eye contact. She felt her heart rate slow.

She felt an urge to say something to it.

That's stupid. It can't speak. You'll spook it.

Court rolled over, still asleep, and the moose's head twitched. It snorted and walked away, tree branches snapping as it went.

Court jolted awake.

"What was that?" he whispered. "Why are you smiling?"

"We had a visitor."

"What kind of visitor? Why didn't you wake me?"

"I think it was a moose."

"A moose can be nacking dangerous."

"It seemed gentle enough to me. I think it was a good sign."

"A sign?"

"It didn't see us as a threat. I think it recognized that we're a positive force."

"A positive force? Are you feeling alright? Did you eat something I didn't see?"

She laughed at that.

"It's just something Master Zheng used to say."

"Who's Master Zheng?"

"No one. Never mind."

She got up and rolled her blanket. Letting Master Zheng's name slip out was foolish. She'd let her guard down. She was getting too comfortable around Court and had to be more careful. Going back into civilization wasn't safe for her. She didn't know how long their fates would be intertwined and she didn't want him knowing any more about her than necessary—it was risky for both of them.

Court followed her lead and rolled up his own blanket. He didn't press the Master Zheng issue and she appreciated that. He was a decent person, she'd decided that already.

Once I know where I'm going, I'll send him back so he can rebuild his village. That's where his heart is.

They ate dried apple slices as they walked the last hours to Chignecto. Court had rationed their food so they'd have at least a day's worth when they arrived. The apple slices helped but her stomach wasn't satiated. She was about to suggest they collect some plants to eat when Court told her they were coming to Chignecto.

"It's just around this next turn." He pointed at the rusted remains of two posts. "Marsh said that used to be a sign for it, from before."

They walked through a cluster of stalls where scruffy-looking vendors competed for their attention. The smell of roasting meats and vegetables was intoxicating and Elle's stomach rumbled in response.

"I'm so hungry," she whispered.

"Yeah, me too. But Marsh always said the bazaar vendors were cheats, taking advantage of people traveling the old roads."

"It smells so good."

"Let's find Moriya first, alright? She'll help us make sure we don't get cheated out of our money."

They weaved through the settlement, drawing stares from a few locals. Court stopped outside a metal trailer.

"This is where she lived the last time I was here. Watch out for the dog."

As if on cue, snarling came from the tall grass but the dog didn't come out.

"Moriya," Court hollered. "Are you home?"

There was no answer and Court's shoulders slumped. A child came near and looked at them with curiosity. Between the long, matted hair and dirty face, Elle wasn't sure if it was a boy or a girl.

"Are youse looking for the Fix-It Lady?" he or she asked.

"A lady named Moriya. Does she still live here?"

"I dunno her name. We jus' caller the Fix-It Lady."

"That's her," Court said. "Moriya fixes up old things and barters them."

"Fix-It Lady's down at the cookhouse."

"Can you take us?" Elle asked.

"What's wrong with your hair?"

"What do you mean?"

"Where's all the color?"

"My hair is this color." Elle ran her fingers through her hair, which was down since she had no one to help her braid it again.

"Can I touch it?"

Court shook his head side to side. "Maybe some other time. Can you take us to the Fix-It Lady?"

"No, I got to play with Jean while she's gone."

"Who's Jean?"

"Fix-It Lady's wolf dog. She doesn't like me visiting Jean on account she's a attack dog but I bring her treats."

The little one pulled a bone from under their shirt that had been stuffed into the waist of their pants. Bits of raw meat still clung to it.

Elle curled her nose at the sight and the child walked into the tall grass calling, "Jeannie doggie, where ares you?"

"Cookhouse is this way," Court said as he started walking.

"Why did you stop them from touching my hair?"

"Lice. A kid with long hair like that is probably full of it."

Elle resisted the impulse to shudder. She'd heard of lice,

of course, but she'd never known anyone to get it. It was just something kids teased each other about when they were young.

"There's the cookhouse."

They drew fresh stares from locals as they went in. A few people were chopping vegetables but otherwise it was empty inside.

A young woman with a scarf tied around her head looked up at them and said, "We're between meals. No lunch for another hour or so. You're welcome to the old eggs there before the dogs get to them."

The woman bent her head in the direction of a pile of dried out eggs in a bowl. Elle's stomach rumbled again.

"Do they cost anything?" she asked.

The woman in the scarf laughed. "If you're willing to pay for that, you must be starving. They're all yours."

Elle grabbed the metal sheet and shoveled food into her mouth with her fingers. Only when her mouth was full did she offer the tray to Court, who declined with a wave.

"I don't recognize the both of you. You new here?"

"Passing through," Court said. "We're looking for someone, actually. Moriya. I met her here a few years back."

"Fix-It Lady. Yeah, she's out back doing dishes. Since your girlfriend there is going to inhale all those eggs, you can take the plate out to her to wash."

Out back, a trio of people swayed side to side between a mountain of food-smeared plates and a collection of clean ones. A broad-shouldered man with white hair was scraping food into a bin then dropping the plates into a bucket of opaque brown water. A short, squat woman was scrubbing the plates in the brown water, dipping them in the less-brown water of a second bucket, and dropping them into a third bucket of steaming cloudy water. A man as short as the woman but much thinner was pulling the plates out with tongs and spreading them across a wide table.

"Excuse me," Court said. "We're looking for Moriya."

All three stopped moving when he spoke. As they turned, almost in unison, Elle realized that the wide-shouldered man was actually a woman. She smiled when she saw Court.

"As I live and breathe, is that Harcourt?"

Surprised, Elle repeated, "Harcourt?"

"It's just Court now. I wasn't sure you'd remember me."

Moriya wiped her hands on her pants and hugged him enthusiastically.

"Remember you? You nearly ate me out of house and home. Hard to forget an appetite like that. You must've been, what, sixteen at the time?"

"Seventeen the last time I was here."

"Right, seventeen." She stood back to look him over. "Well, you've gone and aged into a right fine-looking specimen. But blazes you smell bad. Worse than Marsh did last week. He didn't mention anything about you coming down. It's a treat to get visitors so close together. And who might this be?"

"I'm Elle," she said with a bow.

"You're all dressed up like Marsh's folk but that bow gives you away. City raised, I'm guessing."

Court interjected. "When Marsh was here, did he tell you much about the errand he was on?"

"Now that you mention it, he didn't. Said it might be trouble. He was supposed to stop back in to see me on his way home but he didn't show. Such is life in the new order of things though."

"Do you think we can talk in private?" Court spoke softly, hoping not to offend the dishwashers who were trying to look like they weren't eavesdropping but were fooling no one.

"Yes, yes, of course. Ezra, Suri, you mind finishing without me? You can split my tab credit between you."

The squat woman wiggled her hand to wave Moriya away.

"Was doing some dishes to work off some of my meal tab," Moriya said as they walked. "Fixin' work's been a bit slow of late. Not sure why, but less demand coming up from Alma."

"Has that happened before?" Elle asked.

"Occasionally. Sometimes there's a clamp down on underground trade. The big machine likes to get its piece of the pie, even when poor people are just trading patched up junk to each other."

Moriya shooed away the young one who was still playing with Jean and ushered them inside her trailer.

When the door latched shut, she asked, "Alright, Court, what's going on? I can see in your eyes that something's wrong."

Court paused just long enough for it to be uncomfortable. Elle was about to fill the silence when Court said, "They came for the village."

"Qyntarak?"

"No, humans."

Elle added, "But they had Qyntarak tech. They killed everyone."

"Marsh?"

Court nodded. Moriya collapsed into the old leather chair.

"I need a drink." She opened a compartment mounted to

the wall and reached behind a stack of folded fabrics. She pulled out a bottle that was hazy from scuffs and scratches. Clear liquid sloshed as she drank straight from the bottle. "Do you know why?"

Elle answered, "They wanted a data vault that Dr. Donovan brought to Marsh."

"Donovan? Why does that name sound familiar?"

"He was a researcher with Aldebaran."

"He was a friend of Marsh's, wasn't he?"

"Yes," Court said.

"What was on that data vault?"

Elle locked eyes with Moriya. "Are you sure you want to know? Everyone who's gotten involved has been killed."

"I think I can risk it. Hell, it's not like I've got much longer to go regardless. I'm worn out from just keeping myself fed."

Elle and Court exchanged looks, wordlessly deciding that they would tell Moriya more.

"Apparently, there's a new law coming that's going to take away more rights from humans," Elle said.

"There's hardly anything left to take."

"Dr. Donovan wanted Marsh to help find someone named Nora Barrett, an old friend of theirs."

"Not a name I recognize. Why her?"

"We don't know."

"Where is she?"

"We're not sure," Court said. "But Marsh said she used to work at the University of Toronto. That's where we're headed."

"Toronto?" Moriya laughed and swigged from her bottle. "You going to walk there? That'll take a month, if you survive the trip."

"It's the best plan we have."

"You have any money?"

"We have some," Elle said. "And things to sell."

"We were hoping you'd help us with that part," Court said.

"Let's see what you got." Moriya put the bottle aside and sat forward in her chair.

Elle pulled out the medical supplies and Court dumped the pouch of coins on the floor, the only free space in the cramped trailer.

"Elon's fire. Well, the good news is you won't have to walk."

"How much is all this worth?" Court asked.

"The coin alone would get you room and food for the both of you for a month around here. You won't get a great deal on converting it to qynars but I know some traders who aren't complete scoundrels. The medical supplies you can sell for qynars. More than enough for passage to Toronto."

"What are qynars?" Court asked.

"Currency," Elle said. "Money for buying things."

"Currency of the Qyntarak," Moriya added. "The introduction of the qynar set the stage for their dominance over the global economy, but you aren't here for history and economics lessons. You want to get to Toronto and now we know you have the resources to do it."

"Good," Elle said.

"But can I ask you something? Why do this? Why not stay, keep your head down, and use this to survive?"

Elle unconsciously straightened her shoulders when she answered. "People are dying. The man who raised me was killed over this. He believed it was important that we find Nora Barrett. Maybe it won't make a difference but I'm not going to take that chance. It was important to him, so it's important to me. Dr. Donovan wouldn't have abandoned our life and his work if it wasn't worth the risk."

"And if Marsh was still here, he'd be helping, so that's what I'm doing."

"And even in death, that old bastard is roping me into his schemes." Moriya slapped her hands on her knees and stood up. "We best get moving. It's almost lunch then you two need clean clothes, a wash, and some qynars before we go to Alma and sneak you onto a grav train."

Chapter 24: Court

COURT DIDN'T CARE for the soapy smell or the constricting fit of his new shirt. It was deep purple and held shut with hidden buttons. The vendor had sworn the color and style were very much in vogue. Court had been too embarrassed to ask what "in vogue" meant.

Elle had opted for blue pants and a green top that reminded her of things she had once owned. Moriya had approved of their wardrobes but Court worried the old woman's insight into what was appropriate to wear in Toronto came from experiences at least a quarter century out of date.

After walking an hour to Alma, he'd gained an appreciation for his new clothes, which turned out to be both comfortable and breathable.

"We'll try a man called Polk. I've done a fair amount of repair business with his people over the years. He's our best bet for getting you transport."

When they arrived at their destination, the building was a blackened husk.

More fire, Court thought.

Moriya grabbed the sleeve of a young woman passing by.

"My dear, what happened to The Squid and Whale?"

"Burned down, obviously."

"Yes, I can see that. But what happened?"

"The Qyntarak, I think. One of their small ships set down right in the street. Everyone ran off to hide so no one saw it but I heard they set it on fire."

"And the people inside?"

"They let the customers run away but killed the bartender and the owner."

Moriya released the woman's arm, who scurried off, checking over her shoulder as if worried that she'd get in trouble for answering questions. Moriya looked crestfallen when she turned to face Elle.

"Polk is the only person I knew I could trust. Well, not so much trust as know that he wouldn't do anything to risk future business."

"There must be someone else," Elle said.

"There's a fellow who used to help me get parts for repair jobs. He has a whole brood of kids and always needed the extra cash. Not as connected as Polk for locating things but he has connections. He used to have parts smuggled by train. That's our next best bet."

As they walked through town, Court thought the streets felt emptier than the last time he'd been in Alma and he mentioned it to Moriya.

"I imagine people are scared right now. Alma is nowhere, so to have the Qyntarak show up and murder people, that'll give you pause before you stick your head out into the street."

"It might not have been the Qyntarak," Elle said.

"That's what the girl said."

"She said it was one of their flyers. The people who destroyed Court's village were also in flyers."

Moriya shook her head slowly. "One of the sad side effects of tyranny is that people will turn against their own kind just to survive. But that's not new since the Qyntarak came here. Humans have plenty of dark splotches in their history."

They turned up a lane, little more than two wheel tracks through tall weeds, to a tiny rectangular house that looked like it would fall over in a strong wind. The weeds were trampled flat around the house. Sticks and carved wooden toys littered the ground.

Moriya called from the lane, "Ho. Is anyone home?"

Within seconds, four, no, five children of varying sizes were staring from windows. A woman in a threadbare dress with a toddler propped on her hip appeared in the doorway.

Court hoped she wouldn't step onto the porch for fear it might collapse at any moment.

"Speak your piece," the woman said. "We're still finishing up lessons in here."

"We're looking for Aimar. Is he home?"

"Who is asking?"

"I'm Moriya. This is Court and Elle. We have business to discuss with Aimar. I've worked with him before."

"He'll be back soon. You can wait under the oak tree down the lane. There's a bench."

She closed the door and after a muffled shout, the children looking out the windows disappeared back into the recesses of the little house.

"What did I tell you? A brood of kids. Listen, when Aimar gets here, let me do the talking. You need to walk a careful line with him. He thinks the Qyntarak are a judgement from God and somehow people need to repopulate the Earth with the faithful, which is why he's got more kids than Jean's got fleas."

Sitting in the sun felt unjustifiably leisurely to Court even though there was nothing else for him to do. He was unable to enjoy the mid-afternoon warmth and was feeling impatient by the time Aimar came up the lane.

"Ho, Aimar," Moriya called.

"Moriya? Do my eyes deceive me?"

She held out her palms and Aimar pressed his to hers in greeting.

"It's been a while. How are you?"

"Life carries on. The kids get bigger and so do their appetites, which means extra shifts when I can get them."

"And how's business?"

"What business? It's vanished. The scraps that Polk left for me have all but dried up."

"I hear Polk is out of the picture now."

Aimar shook his head. "So horrific. Perhaps more evidence of the hand of God bringing judgement and justice, I don't know. It is not for us to understand."

"My associates here are looking for safe passage to Toronto. They were in one of the rural villages and their people were massacred."

"More horrors. We live in tragic times."

He moved toward Court and Elle, raising his hands. Court tensed but the man only placed his palms gently against their cheeks.

"Spared by God. How could I refuse? Tomorrow, the morning train will have room. I assume you have no identification."

"They don't, and they'll want to keep a low profile."

"Of course, of course. No identification means more eyes to pay to look the other way. You have payment?"

"They do."

"Do they not speak?"

"I'm their broker."

"Very well. I'll need to go see a friend and get you a price."

"They'll also need a safe place to spend the night."

"Not a problem. I have bunks in my shed. Let's call it a free gift with purchase."

Moriya laughed but Court didn't get the joke.

"Come up to the house," Aimar said. "You can eat with my family while I go. Polk would never have given you such service."

They ate at a sticky and badly stained table amidst the pandemonium of the six children and their visibly weary mother.

"Delicious," Moriya said. She touched the mother's hand. "We'll clean up and watch the kids if you want to go take a nap."

The mother sat frozen in shock for several seconds. "A nap? I haven't napped since, well, I don't know when."

"Go then," Moriya said. "Our small thank you for feeding weary travelers."

Under Moriya's supervision, Court and Elle washed dishes while the children dutifully put them away, anxious to impress the stranger who had promised them a game afterward.

The nine of them were in the yard of trampled weeds playing a game that Moriya called Freeze Tag when Aimar returned.

He looked confused and concerned until Moriya said, "Your wife is taking a nap."

Aimar clutched his hands over his heart. "You truly are angels. Let's go inside to talk."

Aimar waved over the oldest of the children, took his toddler from Moriya, and placed her in the arms of his eldest.

Inside, the four adults sat around the stained table. Aimar steepled his fingers in front of his chin.

"There are two options," he said. "There's a smuggling compartment under the lobster tanks in some of the train containers. It's not a pleasant way to travel but it's cheap. The other option is to pose as a couple who've had their IDs stolen. We can arrange to have new IDs waiting in Toronto. I'm assured that the forged identities are of highest quality. You would travel as regular passengers but be flagged for special ID processing upon arrival. The second option would be more comfortable and you'd have IDs afterward. Obviously, that's also more expensive."

"How much are we talking here?" Moriya asked.

"For which option?"

"Both."

"For IDs and traveling as proper passengers, eight thousand qynars each."

"Sixteen thousand qynars? Are you insane?"

"How much for the lobster containers?" Elle asked. Moriya gave her a sideways glance but held her expression steady otherwise.

"So you can speak," Aimar said.

"How much?"

"Four thousand qynars each."

"Elon's fire, Aimar, that's outrageous."

"Let's go outside," Elle said to Moriya. "We need to confer in private."

The three of them strolled the lane while Aimar waited with his children.

"It's far too much," Moriya said. "A regular train ticket would be three hundred, maybe four hundred, qynars. Eight thousand is exploitative. It's bullshit."

"How much do we have?" Court asked.

"About twelve hundred from converting the copper and silver," Elle said. "What do you think we'll get for the medical supplies?"

"I'm guessing around eight hundred," Moriya said.

"So not even close," Court said. "Half of what we need for one person."

"Time to negotiate," Moriya said. She turned and shouted up the lane, "Thanks, Aimar. We're going."

Confused, Court followed Moriya as she walked away from the house. Within a dozen seconds, Aimar was calling out between gasping breaths as he chased after them.

"Wait. Wait. Moriya, one minute." When he caught up with them, he said, "My friends, where are you going?"

"I brought these two here because I thought you would treat them decently and you tried to swindle them. I want no part of that. And you should be ashamed of yourself."

"Moriya, please, we have known each other for many years. You know I'm no swindler. Things are very hard for everyone. My markup is standard. The prices reflect the work and the risk in a difficult time."

"Two hundred a piece for the IDs. Six hundred each for the train."

"Sixteen hundred qynars? Now who is being outrageous?"

"Then we'll take our chances elsewhere."

"Wait, wait. Four thousand total. I will make nothing but I believe I can negotiate with my colleagues."

Moriya scoffed, "I know what train passage costs, Aimar. I don't believe a fake ID costs three thousand qynars."

Aimar sighed. "The IDs are six hundred each. Those are not negotiable. A syndicate in Toronto does the work. For nine hundred each, I can get you on a train but you won't have a seat. You'll have to wander the train for a few hours since it makes several stops but you'd be onboard. Three thousand total. The best I can do and I'll be left with about one qynar to buy my family a few eggs."

Moriya frowned but Elle said, "We'll take it but we pay for the IDs in person, not upfront."

It was Aimar's turn to frown. "I'm afraid that's not possible."

"Then no deal," Elle said and started walking away.

"Wait, wait. I'll make it work. Yes, I'm sure I can call in a favor somehow."

Elle held her hand out and Aimar put his palm against it.

"We have a deal," she said.

"I need to take these two for a few supplies," Moriya said.

"Then I will take the time to visit with my children. Meet me at the fish market in an hour with your money so we can finalize the details with my contact on the train."

Once Aimar was out of earshot, Moriya said, "What are

you doing? You don't have enough money."

"If we're posing as a couple who were robbed, it would be suspicious for us to arrive with a bunch of qynars. Once we're past the train's security, we'll improvise."

"You're going to get yourself killed. A syndicate that peddles forged IDs isn't going to let you just walk away without paying. Court, surely you aren't willing to go along with this."

"I know it sounds risky but we already have people trying to kill us. Taking action sounds better than waiting around for them to come find us."

Moriya shook her head as she started walking back down the lane. "I don't see how this doesn't end badly."

She took them to an illicit medical clinic where they sold their supplies for 875 qynars. Moriya and Elle seemed pleased with the amount. Their qynar device, which was about the size of one silver coin, showed their new balance as Q2093.

Court had never seen such a device until they'd exchanged their coins for it. When he'd held it, Court realized it was the first time he'd touched a truly alien piece of technology. A wave of anxiety had hit him as he considered how far he was moving away from the world he knew.

They met Aimar as planned and Elle transferred 1800 qynars from her device to Aimar's. He introduced them to a merchant who explained the plan. When the instructions were finished, Moriya wore a grave expression.

She pulled Court and Elle aside. "I don't like this."

"It will work out," Elle said. "I can feel it."

Moriya wrapped her enormous arms around both of them at the same time.

"Be safe and be wise. If you can, send word back to Aimar when you've arrived so I won't have to worry, alright?"

"We'll do our best," Court said, although he realized as he said it that he didn't know how one sends word back from Toronto to Alma.

"Aimar will take care of you from here. I need to be getting back. It's almost dusk and I have an hour's walk ahead of me."

Court reached into his pocket and pulled out a solitary silver coin. "I saved this for you. I know it's not much, but it's all I have to say thank you."

Moriya looked like she might cry when she saw it. "You sneaky bastard. You waited until it was too late to exchange it for qynars so I couldn't refuse, didn't you?"

Court smiled at her and shrugged. "Maybe you can pay off your meal tab."

Moriya gave him another hug. "Marsh taught you well. You'd make him proud if he could see you now."

The compliment made Court fidget uncomfortably and Moriya kept looking at him long enough to take it all in. Then she patted Elle on the shoulder and said, "Take good care of him out there."

"I will."

And with that, Moriya left for her return walk to Chignecto.

They turned their attention back to the merchant who said, "Oh, just one more thing."

Chapter 25: Petra

WILKES HAD HIS feet up on the desk. Petra hated when he did that. With a firm shove, she pushed his utility boots off the work surface.

"Hey."

Petra brushed off the sprinkling of dirt left behind. "Next interview is starting. I need my space."

On one of several active tablet screens, a live video showed Kane leaning over a table and staring into the eyes of a nervous-looking man in a lab coat.

"Dr. Lochlan, you worked with Clint Donovan for almost two years. When is the first time you suspected he was a terrorist?"

It was a ridiculous opening question, but a psychologist had recommended it as an opening salvo for these interrogations. He had argued that it would threaten the scientists' egos to have missed something so significant and that the outmoded word terrorist would evoke emotions from the mostly older contingent of researchers.

It worked on old Lochlan. Flustered, he stumbled over his response until he squeaked out, "I never thought he was a terrorist."

"I see." Kane pretended to take notes on his tablet. So much of an interrogation was theater. Three sentences in and Lochlan was on the defensive, feeling insecure, and worried about his reputation. The man would talk. The question that remained to be answered was whether he knew anything of value.

"Don't get me wrong, I knew he was willing to challenge policies and fight the status quo. Everybody knew that. But kidnapping a patient, that was unexpected."

"And tell me, doctor, why do you think he kidnapped patient L37?"

"I don't know. I mean, I know he loved her like a daughter. It's natural, most of us get attached to our wards. That's why we aren't allowed to be in control of their research programs. Maybe he caught wind of what was in the plan for Elle and decided he didn't want that for her."

"Elle?"

"That's what Clint nicknamed her. Most of the subjects have nicknames, something more personal than their identification number."

"I see." More pretending to take notes. "What was L37's research program?"

"I didn't work with her directly but her L designation means she's in a program for adapting humans to interact with Qyntarak."

"So L37 was part of an experimental group for making humans better at communicating with Qyntarak?"

"Yes, based on her designation. I'd have to pull up her records to tell you specifics."

"No, that's fine. I'll be speaking with the researchers that worked directly with her. Tell me, though, why wasn't L37 reported missing until the staff here was questioned about Dr. Donovan?"

"I don't know. Like I said, I didn't work directly with her."

"So someone working directly with L37 was collaborating with Clint Donovan."

Lochlan held up his hands. "Hold on, I didn't say that. That's a big assumption to make. Look, these aren't rats in a twentieth century lab. They're complex human beings, many of them teenagers, and they have all the same problems as regular teenagers. They get sick, they have bad days, they have fights with their friends, they give people the silent treatment. Nobody gets too bent out of shape if a patient misses a daily check-in every now and then. We worry about trends and the big picture. You have to roll with the punches on a day-to-day basis. Working with humans is messy, you know?"

Kane smiled at that. "Believe me, I know."

It was obvious to Petra that Dr. Lochlan was another dead end. They had seventeen more researchers to interview and several dozen assistants after that. The first seven scientists had provided no actionable intelligence. She knew what would come next—Kane would have to issue an official bulletin looking for L37.

"Thank you, doctor. That's all for now. We may call you back for more discussion."

"Oh, alright then." Lochlan rose from his chair clumsily and fumbled with the door handle. Petra frowned. Having the door locked when interviewees tried to leave was a childish power move but Kane liked people to feel off balance around him.

"Let me get that for you," Kane said.

Beside her, Wilkes tapped on his wrist computer to unlock the door.

Kane followed Lochlan into the hallway and came into the next room where Wilkes and Petra were waiting.

"Another dud," Petra said.

"Donovan must've really been living two lives," Wilkes said, "for seven of them to be clueless."

"Nothing from the sensors?"

"Nothing," Petra said. "Body temperature, pheromone release, sweat production, eye dilation, all negative. No signs of deception, only stress and nervousness."

"And you can't blame him for that," Wilkes said.

"These are scientists who specialize in controlling human physiology. It's not out of the question that they've found a way to suppress their reactions. But we don't have time to waste on that. We need to put out a bulletin for L37. High priority facial recognition analysis on all video feeds. Voice recognition in all transportation stations. Confirm that we have triggers on her identity, all her bank accounts, and her data files. Any sightings, any access, we move. Instruct local authorities to apprehend and detain with prejudice, treat as dangerous and hostile."

"You got it, boss," Wilkes said.

"I'm going to take a break. You can both take fifteen as well, as soon as you get those bulletins out."

When the featureless gray door closed behind Kane, Petra asked if Wilkes wanted help with the bulletins.

"Nah, will only take a couple minutes."

"Alright, I'm going to get a little sunshine and a cup of tea. You want something?"

"Coffee would be great. Thanks."

Petra noticed her hands were shaking as she reached for the door. She shoved them into the pockets of her slacks as she walked. Once outside, she moved behind some shrubs where she knew there were no cameras aimed and put her hands on her knees while she fought to get her pounding heart under control. When she stood up again, her palms left sweaty prints behind on her pants.

Chapter 26: Britt

BEAR FROWNED AS he delivered the news about their last shipment.

"All of it?" Britt asked, still not believing the report.

"All of it. Tea, coffee, and medicine. So not only is no medicine going out, we won't get paid for the tea and coffee either."

"Well, nacking sour split."

"Such language."

"Not ladylike enough for you?"

"You just don't hear old human profanity mixed with Qyntarak metaphors very often."

"What can I say, I'm a cultural bridge builder."

"Not enough of a bridge builder to keep our shipments from being seized."

"Our illegal, undocumented shipments, you mean?"

"Yes, those."

"You know as well as I do that it happens. I'm glad to see

you're worked up about it, though. It means you haven't lost your heart."

"People are going to die without that medicine. I'd say you're not worked up enough."

She exhaled a slow, weary sigh. "I learned a long time ago that this is a game of averages. Losing the occasional package is a cost of playing the game."

Bear's frown intensified.

"Blazes, I'm not happy about it. You don't have to frown for the both of us."

"There's more. The reason I came to see you in person. Novak's disappeared."

"That's inconvenient. Where was he transferred?"

"Not transferred. Not fired, either. Just disappeared."

"Shit."

"The timing can't be a coincidence."

"I'd say not. Could be one of the syndicates making a play for control of the smuggling routes."

"But why eliminate Novak if he was already bribable?"

"I'm not sure. What do we know about who is replacing him?"

"Nothing yet. I'm having drinks later today with some managers. I'll see what I can glean."

"Good. Thank you. Time to get more serious in the hunt for alternate drop sites in case Novak's replacement is a tight ass."

"What about the *Willow Wisp*? Is there any way..."

"I wish there was, but if we had a way to get things into a launch later in the process, we wouldn't be sneaking containers onto cargo trains."

"What about a smaller crate? Enough for their worst

cases?"

Britt closed her eyes and shook her head.

"I'm sorry. I know you have people up there."

"The last message was…"

"Heartbreaking. I know. I'll transmit a message to let the *Wisp* know that the shipment isn't coming. We'll just have to hope they can keep the virus at bay for the next six months."

Chapter 27: Elle

ELLE RUBBED HER hand over her scalp again after they sat down in the dining car. Her head felt cold.

"You have to stop doing that. It's making you look nervous."

"I can't help it. It feels so weird."

"You'll get used to it. I shave my hair all the time. Besides, it'll grow back."

"Except growing it back means it won't match the new ID photo and we can't do anything that gives anyone a reason to look closely at our IDs. So it might be like this for a while. I just hope that guy was right that this is in style in Toronto."

"For what it's worth, it looks good on you."

She smiled and turned to study her reflection in the window. The style was simple with most of her hair trimmed so short it was barely visible. Only a narrow strip of longer hair curved from the front right to the back left.

She had a sunburn from so much time outside. The

merchant who took her ID photo promised he would alter it to reduce the redness so the picture would better match her natural coloring when the sunburn faded.

The dining car was utilitarian with tables bolted to the floor and plain, ivory-colored benches that weren't comfortable enough for the three hours they'd be on the train. Physical discomfort was quickly becoming a theme of her new life.

Wall-mounted displays alternated between photos of the daily specials and instructions for ordering food from wrist computers or personal tablets. Since they had neither, it was unlikely they'd be eating any of the train food, which was for the best since the prices would cut heavily into the 286 qynars they had left.

"Shouldn't the train be leaving?" Court asked.

"Soon, I think."

She kept staring out the window. He fidgeted with his fingers while they waited.

A heavyset woman in a uniform with the train company's logo barreled into the car. "You two need to go to your seats until the train departs."

"Why?" Elle asked.

"Policy, safety, it doesn't matter. It's the rules."

"When does the train leave?"

"In a few minutes. You need to go now."

The woman stood there waiting for them to leave. Elle started to give her a dirty look but thought better of it. They couldn't afford to draw any extra attention to themselves.

"Come on," she said to Court and grabbed his hand to pull him after herself.

"Where are we supposed to go?" he whispered.

She didn't answer, just led him through the next passenger car and into a lavatory. Court surveyed the cramped space, confused at first.

"Is this for, you know…"

"Yes," she whispered. "Stop talking."

Being so close to him in the tiny space, she noticed the lingering scent of soap. For the first time since they'd met, he didn't smell like dirt and old sweat.

A series of chimes played followed by a gentle vibration.

"I think that means the train is moving," Elle said. "Let's go."

They squeezed out into the hallway. A man who didn't look much older than Court grinned and winked at them. Elle rolled her eyes as they passed him.

They went back to the dining car, which didn't remain empty long enough for them to talk.

Elle said, "Come on, let's see if they have any public tablets."

The train traveled at 900 kilometers per hour, floating above the trees using Qyntarak gravity technology. It wasn't a train like the old ones that she'd heard stories about, more like a long grav flyer or a floating building. Only when Elle looked out a window at the landscape racing by beneath them did she have any sense of the incredible speed. Passengers inside the train had no other perception of it, which made it easy to walk through the cars.

They passed through passenger cars of varying comfort levels until a locked door halted their exploration.

"No passengers beyond this point," a disembodied voice said.

"Computer security system. We had lots of those in the

center."

The door slid open before they could turn around, and the heavyset woman in the train uniform stared at them.

"Look who it is. You two really don't like staying in your seats."

Elle wrapped her arm around Court's. "It's our first train trip. We want to see the whole thing while we can. What's back there?"

"Cargo starts here. No passengers allowed."

"That's a shame," Elle said. "Say, since we've got you, we were wondering if there are any public tablets anywhere onboard."

"You don't have your own? I don't see many young people traveling without wrist computers these days."

Elle forced an excessive level of cheerfulness into her voice. "Oh, we sold ours. We're buying upgrades in the city when we get there. Kind of part of the whole experience for us."

"There are network terminals in the observation car, near the front of the train. Just between you and me, though, they're overpriced considering how slow they are, but that's all we've got."

"Thank you," Elle said.

They retraced their route and carried on to the observation car, which they found unoccupied. Elle selected a terminal screen that wasn't visible from the doorways.

"Ten qynars for thirty minutes. We're burning through our qynars pretty fast."

"What exactly are we doing?"

"I'm going to use this network terminal to figure out how to get from the train station to the University of Toronto."

"Assuming we can get out of the train station. You're forgetting the little complication of the people expecting us to show up with money that we don't have."

"Right, so I should try to find the layout so we can make an escape plan."

Court looked bewildered. Elle got a sick feeling in her stomach, comprehending for the first time the risk of Court's ignorance about the world. She had grown up sheltered enough. He was completely out of his element.

When he said nothing, she added, "We also need to find a cheap place to stay tonight."

The terminal dinged when she tapped her anonymous currency device against it to confirm the fee for thirty minutes of use. Elle worked quickly but the terminals were sluggish. She tried to keep Court abreast of what she was doing but partway through the second half hour, he drifted off to sleep in his seat.

Before her third half hour expired, she woke him to look at a map of the station. She pointed at locations as she explained her plan.

"The train arrives at what used to be an airport. There's a security checkpoint where they scan IDs as people leave. Since we don't have IDs, we go to a special processing area here. Then there's a hallway to bathrooms that connects to the luggage area."

"What's a luggage area?"

"It's where you pick up your bags. You know, suitcases and stuff? It doesn't matter right now. Just look here. I'm pretty sure we can get our IDs checked then go down the hall and blend in with the other passengers as they leave."

"And then where do we go?"

"It's about twenty kilometers to the university."

"That's a long walk."

"Yes, I thought the same thing. So we go here and get on a public transit shuttle."

"I don't know what that means."

"It's like a miniature version of the train. It'll cost us another forty qynars. We should be able to get to the university before it closes."

"I thought the university was closed years ago."

"Most of it was shut down, but there's a small part still operating. I mean before it closes for the day. Maybe we'll get lucky and find a clue. And I found a place nearby to sleep that will take anonymous payment."

Court rubbed his hands over his own freshly shaved scalp.

"Now you look nervous."

"That's because I am."

"We're going to make it work. The people we loved died over this. We're going to find this Nora Barrett person and we're going to find out what A2 jackets have to do with this suit and why that matters so much."

She prodded the bag at her feet that held the suit. The bag was new to them but definitely not new. Elle hoped something that looked so worn out wouldn't attract any special attention. And it had only cost seven qynars, an important consideration in her purchasing decision. She'd never had a reason to worry about money beyond the little bit of personal spending allowance she used to get from Dr. Donovan. Now she found herself worrying about what they would do if they didn't find Nora Barrett right away.

They'd have 216 qynars left when they reached the university. If answers didn't come soon, they'd be broke and homeless in a strange city.

Chapter 28: Court

"Our IDs were stolen. Someone was dropping off new ones for us. Do you know where that would be?"

Elle did a sickly sweet voice, making herself sound more like a naive teenager than a nervous fugitive. The guard grunted something unintelligible in response and pointed at a SPECIAL PROCESSING sign.

"I thought you knew the way already from the map," Court whispered.

"I do but we need to look believable. The good news is that so far the layout matches what I saw."

They told their cover story again to the bored-looking clerk at the special processing counter, who fished their ID bracelets from a box.

"You all should get these implanted since you're old enough," the clerk said, tapping his own forearm. "A lot harder to get your arm stolen."

Elle continued with her faux sweet voice. "Oh, I know. I've

been saying that for months. I think this'll be the thing to get us off our behinds and get it done."

The clerk scanned their IDs almost absentmindedly, focusing more on Elle's smile than whatever displayed on his tablet. Court couldn't blame him. She had an enchanting smile when she let it show.

"You all have a nice day." The clerk didn't look at Court when he said it.

"I need to use the lavatory," she said, grabbing Court's hand and leading him to the hallway. She kept quickening their pace the further they got from the security checkpoint.

"Keep your head down. Don't look around," she said.

Court did as she instructed. The throbbing of his heart pulsated in his ears. This was the moment of truth. He didn't want to find out what happens when you skip out on ID forgers in a big city.

The clerk called after them. "Ms. Sir. Just a moment. Hold on a second."

"Keep moving," Elle said.

They pushed into a throng of several dozen people streaming through the luggage area. A meaty hand pressed on Court's chest.

"Our friends from Alma," the man said. He was big, too big for Court to brush aside. "Where are you off to in such a hurry?"

"We need to go," Elle said.

"Not yet. We haven't concluded our business."

"Yes, we have."

"You still owe us."

"We paid in Alma."

"No, you didn't. And here we charge extra for cash on

delivery."

Court could hear the clerk shouting after them from the hallway, his voice growing closer.

"Help, security," Elle screamed. She waved frantically at a nearby security guard. "He's trying to rob us. Help."

The guard began moving in their direction. The big man took his hand off Court's chest, his eyes darting around the room, assessing. People had slowed and stopped walking to stare at them. From further away, several people started running. Two were dressed like the security guard, one was not. The closest guard pulled a stick from his belt. It looked like the Scorpion baton that had killed Marsh.

Elle kicked the man in the groin. He yelped and doubled over.

"Run," she said.

Court chased her toward an outside door. The security guard yelled something at them as they ran past. Court glanced over his shoulder and saw the guard attempting to talk to the man Elle had kicked.

They barged through a glass door into the warm Toronto air. Elle yanked a headscarf off a woman waiting outside.

"Sorry," Elle said as she ran off with the scarf.

"Where are we going?"

"Working on that. There." She veered toward a sign that read TOUR CARS.

Court followed her into a bulbous black machine. Its door closed behind them automatically.

"Downtown," Elle shouted. "Hurry."

"Please state your destination," the machine said.

"Downtown," she repeated.

"Please state a specific destination."

"Uh, the CN Tower, or whatever it's called now."

"Destination accepted. Please approve payment."

Elle fumbled with her bag and slapped the anonymous currency device on a scanner.

"Payment authorized."

"Hurry. Please," Elle said, the panic undisguised in her voice.

As the machine moved away, Court saw a security guard, the clerk, and one of their other pursuers swinging their heads back and forth, unable to determine where Court and Elle had gone.

"Here," Elle said. "Help me get this headscarf on."

Court held the fabric while Elle wrapped it around her head.

She pulled the ID bracelet off her wrist. "These IDs are obviously useless. Good thing we didn't pay for them. Open window."

The computer responded to her command and part of the shell of their moving bubble retracted, letting in fresh air and wind noise. Elle threw her ID bracelet out the opening.

"Yours too."

Court tossed his after hers.

"What's at the CN Tower?"

"Nothing. It was the only landmark I could remember, and we should be able to walk from there. It's just far enough away that even if they track this car, they won't know where we've gone."

"Are you sure?"

Chapter 29: Petra

PETRA WATCHED THE video feed as L37 and her unknown male companion exited a car near the base of the CN Tower. L37 was smart to cover her face with a scarf but it was pointless unless she was going to separate from the guy. His face was in the database now and the facial recognition systems would flag him whenever he showed up on an accessible video feed.

Petra had gotten lucky with the car's video after L37 showed up on multiple cameras in the train station. If they went on foot now, she'd lose them. The old Toronto downtown was a hive of squatters and drifters. Camera installations didn't last a week in a place like that, not even modern models that were almost invisible and difficult to detect. Some people had strong feelings about being watched.

She couldn't blame them.

With the car door open, the sun glare overwhelmed the camera and she couldn't tell which direction the pair was going. A moment later, a grime-smeared man with a wild beard and toothless grin took over the car's interior. Petra shut off the video as he started unbuttoning his shirt. She couldn't help a small smirk—the car company would be spending its profit from the previous fare to clean the interior.

Time to tell the team.

She was taking a risk waiting so long. If she was lucky, they would mobilize without asking questions and no one would ever compare the time stamps on the video archives with the time she raised the alert. She could only hope it would give L37 enough time to get well hidden. Petra tapped a button on her wrist computer.

"This is Petra. L37 is in Toronto."

"Roger that," Wilkes replied. "Boss, you copy?"

"Copy," Kane said. "Everyone to the flyers. Petra, transmit details. We leave in ten minutes. Let's go get our little runaway."

Chapter 30: Court

COURT FELT DIZZY looking up, trying to comprehend the incredible height of the buildings that seemed to reach to the clouds.

"Is this what all cities are like?"

Elle shrugged. "Some of them, from what I've heard and seen in pictures. I came here once but not to this part. That's how I knew about the CN Tower. Dr. Donovan pointed it out to me when we flew in. You used to be able to go up there to eat."

"Why would anyone want to climb up there to eat? How does the food even get up there?"

"You didn't climb. It had these boxes that pulled you up."

"People used to do weird things."

"We should get moving. It's a couple kilometers to the university."

While they walked, Elle showed him the display on their anonymous currency device.

"Only 182 qynars left. That private car ride wasn't cheap."

"How much money are we going to need?"

"Hard to say, but 182 isn't much."

"What do we do when we run out?"

"I don't know."

The streets were empty of people but piled high with garbage. It stunk like urine and decay. Tall weeds and small trees were taking hold wherever they could, some even sprouting up from the tiny hills of things discarded by humanity.

They came upon a little girl, filthier than Court would have thought possible. She was pawing through a pile of garbage and didn't hear them. She recoiled in surprise when they came up beside her.

"Sorry," Court said. "We didn't mean to scare you."

The girl snarled.

"You should be careful digging around there," Elle said. "If you cut yourself, you could get an infection."

The girl scrabbled around the trash mound, using the pile of detritus as a barrier.

"She looks half-starved."

"She's feral," Elle said. "Living like an animal. Probably doesn't have a family."

"We should help her."

"How? We don't have anything to give her. In a few days, we might not be much better off than her."

"But she's just a little kid."

"I know, but there's nothing we can do."

Elle took his hand and led him away. Court looked back repeatedly. The first few times, the girl was watching them go. Then her attention returned to the pile of trash. The last time he looked, she was holding some small discovery up to the sky to examine it.

When Elle released his hand, Court felt a tiny pang of disappointment.

"So people used to live in these buildings?"

"Some of them. They also used to work in them."

"What kind of work requires being in a giant building?"

"I'm not sure, I just know that's what they used to do."

"It's all so massive. I mean, my whole village could fit in one."

"In a small part of one."

"It's hard to imagine so many people."

"Imagine how hard it is for people like Dr. Donovan or Marsh who remember it."

Court's chest tightened at the mention of Marsh and his breathing grew shallow. He stopped walking and put his hand against a building. It felt rough and cool in the shade.

"Are you alright?"

He waved his hand at her, trying to tell her to give him a moment, but she didn't understand.

"Breathe, Court. Just breathe."

He tried to calm himself but couldn't. Images of the village swirled in his mind. He saw Marsh falling to the ground, over and over, then the memory of Walker, a bloody hole in his chest and his legs burnt black. The memory of the smell came with the images and he convulsed until he coughed up the contents of his stomach, the morning's breakfast oatmeal still recognizable all those hours later.

His hand shook as his wiped his lips with the back of his hand.

"Sorry," he said, stammering a little.

"Let's sit down for a minute."

She led him across the street to steps that went into an alcove at the base of a building where they would be in the shade.

"Are you sick?"

"I'm not sure. I couldn't breathe and then everything just went kind of funny in my head."

"It's not much further to the university and then we can find a place to stay for the night. You should drink something but I don't know where—"

The sound of a door opening behind them broke her train of thought. They both turned, the quick movement making Court's vision unsteady for a second.

The man in the doorway was rail thin with eyes that protruded from his face so much they looked unnatural. The red-handled axe dangling from his hand accentuated his unfriendly demeanor.

"Move along."

"My friend was ill. We just need—"

"I saw him emptying himself over there. Whatever disease he's got, we want it away from here. Move on. Now."

He swung the ax up and grabbed the handle with both hands, instantly escalating his posture from intimidating to dangerous.

"Let's go," Court said, his voice cracking.

Elle furrowed her brow but got up and helped Court to his feet. He was still shaky but the short rest had made him feel a little better. He found he could walk with only a hint of lightheadedness.

"Nice neighborhood," Elle said.

He tried to chuckle but it made him cough, the taste of

bile still stuck in the back of his mouth.

They walked without talking. Court focused on moving his feet and keeping his mind away from his memories. The scale of the buildings and streets made it difficult for him to judge distance but it didn't seem to take long for them to reach a sign proclaiming University of Toronto St. George Campus.

"We're close," Elle said. She closed her eyes for a moment then said, "It should be just ahead and over."

Unlike the streets they'd been walking through, they found an area surrounding several buildings that was clean and not overgrown. The buildings were shorter and made from stones and brick, a stark contrast to the earlier buildings made from inconceivably large slabs and that seemed to stretch up to infinity.

"That's it." She led Court up the stairs and through a heavy set of doors carved from polished wood. "I'm surprised the doors are just unlocked like that."

There was no sign of people inside, just a corridor that stretched out to the left and right.

"Do you know where to go now?"

"Not exactly but there's supposed to be an administrator's office close to here."

The clacking of shoes echoed in the hallway, the sound of the footfalls suggesting an urgent walk but not a full run. A woman emerged from the dim hallway into the brighter confluence of the doorway and the corridor. She looked a few years older than Court, although it was hard to be certain in the low light. She moved with a confidence that made Court believe she was more than comfortable with the assortment of weapons she carried. Despite her hurried approached, she seemed calm, as if rushing to them was out of responsibility and not trepidation.

"Welcome to the University of Toronto. What do you seek?"

"We're looking for someone," Elle said. "A professor here."

"You're a little late for that."

"Aren't you open for a couple more hours?"

"I mean you're about a decade too late for finding professors. There hasn't been a real university professor here since I was a teenager."

"We're trying to locate someone who used to be a professor here," Court said.

"What's wrong with him?" the woman asked, using the bow in her hand to point at Court.

"We've had a long day and his stomach is a bit upset."

The woman took a step back.

"Sick? What other symptoms?"

"Not that kind of sick," Court said, trying to sound like he was fine.

"I think he's just dehydrated."

"I can fetch him clean water but he stays there. We can't risk spreading viruses to the people here."

Court sat on a nearby bench. The woman returned with a glass jar filled with remarkably clean looking water.

"Mind the chip in the glass," the woman said. She set it on the floor and pushed it closer to Court with the bow. "Can't be too careful when it comes to disease."

"Thank you," he said.

The water was tepid and not refreshing like the well water back in the village, but it still felt wonderful as he drank and washed away the awful taste still in his mouth.

"You two stay here for now. If he's only dehydrated and the water helps, I'll believe you that he's not sick and you can come in."

The woman went back down the hallway. When she was gone, Court offered the last of the water to Elle but she refused.

"What do we do if they don't let us in?" Even whispering, he worried that his voice would carry down the long hallways that seemed to amplify the tiniest of sounds.

"I'm less concerned with that and more concerned about them not having any information we can use."

They sat quietly for a while and Court started to feel a little more normal, although he was hungry. Elle had assured him they'd be able to get a place to stay and some food with their money, but he didn't know when that would be. A craving for dried apple slices came over him and he stood up abruptly, not willing to let his mind drift back to thoughts of village life.

"I'm feeling better," he called.

The woman returned. With his eyes adjusted to the light, Court could see her weaponry more clearly. Two daggers tucked into a belt were plain with simple handles; arrows protruded from a green-and-gray quiver strapped across her torso; the ornate hilt of a sword poked out above one shoulder; and what appeared to be the handle of a decorative dagger was strapped around one leg.

"Jump in place ten times," she instructed.

"What?"

"Jump in place. Prove to me you're not sick."

Court shrugged and started hopping.

"You too," she said to Elle.

Court felt foolish, but he counted out ten jumps and then did two more so he finished at the same time as Elle.

"Good enough. Come on back with me. I'm Ursula, sergeant-at-arms for the university."

Both sides of the corridor were cluttered with artwork, shelves full of real paper books, and even a mounted skeleton of a small animal. A lizard, Court guessed.

"Right in here," Ursula said. "This is Maud."

The woman behind the desk wasn't tall when she stood, which seemed to require considerable effort. She was a round woman with graying brown hair cut short in a way that made her head look even rounder. She was almost as pale as Elle had been the day she arrived in the village. Ursula carried herself as a fighter; this woman had the air of someone who avoided action.

What was the word Elle had used? Administrator?

"Greetings," Maud said with a wheezy voice. She extended a hand and Elle pressed her palm against it.

A blocked of carved wood on Maud's desk announced Superintendent.

"Ursula tells me you are in search of a professor."

Court turned to look at Ursula but she had gone.

"That's right," Elle said. "We know she used to work here but we're not sure where she went after the university closed. We are hoping you might have information on her whereabouts."

"Au contraire," Maud said indignantly, "this university is not closed."

"No, of course not. I mean from before, I guess."

"You guess?"

Court decided that he didn't like this Maud woman very much. She could stand for some of Marsh's instruction on the basics of pleasant conversation.

"All I mean is, we were told that she was a professor here and we're trying to find out where she is now."

"I see. Unfortunately, young lady, the university does not make a practice of giving out personal information about staff, present or previous. It can create delicate situations for us. Expensive situations, if anyone were to pursue us in the future for sharing things we ought not to have disclosed."

"We aren't here for any nefarious purpose, just delivering some sad news."

Nefarious, Court thought. He knew that word, it had been in something Marsh had given him to read, but he couldn't remember the meaning. It was good that Elle was handling the conversation, he wouldn't be able to verbally spar with Maud.

"Sad in what sense?"

"An old friend of hers died. We're trying to locate her to let her know."

"I can assure you that anyone old enough to have been a professor here is accustomed to old friends dying unannounced. Or even disappearing without a trace."

"Be that as it may, delivering the news was a dying request of her friend. We're trying to respect that. And you did say that you don't make it a practice to give out information but surely that means there are exceptions from time to time."

"Yes, that is true. From time to time, as you say, for benefactors and patrons of the university."

Benefactors and patrons were words that Court didn't

know.

"How much?" Elle said.

Maud put a hand to her chest, feigning offense.

"My dear, our confidential staff records are not for sale."
Maud drawled the last two words with disdain dripping from
each syllable. Then she reached into a drawer and slid an
anonymous currency device across the scuffed wooden
desktop. "But if you care to make a small donation to the
university, you will be helping to continue the traditions of
this grand institution that stretch back to 1827."

Elle's lips narrowed and her eyebrows squeezed together
as she took out their anonymous currency device. Court saw
her dial it to twenty and tap it against Maud's.

Maud clucked and shook her head side to side. Elle's lip
curled on one side, exposing some of her teeth. She tapped
the device again.

Maud only sighed.

Elle dialed twenty a third time and tapped. Maud's
expression stayed blank. Despite a lifetime of being taught
that violence was rarely the best course of action, Court had
an intense urge to introduce Maud's forehead to the top of
her desk. The thought of Ursula's bow and sword in the
corridor helped him keep his impulse at bay.

When Maud realized that Elle was not going to offer up
further qynars, she said, "Thank you so much, my dear, for
supporting the University of Toronto. Your donation is
greatly appreciated."

Through gritted teeth, Elle said, "Now what about the
professor?"

"Oh, I'm sure we can relax the rules this one time. What is
the name?"

"Nora Barrett."

"Let me just check."

Maud returned the anonymous currency device to her desk drawer and took out a small tablet. She consulted with the tablet then excused herself to the next room. She returned within a minute with a paper file.

"We keep hard copies of our records to ensure nothing gets tampered with. Plus there's something magical about physical things, don't you think? That's a big part of the raison d'être for the university these days. But I digress. It says here that Nora Barrett was a full university professor then resigned eleven years ago, which was before…"

"Before things changed," Elle said.

"Yes, a good way to put it. About a year before. No doubt she heard rumors and got out early. Regardless, I'm afraid that's all the help I can be."

"What?" Elle said, almost shouting.

Court heard a rustling outside the door; he guessed it was Ursula preparing for trouble.

"According to our records, Dr. Barrett went missing shortly after she resigned. She is presumed deceased."

Elle shrank back into her chair.

"Not an answer you were prepared for? She wasn't a young woman, you know, not even eleven years ago. You shouldn't be surprised."

"Isn't there anything else you can tell us?" Court said.

"That's all I have. But if you want to leave your names and a way to contact you, I'll keep my ears open."

Maud smiled at them. It was an awful smile to Court, like the twisted smile he imagined the Big Bad Wolf made when it met Little Red Riding Hood. Marsh hadn't approved of that story but it circulated through the village year after year regardless, usually told by the teenagers to younger kids around the campfire. Sometimes one of them would hide in the shadows and howl at just the right time. Court remembered a time when he jumped in his seat, even when he knew the howl was coming. He had been too old to be scared by a campfire story. Paulo had nearly pissed himself laughing.

"Your name?" Maud asked again, breaking Court from his memory.

Elle grabbed his forearm, her nails digging in so hard that it hurt.

"Let's go. Now."

She yanked his arm and he followed her out the door. They rushed past Ursula and hurried down the hall.

From behind them, Maud's voice came in a loud wheeze, "You didn't leave a way for me to contact you."

They burst out of the stone building and into the sunlight.

"What was that all about?"

"I panicked," she said. "Something about that woman. I don't trust her. I don't want her to know anything about me. About us."

Elle moved briskly and Court had to force his legs to keep pace even though they were several inches longer than hers.

"Where now?" he asked.

"We need a place to stay. That leech weaseled sixty qynars out of me. And for nothing. We couldn't afford that. We should..."

"What?"

"We should go demand our money back. She hustled us. I bet she already knew that Nora Barrett was dead."

"Did you not get a good look at Ursula? You'd lose a limb storming in there."

Despite himself, Court let the vision of Maud's head hitting her desk play in his mind's eye for a moment. Marsh would say that such thinking was neither helpful nor healthy.

"I know you're right," Elle said. "It's just wishful thinking."

The condition of the city deteriorated as they moved away from the tiny cluster of university buildings. Piles of garbage reappeared. A trio of mangy dogs darted between buildings. Court instinctively reached for his mag gun before remembering they had left it behind in Alma. The dogs reminded him of how hungry he was.

"That's where we can rent rooms." Elle pointed out a wide building. "It used to be housing for students at the university. From what I read, it's been well maintained since the university was gutted."

Behind a metal door, they found a lone man waiting behind a counter in an austere room. Plain black letters declared HOTEL RESIDENCE.

"Good afternoon. Checking in?"

"How much for two rooms?" Elle asked.

"It's ninety qynars per night. Each."

"Ninety each?"

"That's correct."

Elle looked at Court. If pressed to describe the meaning of the look, he would have said despair.

"We can't afford that," she said.

"You could share a room. Two people in one room is only 135 qynars."

"We can't afford that either. Is there someplace cheaper

that you could recommend?"

"There are other places but not that I would recommend. The security and cleanliness of Hotel Residence is the best you will find in the old city. In good conscience, I cannot recommend accommodations where you run the risk of your room being robbed of everything but the bed bugs."

The hotel man had a smug look on his face as he alone enjoyed his joke.

Back in the waning sun of the late afternoon, Court said, "My impression of Toronto isn't great so far."

"That asshole in there isn't wrong. This is the only place I found that sounded reasonable." She collapsed on the steps. "Shitty sour split."

"Language, language. Language, miss." The voice came from a nearby tree.

Leaves rustled and a body landed on the ground with a thud. The source of the voice was a shortish man, maybe five feet tall, dressed in layers of brown fabrics. There was no telling what the original colors might have been.

Reacting purely on instinct, Court moved between Elle and the stranger. Elle nudged him aside so she could get a good look.

"Why were you in that tree?" she asked.

"Shhhh," the man replied. "Keep your voices down and don't use their profanities. They are listening."

Elle rolled her eyes.

"You don't think after fifty years that the Qyntarak haven't gotten used to humans saying sour split?"

The man covered his ears and searched the sky.

"Please," he begged.

"We'll make you a deal," Court said. "She won't say it

again if you'll tell us the best place to get a clean, safe place to sleep for the night."

"My tree is best but you can't have that."

"We were hoping for something more indoors," Elle said.

"Then the Hotel Residence, right there."

"We can't afford it." She looked down at her feet and Court thought it was odd that she would feel embarrassed in front of a man living in a tree.

"Then you want the Rofchild. Very clean, most people only stay a few hours, not enough time to get dirty. And no bugs. Best place to go for no bugs."

"Why would people only stay a few hours?" Court asked.

Elle looked at him in surprise. Neither she nor the tree man answered his question.

"How do we get there?" Elle asked.

The man pointed and said, "Go that way until you see the orange pizza store then turn left and you will find the Rofchild."

"Thank you," Elle said.

The man's expression grew somber. He grabbed Court by the shoulders.

"Go quickly and get inside. They're watching us, from the skies. I saw them just today. It's not safe. It's never safe."

"Alright," Court said and wriggled free of the man's bony grip.

"Beware the skies. They're flying today."

Chapter 31: Britt

"No information on Novak's whereabouts," Bear said.

"What about the new dock supervisor?" Britt asked.

"Vidonia Kraft, age thirty-seven. Formerly a logistics coordinator at another dock. Doesn't know her father, her mother died in an accident six years ago. No siblings, no children, no record of negative encounters with any Qyntarak-linked businesses. Below average debt load. This is a promotion so she'll be making more money and feeling good about her life. I just don't see any avenue to approach her. I think this dock will be cold for the foreseeable future."

"What does that mean for us?" Wilm asked. He was sitting cross-legged on top of a crate.

Sitting like that would be murder on my hips, Britt thought. *Am I too old to be thinking about starting a new site? Maybe time to pass the torch...*

Without moving her head, she shook the thoughts away.

No, I don't give up because things get a little challenging.

She looked from Wilm to Bear. They were believers in the cause and they believed in her leadership. Time to be a leader.

"It means we prioritize finding a new site. We still have legitimate inventory we can sell and ship from here. We'll use those proceeds to bootstrap another location."

The men nodded in agreement.

"Bear," she continued, "I know you just started looking, but any leads on potential locations?"

Bear shook his head.

"How long—" Wilm began to ask but stopped when the latch of the door clicked open.

"Sorry I'm so late," Ainsley said after the door had closed behind her.

"We started without you," Britt said. "The short version is that this dock is cold and we need to scout for a new location."

"There's something else. The reason I'm late. Someone is looking for Nora Barrett."

Chapter 32: Elle

ELLE WRINKLED HER nose as she examined the bedsheets in their room.

"I suppose I shouldn't be surprised that the cleanliness standards of a person living in a tree would be questionable."

"It's better than the street, isn't it?" Court said.

"Marginally. I think I'll sleep on the floor."

The space was tiny. A toilet, a ten-liter jug of water, and a small counter took up one wall. A bed for two lined the other. The door couldn't even open all the way, but it had only cost twenty qynars for the night.

"There's not much room to sleep on the floor."

"All the more reason for me to sleep there. I'm smaller."

"Not for long if I don't eat something."

"Right," she said and handed him a pouch. "By the way, this is food."

Court tore open the packet. The bewilderment on his face was unmistakable.

"What, exactly, is this?"

"Food."

"You said that. But what is it made from? It doesn't look real."

"I'm not sure but it's all we have, so you'd better eat it."

He scrunched his face as he took a tentative bite.

"Well?"

"You were right about one thing. It's not as good as apples or rabbit."

She laughed and they both ate. She felt better almost immediately and thought she saw an upswing in Court's mood soon after, even if he hadn't enjoyed the taste.

"Do you think that water is safe to drink?" Court asked.

"For twenty qynars a night, I wouldn't risk it. We should have bought clean water, I didn't think about that."

"I can wait until morning."

"Good. Because I'm exhausted."

She lay in the narrow space on the floor, her feet by the toilet and her head near the door. A third of her body was under the bed frame. She closed her eyes and tried to pretend she hadn't seen the sea of dust beside her.

"Any idea what we'll do in the morning?"

"No." She could hear the weariness in her own voice—and the defeat. They'd hit a dead end. They had no clue about how to proceed and very little money left to survive on. "Hopefully, a good night's rest will provide some clarity."

Sleep took Elle quickly but kept a loose hold on her. Footsteps and giggling in the hallway woke her several times. When the Rofchild grew quiet, her dreams tormented her. Vaidehi being shot from the sky. An apple tree bursting into flames. The crazy man from the tree falling from its burning branches, his face turning into a giant mouth full of tiny, pointed teeth.

The giant mouth kept repeating, "Beware the skies. They're flying today."

Something jolted her awake. Their room didn't have a window so she couldn't tell how late it was. She squinted, trying to judge whether the light coming in under the door was brighter than the last time she woke up. A shadow moved in unison with a creak.

Someone was outside the door. She looked up, straining in the dim light to confirm that the chain lock was in place.

It was.

The electronic lock clicked, and the door cracked open. Elle held her breath and reached up to grab Court's arm. He grunted and rolled out of her reach. The door opened further.

She realized her head was close enough for someone to see her, and maybe even grab her, through the opening. She pushed herself away, twisting so her legs slid under the bed and bunching her torso and arms by the toilet, its stink making her nose curl.

The chain jingled and pulled taut. Then the door shut with a soft click.

Elle pulled herself up beside the bed, clamped her hand over Court's mouth, and shook him with as much force as she dared, hoping she didn't make enough noise to leak past the door.

His eyes went wide and he struggled until he registered her shushing him. She pointed at the door and the light coming in underneath it. The shadow was gone.

"What's wrong?" he whispered groggily.

"There's someone out there. They just tried opening our door."

"Looks like they've moved on," he muttered then lay back down and closed his eyes.

Elle sat on the edge of the bed watching the light, making sure the shadow didn't return. Her heart was racing. She concentrated on taking slow, intentional breaths.

A loud knock on the door made her flinch and forced Court awake.

"Housekeeping," a man said from the hallway.

They didn't answer him. More knocking.

"Housekeeping," the man repeated. "I'm here to clean the room."

The electronic lock clicked again. This time the door opened to the limit of the chain. Court jumped up and tried to push it shut but there was a boot between the door and the jamb.

"Can you come back later?" Elle said.

"Sorry. Can't."

Something swung through the opening in a blur and pieces of the chain clattered to the floor. The door burst open, slamming into Court's nose. He fell back on the bed, his legs trapped between the mattress and the door. The man came into the room and pressed the end of a Scorpion baton into Court.

"Don't move." He had a gun in his other hand. Elle recognized the model from her training—a Morris S7 stun gun, powerful enough to put her in a coma at full strength. He pointed it at her. "You either."

Chapter 33: Court

THE BATON BITING into his chest made Court think of Marsh lying dead in the village.

"You either," the intruder said, pointing his gun at Elle.

His focus was off Court for a fraction of a second and Court took the opening. He grabbed the baton with both hands and rolled his whole body, pulling the man off balance. The gun went off with a crack, a shower of sparks jumping from where it struck the wall.

While the man tried to right himself, Elle kicked at his knee. With the fourth kick, he bellowed. When he shifted his weight to his other leg, Court got an elbow to the man's stomach. He grunted and rolled away from Court toward the corner of the room. In a blur, the gun snapped again and Elle collapsed.

"No," Court screamed. While he watched Elle convulse, he heard another snap and the room burst into a thousand brilliant colors before everything went black.

Chapter 34: Elle

WHAT IS THAT ringing?

Elle tried to open her eyes but it hurt. The light was so bright. And the ringing...

Where am I?

Her lips were parched.

When is it? Why am I so thirsty?

She heard nothing but the ringing. No voices, no movement.

Elle cracked her eyes open more slowly. There didn't appear to be anyone in the room with her. She tried to get up but was tied to a cot.

Trying not to panic, she studied her surroundings: white walls, no windows, no decorations, and no signs. A tube with a blue sticker that read WATER hung near her face.

She rolled her head further and got her lips around the tube. She sucked but there was no liquid.

A water tube with no water? What is wrong with these

people?

She remembered the room at the Rofchild. A man had forced his way in.

Court... Where's Court?

She had to get out. She had to find Court.

The ropes gave no promise of slackening as she twisted and strained; defeated, she let her head fall back for a reprieve from the pointless exertion. It wasn't going to work. She wasn't going anywhere.

Out of her line of sight, she heard movement.

"Oh, you're awake. Good. I was just bringing you some water in case you were thirsty when you came to." A woman hung a blue bag of liquid on the bed frame and attached the hose to it.

"Just sip through the straw if you need a drink."

Elle hated to show weakness in front of her unknown captor but she was desperate. She drank enough so she could speak clearly.

"Where am I? Who are you?"

"Hold those questions for just a moment." The woman called out, "The girl's awake."

"Finally," a man said.

The voice sounded familiar, but from where? When his face came into view, she understood. It was the man from the Rofchild, the man who'd broken into their room. She should have expected that but her head was so foggy.

"Who are you?" Elle demanded.

"I had the same question for you. No implanted IDs that we can detect. No ID bracelet on you or your friend."

"Where is he?"

"Don't worry, he's fine."

"If this is your idea of fine, I beg to differ."

The man laughed. "That's a funny expression, isn't it? I beg to differ. I suppose it was meant to sound polite once upon a time. It's a really old-fashioned saying. Makes me wonder where someone your age picked it up."

Keep quiet, she told herself. *He's trying to goad you into talking.*

"Look, we don't want trouble with you," the woman said. "Just tell us who you are."

"If you don't know who we are, why did you break into our room? Sort of makes it seem like you do want trouble."

"Was that a threat? Did she just threaten me?"

"Would you knock it off," the woman said. "You were asking about Nora Barrett. How do you know that name?"

It was like a spark ignited in Elle's brain.

They know about Nora Barrett...

"Did you know her?" Elle asked.

The man laughed. "You could say that."

"Nora Barrett vanished quite a while ago. We're interested in any information about her. Why were you looking for her?"

"I'm not inclined to sharing with people who've kidnapped and tied me up."

The man let out a frustrated sigh.

"She's right," the woman said. "We haven't given her any reason to trust us."

"She tried to dislocate my knee."

"After you broke into her room."

"Right, I see your point. I'll untie you. We only want to talk."

He untied the ropes and gave Elle room to stand up. The

man was even bigger than she'd realized. He towered over her.

Once free, she located an unconscious Court tied to a chair and rushed to him.

"He's not hurt, only stunned from a neuroelectrical inhibitor slug. He'll come around soon. You came to faster than normal," the woman said.

Elle rubbed the spot where the slug had hit. It was tender.

"You'll have a nasty bruise there. Maybe a welt. Sorry about that," the man said.

"Can you wake him?"

"No, it's best to let his body revive itself at its own pace," the woman said.

"And what happens if I tell you why we were asking about Nora Barrett?"

"That depends on what you tell us," the man said.

"Are you trying to be an asshole or is it just coming naturally?" the woman said to him. "Nothing's going to happen to you. I guess you could say that we're concerned about her legacy."

The statement didn't make sense to Elle but the word legacy caused her to think of Dr. Donovan, which made her remember the suit.

"Where's my bag?"

"We have it," the woman said. "Surprising to find it full of Aldebaran tech."

"It belongs to me. I want it back."

"Belongs to you?" The man laughed. "You mean you stole it from somewhere."

"Give me my bag, and the suit, and I'll tell you what you want to know. Then you let us go. Deal?"

"Fine." The woman retrieved the bag from the next room and returned it to Elle. The helmet, the suit, and her anonymous currency device were all inside.

"Well?"

"We're delivering a message. An old friend of hers died and asked us to let her know."

"We already know that," the man said. "That's what you told the superintendent at the university."

"Who was the friend?" the woman asked.

"You're not Nora Barrett," Elle said. "That news is for her."

The man snorted. "And I'm the asshole?"

A voice came from the adjoining room. "Enough of this bullshit. Ainsley, Bear, you're just going in circles. Let's cut to the chase." Another woman, much older than the first, came in with palms extended. "I'm Nora Barrett."

Chapter 35: Petra

KANE'S FACE WAS a bit bigger than life-size on Petra's oversized tablet screen. She could see spittle spraying as he yelled.

"We've been here for nineteen hours. You had them on video. How can you not have any idea where they are?"

"They went into the old Toronto financial district on foot. There was no way to track them."

She noted a vein that bulged on Kane's forehead. She didn't remember seeing that before. Then again, she'd never seen him this visibly upset.

"We have access to every video feed. We have the most sophisticated systems in the world for facial recognition, gait analysis, voice analysis. We have grav flyers patrolling the streets that found their forged ID bracelets on the side of a road from seventy-five meters. This is unacceptable."

Panic started to grab hold in Petra's gut. Her little, windowless control room suddenly felt much too small. She'd pushed it too far. Kane was going to conclude that she was incompetent.

I'll be off the team. My mission will... it'll... I'll be scrubbed.

A screen to her left flashed. She glanced that way involuntarily. Even on the brink of being fired, she couldn't stop herself from doing her job.

"Am I distracting you from something, agent?"

"Wait one." She tapped and swiped through the incoming data feed. "We've got a lead. Ninety minutes ago. The Rofchild, a rent-by-the-hour establishment within walking distance of their last known location. An assailant stunned the front desk clerk and broke into a room. Occupants were a man and woman matching approximate age and description of L37 and her companion. Signs of struggle, no blood, stunner slugs found in the room. Local authorities are investigating."

"Now we're talking," Kane said. "Pull up the video feed. Let's take a look."

"Sorry, sir, I can't. The Rofchild doesn't have a networked system. Police notes say they're reviewing security footage so there must be an on-site archive. I'll be able to see whatever the police upload to central storage but there's no telling how long that will be."

Kane looked offscreen. "Wilkes, take a couple folks to this Rofchild rooming house in Toronto and look at those recordings."

"Roger that, boss."

"Good work, Petra. Keep searching on your end."

Kane disconnected the video call and Petra flopped back into her chair.

I did what I could for you, L37. You're on your own now.

Chapter 36: Elle

"B-but you're supposed to be dead," Elle said.

The woman claiming to be Nora Barrett grinned. "I look pretty good in spite of it, though, don't I?"

"Prove that you're her."

"You want me to prove that I'm me? Alright, Ainsley, am I Nora Barrett?"

"Yes. Or at least you used to be."

"There you go. I'm Nora Barrett, or at least I used to be."

She wore a charming smile that grew bigger as if her own banter entertained her. Elle didn't reciprocate the smile, maintaining an icy stare and trying to think of what would make her believe this woman was, or was not, Nora Barrett.

"When you were younger, who were some of your friends?"

"A test? Clever. I've had lots of friends over the years. Care to be more specific?"

Elle closed her eyes, trying to remember what Marsh had

said.

They were, what, students together? Worked together?

"You knew some scientists when you were younger. They had a nickname for you."

"Yes, that's true. One of them died recently."

She looked genuinely sad but Elle couldn't let herself be sucked in by the woman's charisma. Too much was at stake and this woman showing up felt too convenient.

"Names?"

"You're talking about Clint and Marsh. They called me the tour guide."

A tingle went through Elle's body that made her shiver. It wasn't definitive proof but Elle knew, she just knew, that this was her. They'd done it. They'd found Nora Barrett. They'd found the tour guide. Everything was going to be fine.

"We brought this to show you," Elle said with a shaking voice. "It's from Dr. Donovan."

Nora didn't take the bag from her.

"I'm afraid I don't understand. Who are you?"

"My designation is L... my name is Elle. Dr. Donovan raised me."

"Why would Clint send me an Aldebaran suit? Why would he send me anything after all these years?"

"Dr. Donovan snuck me and this suit out of the Aldebaran research center where he worked. The Qyntarak killed him. Court found me."

"Who's Court?"

Elle touched Court's arm and he stirred from the contact.

"Court found me and took me to Marsh—"

"Marsh Lapin?"

"Yes."

"Out in the godforsaken woods?"

Elle told them about the village, the data vault, the cryptic message, the massacre of Court's village, and her trip with Court to find Nora Barrett.

Nora covered her mouth in what looked like sincere horror as Elle spoke.

"Hearing what you've gone through, I feel awful about the way Bear brought you to see me."

"It was a justified precaution," Bear said in defense of himself. "She did try to break my leg."

"You broke into our room and shot us." Elle enunciated each word with force.

Court shifted in his chair again.

Ainsley checked his pulse. "He should be awake soon."

"Now that you've delivered this suit to me from Clint, what am I supposed to do with it? I feel like I'm missing a piece of the puzzle."

"There was a recording. The message from Dr. Donovan said for you to compare it to an A2 jacket. We're hoping that means something to you."

Nora tapped her chin. "Interesting—"

"Britt, we've got company," a man shouted from the other room. He rushed in with a panicked expression on his face.

Elle looked at Nora in shock. "Britt?"

"Later," she said. "Wilm, details."

"Three men, armed, in state-issued uniforms but I don't recognize the insignia. One's stationed at the exterior entrance, two are going through the train platform, I assume to use the interior stairs. There's a grav flyer hovering out front."

The color seemed to drain from Britt's face. "Shit."

"We're busted," Ainsley said.

"Yes," Britt said. "Roof evac it is then. Bear, you'll have to carry Sleeping Beauty there. Elle, follow Ainsley and don't forget that suit."

"What about you?" Ainsley asked.

"I'll buy you time."

"No."

"It's alright. I'll be fine. Everyone, hurry, please."

Bear had Court untied and slung over his shoulder when the doors blew open. Ainsley screamed. Bear dropped Court to the floor with a thud and jumped behind the now-empty chair. Something pinged as it ricocheted off the chair.

Bear returned fire with his Morris S7. The stunner slug sparked against the body armor of the intruder, illuminating the word WILKES over his left breast.

Wilkes fired again and a hole burst open in the padding of the chair where Bear had been taking cover a fraction of a second earlier. Wilkes tracked Bear's movement and ignored Elle, either deeming her a lesser threat or having not seen her yet. Elle spun into a sloppy roundhouse kick, her inner thigh burning after weeks without practice or stretching, but she connected with Wilkes's hand and sent the gun clattering.

Wilkes tackled her before she had regained her footing from the kick and crashed on top of her. The impact knocked the air from her lungs and he slapped her across the face with the back of his left hand, the one she hadn't kicked.

"Stupid bitch," he said with a snarl and slapped her again.

"Don't move, asshole."

Wilkes turned to see Ainsley pointing his own gun at him. He rose from the ground by pushing off Elle, grinding her shoulder blades into the cold floor. The gun shook in Ainsley's hands and Wilkes lunged at her. She pulled the trigger but nothing happened. He laughed and punched her in the nose, sending her stumbling backward as blood poured over her lips and chin. He pulled the gun from her hand.

"It's paired to my ID, you dumb shit." He shot her in the leg. Ainsley screamed and collapsed. Without looking at her, he pointed to Elle and said, "Stay down."

Elle craned her neck to see what he was looking at. A second attacker had a gun to Britt's head. A terrified Wilm stood with his hands raised and his eyes locked on the gun.

The third attacker was exchanging blows with Bear, the big man's bulk letting him go blow for blow with the smaller opponent despite his body armor.

Elle couldn't see Wilkes's face but she imagined a sadistic smile on it. He unclipped the Scorpion from his thigh and pressed his thumb into it. Blue sparks shot from the end. Before he could reach Bear, though, Wilkes fell to the ground. When Bear stepped back to dodge a swing, he stumbled over the fallen Wilkes. In the momentary chaos, the Scorpion's live end hit Bear's attacker in the leg and he shook violently before crumpling.

The attacker with the gun to Britt's head swung his arm and aimed at the pile of bodies. Elle scrambled backward away from the line of fire. The gunman swung the gun toward her then back to the group on the floor.

That's when Elle saw Court gripping Wilkes's legs. That's what had taken him down.

Britt turned and drove her knee into the gunman's groin. He grunted but his body armor absorbed most of the impact.

He raised his arm to strike her and Wilm rammed his shoulder into the man's torso, driving him back into a metal wall that rattled from the impact.

The gun clanged and fell.

"You're dead," the gunman said.

"Britt, the door," Wilm yelled.

Wilm held the gunman pinned against the wall even while he pounded on Wilm's sides with his fists.

Lights flashed and a klaxon rang out. The metal wall opened outward at an angle. Wilm kept pushing him back until the intruder had no more floor under foot and he slipped through the opening. Wilm dropped to his stomach, trying to decouple himself from the falling man who was desperately grasping at Wilm's shirt.

The man's bulky armor caught on the lip of the floor and the slack gave Wilm enough opportunity to roll out of reach. The man clawed at the floor but it was too smooth to grip. A moment later, he plummeted from sight.

Court was still holding on to Wilkes's legs while Wilkes swung his Scorpion, using it like a club on Bear. They were all shouting incoherently at each other.

A gunshot reverberated through the room.

"Enough," Britt said.

All eyes turned to her where she held the gun of the unconscious intruder next to his limp arm so his ID would activate it. Wilkes stopped swinging. After several seconds, he let his Scorpion baton drop from his hand.

"Get his helmet off," Britt instructed.

Bear moaned as he rolled to a kneeling position and forced the helmet off. The face underneath was pockmarked, and the man's hair was soaked with sweat.

"Who are you?" Britt demanded.

"Kiss my sour split," Wilkes said.

She kicked him in the mouth.

"That close enough?"

"I'm going to flay you open, you old cunt."

"Charming. Wilm, you alright? Can you check on Ainsley? As for you, Mr. Wilkes, assuming that's your name, strip down to your underwear."

Wilkes spit blood from his gashed lip at Britt's shoe.

"Fine. Bear, you can do it. No need to be gentle."

Elle got to her feet and went to Court.

"Hey, you're awake," she said with sarcastic playfulness in her voice.

"What is going on?"

"Hold on," Britt said. "Let's save it for when the trash is put away."

When Bear had Wilkes stripped down to his tight-fitting, knee-length underpants and nothing else, Britt waved him toward the storage room full of crates.

"One last chance to talk," Britt said, "before we lock you in here."

"Go to hell. My team'll have me out of here within an hour and you'll be picking through garbage on red ships."

"When you look back on this moment, I want you to remember that we gave you a chance to be a decent human being. Go ahead, Bear."

Bear slammed the inactive end of a Scorpion into Wilkes's nose. He stumbled back against a crate. Bear flipped the Scorpion around and jammed the active end into Wilkes's bare stomach, causing him to fall back against the crate and then roll to the floor. Bear stripped Wilkes's unconscious associate and dragged him into the storage room as well.

"Leave them some water and open an air vent. With their grav flyer floating outside, someone'll be here for them soon enough," Britt said.

Bear moved a pair of four liter jugs into the room and locked them in.

"This was such a great location," she said with a sigh.

A pulsing chime played outside.

"Train's arriving," Bear said.

"Perfect. Throw their clothes out before it gets here. If we're lucky, it will sweep them away and maybe buy us some extra time."

While Bear did that, Britt checked on Ainsley, who had been moaning since Wilkes shot her.

"She's going to need a surgeon," Wilm said. "I'll give her something for the pain but we don't have anything strong enough for this."

"I know someone who can help. We'd better get moving."

"Elle, what is going on?" Court asked.

Britt stepped toward him and put out her palm. "We haven't met yet. My name used to be Nora Barrett. You can call me Britt."

Chapter 37: Petra

PETRA WATCHED THE text messages flash on her tablet screen as a conversation went back and forth between two devices that the owners believed to be anonymous and secure.

In a bad box. Bushwhacked at the teapot. Need help shaking up a sawbone.

For?

Crew stoved up by barking iron in prayer bone.

Just one?

Yes.

Burning the breeze to your shack.

ACK. Will find a sawbone.

It wasn't fair for her to be too judgmental. For amateurs, they were doing a good job. Bots would never single out their old cowboy slang from the noise of the network. But she was no bot and she sure as hell wasn't an amateur.

She deleted the notifications from her tablet.

The camera feed from the grav flyer had just shown L37,

the unidentified male, and four brokers leaving the building that Wilkes and team had entered. One of them had a leg wound. The coded message reinforced her conclusion: barking iron in prayer bone had to mean a gunshot in the knee.

They were going to see the head of security at the University of Toronto, a known Reclamationist. Since Petra wasn't going to tell Kane where L37 was headed, she and her companions would be safe for now.

She tapped on another tablet and waited for Kane to answer. He was going to be pissed, but at least he'd be pissed at Wilkes this time.

Chapter 38: Court

THEY WERE IN old human-driven cars. Court rode with Elle and Britt. Ainsley, the injured woman, rode with the two men.

Britt turned around from the front seat to face them. "Black market taxis," she said. "No ID records, no tracking, and anonymous payments accepted. Gotta love em."

The cars left them outside a building that looked abandoned. From behind a mature tree trunk, Ursula stepped out from the shadows. The sun glistened off the decorative sword hilt when she raised her hand in greeting.

Without conversation, they followed her inside. Ainsley grunted as she limped, supported by the shoulders of Wilm and Bear. Her pant leg was dark with blood. In the village, that kind of injury would be life-altering.

Ursula took them to the lowest level of the building and down an unlit corridor. The darkness seemed to swallow up the meager illumination from her handheld light.

"These underground walkways connect the university buildings. I make sure the cameras stay vandalized around the entrances so I can get people in and out discreetly if need be."

The dark walkway felt like a tunnel to Court. It ended at a nondescript metal wall. Ursula squatted and slid her hand into a gap at its base. Something clicked and she pulled the wall panel open like a door.

"Added this myself. It's not fancy, but it keeps riffraff out."

Behind the false wall was a storage space filled with shelves and boxes. Ursula stuck her fingers under another wall panel and it popped open to reveal a well lit hallway.

"We're underneath the main university building now. I have a spot ready for you."

They took Ainsley into a tiled room where the fumes from disinfectant cleaners burned Court's nose.

"What about the surgeon?" Britt asked.

"Dr. Barton. On her way. She's bringing a field surgical bot. It's what I could manage under the circumstances. I sterilized everything as best I could. I need to go back to meet the doctor."

Ainsley groaned as Bear helped her onto a metal table. Court took Elle by the arm and pulled her away from the others. Since he'd woken up, he'd been following her lead in the interest of basic survival but he needed to understand what had just unfolded. Britt had insisted they not talk in front of the taxi driver, so now was his first good opportunity for explanations.

"Who are these people?"

Elle kept her voice low to match his. "They're... actually, I don't know any more than you yet. We hadn't gotten much further than establishing that Britt is Nora Barrett before those people showed up and tried to kill us."

"Why did the big guy attack us?"

"They wanted to know why we were looking for Nora Barrett."

"They could've just asked."

"I don't get the feeling their world is that straightforward." Elle squeezed the bag with her suit against herself. "Once the situation calms down, we'll talk it through with Britt, we'll leave the suit with her, and hopefully they can help you get back home."

"The way you said that, it sounds like you aren't going back. I thought... I mean, I assumed that... I don't really know what I thought. What are you planning to do?"

"I still have friends back at the research center. They're the closest thing to family I have. Maybe some of them will want to escape with me. Live life on our own terms, you know?"

The last few days, he'd come to think of her as the only family he had left. He'd just assumed they'd stay together, that their experiences would connect them permanently, or least for much longer than a few weeks.

The bruises forming on her face looked more pronounced under the harsh, artificial light in the room. He reached his hand toward her, letting it hang in the air close but not touching.

"Your face, does it hurt?"

"Yes, quite a bit, but I can't complain compared to her." She tilted her head toward Ainsley, who was moaning on the metal table while Wilm cut away the blood-saturated leg of her pants.

"Those were the same people from the village, weren't they?" Court said.

"Maybe. They were dressed the same."

"I would've liked a few answers from them."

Britt stood over Ainsley running her fingers through her hair, her gentleness a dramatic change from when she'd kicked a man in the face less than an hour earlier. Her hands were steady, unlike Court's hands that had been trembling since the taxi.

The door's hinges creaked as Ursula led in a blindfolded woman pulling a metal case on wheels.

"Everyone out," Ursula said.

Only when Britt nodded did Bear and Wilm move from Ainsley's side. They gathered in the hallway just outside the door. Ursula joined them a minute later.

"Doc says it's bad but the bot can clean it out and rebuild the knee with restin. It won't be as good as new but she'll be able to walk instead of losing her leg."

"Thank you," Britt said.

Ursula pointed at Court and Elle. "Didn't take long for you two to find trouble, did it?"

"Ursula, is there a place to talk?" Britt asked. "There's much to discuss."

"Follow me. I have a secure room."

She took them down a concrete hallway to a door marked ARMORY 2. She keyed in a long passcode, scanned her eyeball, and waved her forearm in front of a reader. There was a single table inside with eight mismatched chairs, a cot, and a barrel labeled WATER with a mug sitting on its lid. The faded letters on the mug read UNIVERSITY OF

TORONTO PARENT. At least a dozen tablets and other electronics that Court didn't recognize were scattered across the table.

"Excuse the mess. I wasn't expecting company."

"Not exactly an armory," Bear said.

"On the contrary, these are the most important weapons we have. Sadly, I get very few opportunities to use Janice."

"Janice?"

"My sword. That's her name."

"You named your sword?" Wilm asked.

"Your sword is a female?" Bear said before Ursula could answer.

"Of course. She's sleek and well-balanced. Why wouldn't she be female?"

"I just thought—" Bear started to stay something but seemed to think better of continuing.

"I wonder what Freud would say."

"Who's Freud?" Court asked.

"Enough of this," Britt said. "We have serious matters at hand. Elle, let's take a look at that suit. Maybe Ursula can help."

Elle pulled her suit and helmet from its bag. Ursula moved the electronics to one end and helped Elle lay the suit out on the table.

"Aldebaran. How'd you get this?"

"Just a minute," Court interjected. "Can we back up a few steps?"

"I'm sorry," Britt said. "Court's right. Introductions are in order. Everyone knows me already. I used to be a professor here at the University of Toronto. For the last ten years or so, I've been a broker, getting supplies from Earth to the ships that hold people sent off planet during the expulsions. Bear, Wilm, and Ainsley help with that."

Elle looked to Ursula. "And you're obviously more than just the head of security here."

"That's my official job, but it's not all I do."

"And who were the men who attacked us?"

"We're not entirely sure," Wilm said. "They're state security of some sort but beyond that, we'll need to ask around."

The introductions hadn't told Court anything useful. Knowing their names didn't mean he knew them, but he didn't have any alternatives. They'd narrowly survived an assault from government gunmen. They had nowhere to go and even if they did, how would they get there safely? Elle, at least, seemed satisfied for the moment.

My job was to make sure she got here alive, and she's here. The thought triggered a wave of guilt for her cuts and bruises that were swollen and turning more purple with each passing minute.

"And who are you two really?" Ursula asked.

Court and Elle shared the sequence of events that had brought them to Britt.

"Where did this happen? I'm surprised I haven't heard any rumors about it."

"It was out east," Britt said.

"There were almost two hundred people there," Elle said. "It was awful. Whatever made Dr. Donovan leave, it's important. A lot of people have died because of it."

"Which brings us to this suit. We need to find what secrets it's hiding." Britt ran her hand along the suit as she spoke. "Pilots wore A2 jackets in the 20th century. They often had maps sewn into them. The map helped them find their way to safety if they were shot down in dangerous territory."

"There's a map hidden in the suit?" Court asked.

"Maybe not a map but something. That's my hypothesis."

Ursula leaned in to examine the suit. Wilm and Elle did as well. Court watched and felt useless with his lack of knowledge of all but the most rudimentary technology.

After several rounds of examination, they had made no progress.

"What about the helmet?" Ursula asked. "Does it have a HUD?"

"A what?"

"A heads up display."

"Oh, yes, but only with basic information like temperatures and battery level."

"What about a hidden menu?"

Chapter 39: Elle

ELLE PUT ON the helmet and the screen inside lit up.

"What do you see?" Britt asked.

"It says the power is at sixty-four percent, the air temperature is 20.4 degrees Celsius, and the suit is inactive."

"There must be something else," Ursula said. "Can you operate it with eye movements?"

"The controls are on the sleeve."

Elle felt someone pushing the suit into her arms and guiding her hand to the control pad. She tried swiping her finger in the pattern for activating the suit and the screen displayed a warning message.

"Suit and helmet not attached," she read aloud. "That didn't work."

She drew the deactivation pattern and saw another warning message. Then the screen changed.

"It's asking me if I want to access the help menu." She tapped twice for yes and a set of topics appeared on screen.

"There's an option for a tour."

"That sounds promising," Britt said. Elle was sure she heard excitement in the older woman's voice.

Elle swiped and tapped. The screen showed an outline of the suit with red dots. As she swiped, a different dot would pulse from light to dark. When she tapped, a box appeared with details about a feature.

"I don't understand," she said as she selected the last pulsing dot. "The tour's a dead end."

Elle tapped to clear the final pop up and a red dot appeared next to the helmet on the screen. She selected the new dot. The box that appeared asked a question.

What is your designation? -CD

There was no obvious way to enter an answer—no on-screen keyboard display, no buttons or menus she could select. But she was on the right path. CD for Clint Donovan. The answer was her designation from Aldebaran, the identification number they'd given her. One higher than the person before. One less than the person who'd come after.

"I found something but I don't understand how to continue."

The background color of the screen switched to red, and a message appeared along the bottom.

Incorrect or invalid response.

It's voice controlled, she thought.

"L37," she whispered.

The background of the screen flashed green, and the message changed again.

"Compartment open," she read. "It says a compartment is open. Does anyone see a compartment?"

"Yes, we see it." This time the excitement in Britt's voice

was undeniable. "Wonderful work, Elle. Just stay still for a moment while we look."

She felt people brushing up against her and the screen snapped back to its original display.

Elle removed the helmet, and Britt showed her a foam block, no bigger than a fingernail, in which a miniature capsule was embedded.

"Another data vault," Elle said. "Isn't it? It looks just like the scans from Dr. Donovan's leg."

Britt turned the block over in her palm and showed Elle the bottom on which "A2" was hand-written in silver.

"Do you have a way to read the data?" Elle asked.

"I have no idea," Britt said. "I don't even know what this is."

"There was an Aldebaran data vault embedded in Dr. Donovan's bone when he died. Marsh found someone who could read it. This might be the same thing."

"Give it to me," Ursula said.

Chapter 40: Britt

BRITT COCKED HER head to the side and considered Ursula for a moment. They didn't know each other, not really. But people she trusted trusted Ursula. That would have to be good enough. She dropped the foam block into the open palm of the younger woman.

Ursula looked through the collection of devices on the table until she found one that seemed to satisfy her. It was a mid-size tablet, maybe nine or ten inches along the diagonal. When Ursula turned it on, a stylized letter A glowed on the screen.

Britt recognized it as the Aldebaran logo. "Is that—"

Ursula interrupted her. "An Aldebaran tablet, yes. Someone bartered it for old university equipment. It's not connected to the network and no wireless signals can get out of this room. Don't worry, it's safe."

"Why do you have it?" Bear asked.

"I just told you."

"I mean why do you personally have it. For that matter, why do you have so many devices here?"

"It's a complicated story but the short version is that Maud upstairs runs what's left of the university. She has a lot of discretion over what gets sold off and what constitutes valid payment. Occasionally, she accepts barters and I take them from her as wages instead of qynars. It's a convenient way to accumulate some much needed tech discreetly."

"Much needed for what?" Wilm asked. "And how do you eat if you keep taking tablets instead of money?"

Ursula gave Britt a confused look.

"I didn't tell them anything about your operation."

"Wow, you all are a trusting bunch to come here blind."

"We trust Britt," Bear said.

"Well, let's just say that running security here isn't my main source of income and the tech comes in handy. Such as right now."

She set the foam block on the bottom of the tablet with the data vault facing down. The tablet screen came to life.

"It wants a password."

Britt saw from the looks on Elle's and Court's faces that they didn't have the password, or at least didn't know that they had it.

"Well?" Ursula asked.

"We don't know," Elle said.

"The first data vault needed the lyrics to an entire song to get into it."

"Try L37," Elle said. "That was how I unlocked the suit."

Ursula tried it but the tablet screen flashed red and displayed a new message: Failed attempt 1 of 5. After 5 failed attempts, the vault will lock for 24 hours. Hint: Stickiest place for a concert.

"What's L37?" Court asked.

"Let's talk about it later."

Britt could see in the girl's face that a lot of secrets were hidden behind that deferral. She wondered if it was obvious to Court. She didn't get the impression that these two knew each other all that well.

"Only four more guesses," Ursula said. "Anyone know the stickiest place for a concert?"

Britt laughed and warm memories bubbled up, memories from a happier time, before life got complicated—memories of cold beers on sidewalk patios during humid summer evenings; the smell of greasy food, everything fried, golden, delicious, bad for everyone's health; and the laughter, which was most definitely good for their health.

"The Horseshoe Tavern," she said. "I haven't thought of that place in ages. It's not even very far from here, or it used to be. It must be long closed by now."

Watching over Ursula's shoulder, Wilm said, "That worked."

Bear and Wilm squeezed against Britt's left side while Elle and Court pressed in on her right, everyone trying to get a look at what secrets would be revealed.

Ursula snapped at them. "Alright, everyone just back up a step. Personal boundaries, people. Ever heard of them?" She slid her seat back and offered it to Britt. "Here, you can drive."

A wordless look from Elle told Britt that she approved.

It took a moment for Britt to orient herself with the structure of the data vault's contents, but she soon found a partition labeled NORA, and in that partition was a video titled Nora Overview.

Elle gasped when Clint Donovan's face appeared on the screen.

"Nora, greetings, my dear friend. It has been far too long. I've been telling myself for years that I should come visit you, but I don't need to tell you how hard that type of travel is these days. And now, if you're watching this video, it means something has happened to me and it's too late."

He hesitated for a few seconds, presumably to keep his emotions from getting away from him. Britt felt a tingle in her left eye, an early warning sign of her own tears threatening to spill out without much further provocation. Britt preferred to maintain a strong facade, so she was relieved when Clint jumped straight to the point.

"But there are bigger issues at play. The Qyntarak are moving to strip humanity of our remaining freedoms and many of our rights. I have cultivated friendships and forged alliances with a number of influential Qyntarak who oppose these changes. This data vault contains interview notes, transcripts of Qyntarak leadership meetings, and drafts of legislation going before the Akarrak. The end result is bleak.

"The new laws will allow for ownership of humans, which I realize is not a new idea on our planet. In the latest proposals I've seen, creditors would be allowed to make a claim for the offspring of a debtor if an adjudicator rules that the debtor's lifetime earning potential makes them a high risk for default.

"I'm sure you're familiar with the increasing debt load of most humans. The Qyntarak are ruthless and greedy. Large syndicates have the majority of humans on and off Earth buried under inescapable debt loads. The statistical models presented to the Akarrak predict that three-quarters of humanity will be owned within three generations.

"Once that many of our kind are property instead of free people, we will have lost the ability to resist politically or economically. We will have sold ourselves to the Qyntarak. And then..."

Clint's voice cracked and the video glitched. The lighting was different after the glitch and Clint's red-rimmed eyes were puffy. He had stopped the recording to cry.

"Sorry about that. It's hard not to get emotional about this. As I was saying, once Qyntarak own our future generations, we will be powerless to stop what comes next. Most of the Akarrak council members are in the pocket of one or more of the syndicates, and a couple of the syndicates are keenly interested in a new export business. They want to ship humans to their home world and colony planets where we can be sold as food."

There was another long pause. The video didn't glitch. A single tear ran down Clint's cheek.

"Although it's rare and illegal, some of them already eat human meat and consider it a delicacy. They believe they can create a profitable market for humans as food on their planet. One of my allies claims that a motivation for the expulsions was to create the need for a research program to identify potential issues for humans during multi-year space travel."

Britt paused the video because the tablet's little speakers could not compete with the string of profanities coming from Bear. He pounded his fists on the table.

"No. No, no, no. We're a sentient species. They can't just start eating us. That's got to violate some universal law or something."

Britt snapped at him, "Bear, calm down. We need to finish listening to Clint first then we'll be outraged and decide what to do next."

Bear grunted and shrunk back at the rebuke. The two of them had been working together for years. Britt rarely saw him lose his cool like that so she knew he was shaken. Hell, she was shaken.

She resumed the playback.

"But all is not lost. Not yet. That's why I need your help, Nora. In addition to the evidence, this data vault holds a wealth of technical specifications and data that, if placed in the right hands, can be used to fight back and to reclaim our planet."

Clint seemed to sit up straighter in his seat when he said that last part.

"First is all the information I could gather about human health and survival in space. The Rohindian Virus is a red herring. The Qyntarak designed it to keep humans weak and afraid. They sell expensive antiviral medication to ensure the people on those ships stay in debt so they can be controlled. An inoculation formula and procedures for low-radiation treatment are on the data vault.

"Second, there are instructions for commandeering those ships and returning them to Earth, including navigational data and landing procedures. With the right leadership and organization, humans can take control of the red ships and bring our people home.

"Third, technical specifications for creating and controlling the temporary black holes that the Qyntarak use as weapons. With this technology, humanity will be able to defend itself.

"Finally, there are instructions for communicating with the Qyntarak home world. My sources here tell me that the behavior of the Qyntarak on Earth is not consistent with the philosophies and lifestyles of most Qyntarak. Like humans, they have many factions and ideologies in a constant struggle for dominance. Being spread out over several planets and moons exacerbates the problem, making it that much harder to find a unified position on almost anything. Sending word about how humans—and Earth—are being mistreated may gain us sympathy from other Qyntarak, maybe even leading to assistance or at least their refusal to buy exports from the ones who are here now.

"Everything included on this data vault is the culmination of years of earning the trust and confidence of several influential Qyntarak, including some on the Akarrak. Leaving with this data will burn all my bridges. The Qyntarak will be suspicious of anyone who's ever been associated with me. My allies will need to bury their human sympathies and will be unlikely to risk further assistance. This is a one time opportunity.

"Nora, I am begging you to please help see this through. I know you have connections with the Reclamation movement and the means to smuggle contraband into space. Please, old friend, help save humanity."

The recording went black then stopped. No one in the room spoke.

After a long minute, Bear said, "Drive out a technologically superior alien species and save humanity. He doesn't ask for much, does he?"

Chapter 41: Britt

"IF THIS IS true," Ursula said, locking eyes with Britt, "then it's a game changer."

Britt wasn't sure she could speak without her voice cracking. She rested her chin on steepled fingers to look contemplative while she bought herself time to get control over the quaver she felt in her throat.

"The Qyntarak designed the virus?" Bear said. "And they have a vaccine while we're struggling to sneak antivirals into supply shipments to keep people from dying? That's..."

"Immoral?" Wilm offered. "Criminal?"

"Yes, both of those."

"I agree," Britt said. "And I, for one, am going to do something about it. But I won't presume to make that choice for the rest of you. If anyone wants out, now's the time to say so."

She searched the faces in the room, taking in their expressions. Mostly, she saw resolve and anger. Court looked like he might shit in his pants.

"My wife is out there on one of those ships," Bear said. "You know I'm all the way in."

Elle said, "I trust Dr. Donovan and this is what he believed is best."

Wilm raised his hand. "You can count me in. I want those bastards to go home."

Elle gripped Court's hand. "It might make sense for you to go back home. If it all works the way Dr. Donovan says, if everyone comes back to Earth, they will need people to teach them how to survive, to hunt for meat and grow vegetables. They'll need people like you to be ready for them."

Britt thought that Court looked hurt, maybe even insulted.

"No," he said. "The nacking Qyntarak killed my family twice. I only understood half of what he said, but I want to help if I can."

"What about Ainsley?" Wilm asked.

Britt furrowed her brow. "I guess that'll depend on how the surgery goes."

"So what's next?" Bear asked.

"Reclamation leadership is on the *Willow Wisp*," Britt said. "And they're already expecting a delivery from us on the next supply launch."

"But our containers are gone. We've missed that boat."

"We've missed the chance to get full-size crates on the cargo shuttle but something small enough to be carried aboard might still be possible. A radiation-shielded box with a ping locator wouldn't have to be big to hold the data vault. Our person on the shuttle could smuggle it on with her personal items."

"And what? She'll just toss it out the airlock manually?"

"Yes, that's perfect, actually."

"I was being sarcastic."

"I know, but that doesn't mean it won't work."

"The launch is in four days. The crew will go into quarantine by 8pm tomorrow," Ursula said. "That's not much time."

"How do you know that?" Bear asked.

Britt patted his arm. "Ursula is the one who's been providing us with our intel on shipment schedules and crew rosters the last few years."

"I can program a ping locator with the *Willow Wisp* codes," Ursula said.

"We'll need to acquire a transponder," Britt said. "Also, can you make a copy of the data vault? If something goes wrong, we don't want to lose our only copy."

Ursula nodded affirmatively. "I'll put it on an open source device with stronger encryption. I'll use a Reclamation public key and my personal private key so leadership will know it's legit. We can send the copy to the *Wisp* and secure the original here."

"Perfect. You better start that now. As soon as it's ready, we need to move."

Chapter 42: Kane

GOVERNOR TORKANUUX VIBRATED with rage, its upper body moving side to side. Kane knew he had to be careful. His suit was set to translate his physiological reactions into Qyntarak-style temperature changes. He needed to demonstrate an appropriate level of remorse and shame so that the five Qyntarak gathered in the governor's private council pit would see that he understood the severity of his failures. At the same time, he had to project a minimal amount of confidence so they would not judge him to be incompetent. It was a lot of nuance for the suit to get right and Kane worried that he wouldn't have sufficient control of his physical reactions from which the suit took its cues.

Kantarka-Ta was letting its frond antennae waggle, not making any secret of its delight in seeing Kane knocked down a few pegs.

Bastard, Kane thought and then regretted it in case his irritation showed up on the suit.

"Honorable Torkanuux," Kantarka-Ta's translated voice played in Kane's helmet, "if it aligns with your preference, the staff of my office would be able to complete the mission after the failure of your human staff."

Kantarka-Ta didn't say his name. Kane understood the implied slight—Kantarka-Ta was dishonoring him by not referring to him by name. He didn't have an emotional reaction to it the way a Qyntarak would, but intellectually he recognized the insult and knew it would not go unnoticed by the other Qyntarak, including the governor.

Governor Torkanuux clacked its mandibles, a Qyntarak reaction similar to an irritated sigh but Kane's helmet didn't attempt to translate it.

"For the staff of your office to complete the mission aligns with my preference. My preference is for the staff of your office to bring the human Kane and instruct it in the methods of completing the mission with full success."

Kane focused on his breathing. Kantarka-Ta's team taking over the retrieval of L37 was humiliating enough. But accompanying the smug Qyntarak while they did it? That would be torturous.

The governor's upper body moved back and its antennae folded down. Irritation.

"Human Kane, your suit proclaims your inner feelings. You are angry and humiliated by my preference. That is the desired response. Your failure is without justification. Your failure brings shame to me."

"Honorable one of many," Kane said, "I am full of shame and my failure is without excuse. I beg your pardon for how this suit conveys my physical reactions. I am not angry and I mean no disrespect."

Taxranar, the governor's chief advisor on legal concerns, made a snapping noise while its frond antennae swayed side to side, the Qyntarak version of a hearty laugh. "The human Kane is dishonored by having to accompany Kantarka-Ta when it does its work."

All the Qyntarak, except the governor and Kantarka-Ta, joined Taxranar in its "laughter."

Kantarka-Ta swatted Taxranar with the side of one of its long stabbing appendages.

Taxranar continued to laugh and said, "Even the human thinks you smell too much like human to be in proximity to you."

Kantarka-Ta hit Taxranar much harder and made a sound similar to a hand slapping water. Taxranar slid from its resting position into an aggressive standing posture and clapped its grasping pincers together. Kane had never seen this behavior in person but he knew it was an assertion of dominance. Taxranar was reminding Kantarka-Ta of their relative positions in the social and political hierarchies. As a Qyntarak with close affiliation with humans, Kantarka-Ta was looked down upon by most Qyntarak in the leadership circles despite its close relationship with the governor and the governor's fondness for humans.

Kane wasn't an expert on primitive Qyntarak behaviors. He knew them in a work environment where they held their baser instincts at bay. From his rudimentary understanding, the next move would be for Kantarka-Ta to lower its equivalent to a head, the area where its antennae and thermal-optic organs were located, and to recline further in its seat.

Instead, Kantarka-Ta stood and returned Kartar-Kar's

hand-slapping-water sound and clapped its own pincers.

A standoff.

Kane held his breath, part of him hoping that Taxranar would strike Kantarka-Ta down. But anything short of a mortally wounded Kantarka-Ta would be bad for Kane. An embarrassed and humiliated Kantarka-Ta would be merciless in its dealings with Kane while it sought to redeem itself.

"Enough," Torkanuux said. The meek translation in Kane's helmet did not do justice to its menacing body language and the volume of the governor's command. "We are not unkanturanka that have crawled out from the underside of a boulder. The preference of our kind is to conduct our business with the decorum of great beings. Your clanging of fists brings shame to all of the group gathered in this pit. Recoil and recline unless you wish to lose your fists forever."

The translation surprised Kane. "Fist" was not a very accurate way to describe their blunt grasping pincers, but in the context of an altercation, it made sense.

Kantarka-Ta and Taxranar held their positions long enough that it would have been disrespectful to a human leader but they did eventually slink back to their places. Kane's helmet seemed to have trouble keeping up with the flurry of temperature changes surging through the upper bodies of the five Qyntarak around him and he had to dismiss the overlay on his heads up display.

"Kantarka-Ta," the governor said, "you will complete the reacquisition of the human L37 with Kane in attendance for observing. You may delegate tasks to him at your discretion. The success of the mission is now your responsibility. Let us now consider the business of the next topic."

Kane sat silently through the rest of the governor's council meeting and attempted not to brood. He wasn't involved in any of the other matters and the Qyntarak had no desire for his input on their other affairs.

The meeting was over and he was removing his suit when his wrist computer buzzed. The message was from Kantarka-Ta.

We have a lead on human L37. Departure shall be in 7 minutes.

Chapter 43: Court

COURT TRIED TO follow two conversations while they waited for the data vault to finish copying. Ursula was telling Bear about the Reclamation movement, and Britt was asking Elle about growing up with Clint Donovan and the research experiments she had been part of.

"The takeover of the *Willow Wisp* was a carefully orchestrated campaign," Ursula said. "The senior leadership of the Reclamation believed they needed an off-world headquarters that the Qyntarak couldn't raid or eavesdrop on. It took two years of planning to get a critical mass of Claimers and sympathizers on the roster for that ship. Even the two Qyntarak custodians were sympathizers. Or are sympathizers, I suppose. As far as I know, they're still up there."

"And you didn't know anything about Clint's own research?" Britt asked.

Bear asked, "How come the Qyntarak can't just knock

them out with one of their black hole weapons?"

"No," Elle said, "he wasn't allowed to talk about it and he wasn't supposed to know about what I was doing."

"The *Wisp* has the same technology as the other Qyntarak ships. And it's a small ship, so it's hard to detect. Space is a big place, even in our little corner of the solar system."

"Before the Qyntarak came," Britt said, "Clint was heavy into genetic engineering with a particular interest in increasing human resiliency. Tolerance for broader temperature ranges, accelerated healing, and even limb regeneration. Do you know if he continued with that work?"

"Do you have access to rosters for other ships?" Bear asked. "Or information on the passengers?"

"I don't know," Elle said. "We didn't talk about it. I wasn't allowed to talk to the other kids about their experiments either. All I know is what involved me, which was trying to talk with the Qyntarak. I wasn't very good at it."

"The *Wisp* knows about the status of at least some people on most ships. There's a network of Claimers but communication is sketchy so the data is sparse and infrequent. And only essential information is broadcast to Earth since every transmission risks compromising the *Wisp*'s current position."

"A child talking directly with Qyntarak? That must have been terrifying for you," Britt said.

Bear pointed toward the ceiling with his finger. "My wife is up there. She's been gone ten years and I have no idea if she's even alive still. It's why I help Britt smuggle antiviral medications. Just in case."

"I grew up seeing them every week, so it was normal for me. But I couldn't really talk with them. The doctor said my vocal chords, in theory, should be able to reproduce Qyntarak sounds better than most humans but, like I said, I wasn't good at it. I was better at understanding them."

"They separated you?" Ursula said. "That's unusual, to separate a married couple."

"I was working off planet at the time and they took the whole town at once. No one even told me. I came home to an empty house. Thieves had ransacked it. It took three weeks of yelling at paper pushers just to confirm it happened."

Court found it exhausting to follow both conversations and as much as he wanted to hear everything being said, he was relieved when Ursula announced that the copy of the data vault was complete.

"Time to go," Britt said.

Ursula held up a hand. "Wait, a proximity alarm just tripped. Let me check what's going on first... Oh shit. Two Qyntarak in full armor and a grav flyer parked on the lawn."

"Qyntarak?" Court said. "You're sure?"

Ursula gave him an irritated glare. "Yes, I'm sure."

"They're here for me," Elle said. "I'll give myself up. It doesn't matter if they take me now. You have the data vault and a plan to get it where it needs to go."

"No," Court said, "there has to be another way."

"The rest of you can stay hidden here. We can't outrun them. We can't fight them."

"She's right about that," Ursula said.

"It won't work," Britt said. "If they only get Elle, they'll come looking for Court, and probably the rest of us. I will not cower down here waiting for them to come knocking."

"Do you have any other ideas?" Ursula said.

"I do," Britt said. "First, we need to check on Ainsley and

hide the original data vault.”

Chapter 44: Court

COURT WAS NOT enthusiastic about their plan but his opinion didn't matter much at the moment. Britt hobbled up the stairs beside him and Elle followed behind them. His hands were cold and shaking.

According to Ursula's surveillance system, there were at least six Qyntarak and one human. They were walking into their hands, or pincers, or whatever they were called, in order to buy time for Bear and the others hiding in the basement.

"Stop there," a synthesized voice said as they crested the stairs. It sounded similar to the voice of the alien that had killed Dr. Donovan but not identical.

They raised their hands and stopped at the top of the stairs, Elle still partially obstructed behind Britt and Court.

All the Qyntarak wore armor with some parts of their bodies covered in a flexible material and the rest covered in layers of a dull black plating. The one who'd spoken had a gun-like weapon pointed at them. Further back, another held Maud, the university superintendent, with a stabbing tentacle pressed against her ribs. Two more Qyntarak moved toward Court, Elle, and Britt. Their long legs, four per alien, clanged on the old stone floor as they advanced with surprising speed for their size.

One of them jabbed Elle with its pincer-like arm. Was arm the right word? Court wasn't sure.

"You are human L37. This is the accurate reading of your appearance. Do you acknowledge?"

Its voice was high-pitched with a hint of a buzz, like a human trying to talk like a bee. Elle didn't answer. The plan was for Britt to act as their negotiator. Court hoped that was a smart move.

"Who is in charge here?" Britt asked.

The Qyntarak roared, the sound muffled but audible through its body armor. The suit didn't provide a translation of the noise.

"Insolent human, your speech was not requested. Recline in silence," the bee said. It poked at Elle again. "You are human L37. Confirm the truth of this assertion."

"I speak for her. And I demand to talk with your superior."

Court was impressed by the steadiness of Britt's voice. The Qyntarak struck her with the side of its long stabbing arm-tentacle thing. The slap wasn't overly violent but harder than necessary for someone her age. Court's body tensed.

From a distance, another Qyntarak made a snapping noise and its suit's speaker said, "Laughing. Laughing."

The laughing Qyntarak came closer and Court saw it was smaller than the others. It poked Court with its own tentacle-like appendage. Court felt like he was being prodded with a sharpened stick.

"You are upsetting the other human here," the smaller alien said. Its synthesized voice was deeper with a trace of a whistle. "Look at how hot its face has become. Human Nora Barrett with the false name Britt, I am full of curiosity about why you are in the companionship of these two fugitives."

How in the nacking hell do they know who Britt is?

"Are you in charge?" Britt asked.

It leaned in close to Britt. "Yes. And much wisdom it will be for you to answer my questions. We are not here to answer yours."

"They came seeking sanctuary and wish only to be productive members of the economy. We have no quarrel with any being."

"Human fool, this one is the property of Aldebaran. You are all three in possession of stolen property."

"She is a human being and no one's property."

"A matter of semantics. She contains their property. We must return her to her caretakers."

The smallest Qyntarak grabbed Elle's arm with its pincer and pulled her toward itself. She gave a startled yelp, and without thinking, Court grabbed it.

"Let her go."

"Court, no," Britt shouted.

He wasn't sticking to the plan but he couldn't bear to have them drag her off like that. He wrenched on the Qyntarak's tentacle with both hands. It was incredibly solid, like pulling on a tree. Something smashed into Court's side and sent him staggering back. He lost his grip and then his footing when his heel slipped over the edge of the stairs. He fell back and tumbled down them, banging and bouncing too many times to count until he reached the landing where his head smashed against the floor or wall or maybe the railing, he wasn't sure. The room went blurry.

Through a fog, he saw movement but couldn't make any sense of it. At one point, he felt sharp pains in his knees and pressure in his armpits. He might have vomited, but he wasn't certain.

When the fog started to lift, he squinted against light shining into his left eye, then his right eye. He was looking up at someone.

A female voice said, "He'll be fine, I'm certain." He recognized the voice.

Who is that?

He couldn't quite place it. His head was still swimming. He tried to focus his eyes.

The deep Qyntarak voice with the whistle replied. "Maw-ooed, your assessment is noted. It is shameful that your previous service was not as adequately performed."

Maud the superintendent. The alien pronounced her name incorrectly but Court could make out the blurry outline of her face. He started to say something to her, to beg her for help, but felt a sharp poke in his neck. He tried to make sense of what was happening, but everything got blurry again and he felt too sleepy to keep his eyes open.

Chapter 45: Elle

"L37," someone said. "L37, wake up."

She could hear it in the distance. It was a human voice, that was nice. She didn't like those Qyntarak synthesized voices. They didn't do a good job translating. She could do much better. The voice sounded familiar though.

Someone from the woods, right? Someone from Court's village.

Her eyes snapped open. That voice belonged to the man who killed all those people.

He sat in a chair across the room, one leg crossed over the other like he was there for a relaxing social visit.

"Where am I?"

"Ah, there you are. I thought you'd come around faster, given your advantages."

Advantages? What's that supposed to mean?

"You didn't answer my question."

She heard the disgust in her own voice. Her hatred for

this man was palpable, something she could almost taste. She wanted answers and then she wanted to make him pay for what he'd done.

"My name is Kane. I work for the governor. The Qyntarak didn't want to question you personally. Called you horrible names, actually. Some of them are a little superstitious. They believe you are an unnatural creature, an abomination. I think some of them are scared of you."

Something was holding her down. She strained for a second and realized it was fruitless so she spat at his feet.

"I don't care what they think. Or you."

"Tsk, tsk. Hardly polite toward your hosts."

"They drugged me and strapped me to a chair. That's not very hospitable."

"Be that as it may, here you are. And your fate very much rests in their, uh, hands. You are chock-full of intellectual property. Aldebaran has invested a lot in you so it's a delicate situation given that the scientists there feel you are a compromised research subject because of your time away."

"That's their problem, not mine. I never agreed to be their research subject. I'm not a guinea pig. You have no right to hold me."

The bastard laughed at her.

"How do you even know what a guinea pig is? Doesn't matter. You didn't have to agree. You were born a ward of the state. Do you know who owns Aldebaran? The governor is the largest stakeholder. What Aldebaran wants, Aldebaran gets. Including you."

She hadn't known about the governor and Aldebaran.

"The look on your face tells me you understand the precariousness of your situation. Aldebaran doesn't want you back and they don't want you set free. Your friends will face lifetimes of fines and penalties. They'll end up in forced work programs. The question is what happens with you?"

"How can I help them?" Elle hoped that Kane had enough allegiance to his own species that he'd offer her something. She would cooperate if it would help Court and Britt.

"The only person you can help is yourself. I've seen your files. I know what abilities you've shown so far. I know what abilities you could develop with the right training. That's why I'm offering you a job on my team. Special operations for Qyntarak-human affairs."

"That makes no sense."

"Despite your skepticism, I assure you, it makes perfect sense. I have an opening, thanks to you and your friends, and you're the ideal candidate. I know what you are, L37."

"And what is that?"

"The perfect combination of human and Qyntarak."

Elle wanted to respond, to scream at him, to deny what he said, but she couldn't. Some part of her feared that he might be right, that he was telling the truth. She was different, she knew that. Everyone in the center was different. Different from each other, yes, but all of them were different from the instructors, the caretakers, and the staff. But part Qyntarak? Part alien? That wasn't possible.

"Dr. Donovan didn't tell you, did he? You are Frankenstein's monster. Everyone was surprised to learn that the Qyntarak are DNA-based. I say everyone but we think they knew. It was a surprise to humans at least. DNA-based but not closely related to humans. And yet, with the right technology, those mad scientists found ways to create hybrids. They died in test tubes by the hundreds of thousands. But some survived. And a few, a very few, thrived. Like you."

"Enough. Enough," she screamed. Then more calmly, she said, "Don't I get legal counsel or something?"

"That's not how this works. Not with you." He stared like he was trying to read her mind. "You can work for me or you can spend the rest of your days in a cage, occasionally being poked and prodded and studied by bored scientists."

"I'm not interested in those options."

"You're not the first person to be born into a life they'd rather not have, but at least you're getting a choice. That's more than most people get these days. You need to look after yourself to survive. That's what Dr. Donovan did."

"Dr. Donovan was a good man."

"Yes, of course, I'm sure he was. A good man who had to make hard choices. First to look after himself and then to take care of you."

Elle noticed she was gritting her teeth. She didn't like hearing him talk about Dr. Donovan.

"Don't squander an opportunity here. You don't want to end up in a cell or, worse, off planet on a red ship doing forced labor. I've heard stories."

"You're mad if you think I'm going to work for you while you send my friends off to prison."

"Friends? That band of smugglers and traitors? Don't make me laugh. They aren't your friends. They were using you. You're just a pawn to them."

Court's face flashed through her mind. Maybe Kane was right about Ursula, Britt, and the others, but not Court.

"You're wrong. You killed an entire village of people and Court risked his life to keep me safe."

She regretted saying it immediately. It revealed too much and Kane smiled at the opening.

"Yes, that's true, the naive boy from the woods. His only crime was harboring a fugitive who smuggled proprietary technology out of a secure Aldebaran research facility. Then again, how would he know any better? He probably just thinks you're pretty."

He was goading her, and she struggled to keep her reactions under control.

"Tell you what, let's make a little deal. I release your restraints and give you a chance to escape. I can't actually let you go but if you can best me and get out of this room, I'll have the charges dropped for your boyfriend from the wilds. If you can't overpower me in a hand-to-hand fight, well, I won't have any use for you anyway."

She didn't answer. The deal wasn't a good one, not by a long shot, but if there was a chance that she could help Court, she had to take it. Kane didn't wait for an answer, he tapped on his handheld tablet and the metal restraints popped open, releasing her wrists and ankles.

Kane stood, set the tablet on his chair, and stretched, his back popping as he twisted side to side.

A voice in the back of Elle's head warned her that this was a bad idea. He was a soulless monster, not someone to be trusted. But what choice did she have? She sat up and spun in the chair so her legs hung over the side. She still had lingering fuzziness from whatever they'd drugged her with earlier. Reflexively, she reached to the place on her neck where she'd felt a sting right after Court had fallen.

"Court, is he alright?"

"Yes, he's fine. Come on, let's get this started. Since you

were just sedated, I'll give you the first shot for free."

Elle rocked forward and landed on her feet. A newfound desire to attack ignited in her veins. She took a tentative step toward him and he responded by closing the distance.

"Come on," he yelled.

He was close enough that she could see the saliva glisten on his tongue as he shouted.

"Let's see what Master Zheng taught you."

That surprised her. "You know Master Zheng?"

"Yes, I do. He kicked my ass once. Only once."

His smug grin infuriated her. Master Zheng's training showed her dozens of possible attacks, his likely counterattacks, and the results if he did give her the first hit for free. She decided on a crotch hit to inflict fast and serious damage. He deserved it. She let her foot fly, and he caught it as he shifted to one side. She hopped on her free foot to keep from falling.

"Hardly sportsmanlike. Lesson number one: there's no such thing as a free hit."

He twisted her foot, and she jumped awkwardly so the rest of her body would follow the twisting ankle and avoid an early injury. She clipped his face with her boot as her legs spun. He released her and stepped back, rubbing his chin. A tiny smear of blood came away on his hand.

"First blood. Very good. Now we have ourselves a fight." He crouched into a defensive stance and waited for her to make another move.

Kane knew she wanted to attack him. He would use her disgust and anger to his own advantage. She knew it and she didn't know how to stop herself.

For several seconds, her rational brain held her back.

Then he glanced up at the corner where two walls met the ceiling.

She seized on his distraction, lunging and driving her palm up into his chin. His arms swung in defensively and she slapped them down, keeping them away from her head and torso. She kicked at his legs then landed a glancing blow to his groin. Kane stumbled back, and Elle pummeled his stomach with a burst of rapid fire punches.

She didn't relent, staying close until she had backed him up against the edge of the room. He braced himself against the wall and used his extra weight to force her away from him even while she was attacking.

Keep going, she told herself. *Don't give him a reprieve.*

She hurled herself back at him and jabbed at his face. Somehow he got a hand up and slapped her incoming arm to one side. Her fist stopped at the wall. She heard the crunching and snapping of things in her hand before she felt the burning pain surge up her arm.

Kane's other hand sunk into her gut and for a moment she couldn't think straight. He grabbed the wrist of her throbbing arm and twisted. He didn't have much leverage but with his extra mass and her pain, he was able to angle her away from himself. She swung her free arm wildly but didn't connect with anything.

Her leg got tangled with his and she felt herself losing her balance. In a flash of terrifying clarity, she saw how this would play out. He'd found the advantage; she wasn't going to win. Her focus shifted to self-preservation as she weighed options for minimizing injury.

She tried leaning away from Kane but with surprising dexterity, he planted a foot on her hip and sent her stumbling across the room. She crashed into her chair with a sickening thud.

"Pathetic. Maybe you and your sad little forest friend belong together in prison after all."

So many parts of her hurt that she wasn't able to focus on just one. She wanted to stop, to give up.

Court... He wouldn't give up... he wouldn't stop so long as he had breath.

She had to give as much as he would. The thought drove her on. She pushed herself back to her feet and bobbed in a defensive pose. One hand was already starting to swell. Best to avoid using it. Her side hurt with every movement.

Cracked rib, maybe? Need to be careful.

Kane had a disgusting grin on his face.

"Maybe I spoke too soon. Back on your feet after that? Good for you. Master Zheng would be impressed, but I think we're done here."

He brushed his hands down his shirt as if trying to smooth wrinkles or remove dust that wasn't there. He started to reach for the tablet he'd set on his chair but stopped when Elle hollered at him.

"We're not done. Not. Even. Close." Spit flew from her mouth. She couldn't stop now. She'd help Court or she'd be unconscious.

His smile morphed into something sinister.

"Very well."

He came at her like a blur with a volley of fast punches and kicks. She deflected a few and took the impact of even more. One of his swings grazed her injured hand and the momentary distraction of the pain gave him an opening to hook her leg and drop her to the floor. Her side felt like it had been stabbed. She grabbed onto his leg and instinctively curled herself around it to make it harder for him to hit her. The move knocked him off balance and he fell to one knee.

He was over her now and Elle feared she'd made a critical mistake. But then he braced himself with a hand on the floor and Elle saw an opportunity. She stretched her neck and was just close enough to reach his forearm. She bit as hard as she could, forcing back her revulsion as her teeth sunk deep into his flesh.

Kane screamed and pulled his arm away, which caused him to topple over sideways to the floor. Elle rolled over to her back and kicked at him frantically. Her boot scraped over his ear then her other foot hit the side of his face and she heard something crunch. He tried to roll away from her and she kicked the back of his head twice before he was out of reach.

Don't stop, don't stop, don't stop, she told herself because she didn't want to keep going.

Kane's face was scratched and a line of blood was hanging from his mouth. He pulled himself up using her chair, which she saw was bolted to the floor.

His confident expression was gone, and he seemed to struggle to look at her. He was almost to his feet, and she realized with newfound panic that he was going to attack again. Her legs flailed as she tried to get back up without using her bad hand or aggravating her burning ribs. Kane flinched at her motion and lost his balance. His face bounced off the armrest of the chair then his head cracked against the floor. He rolled from side to side on the floor briefly and moaned. He didn't get up.

Elle ran for the door only to discover that it didn't have a handle or control panel. There was no way to open it.

"No," she shouted.

She grabbed his tablet, which was lying on the floor cracked but functioning. She tapped and swiped but it repeatedly flashed UNAUTHORIZED.

"No, come on, something has to work."

She tapped harder then started slapping the screen with her palms.

Settle down, L37. Work the problem.

She took a few centering breaths and looked at the screen with more focus. The door clicked before she'd pressed another button and exhilaration washed over her. She glanced at Kane on the floor and made the split-second decision that she would run. The door slid open and for an instant she saw the spark of a Scorpion before everything flashed white then stopped.

Chapter 46: Court

A GRAY-HAIRED man with a frazzled look about him rushed into Court's holding cell without preamble or introduction.

"Court," the newcomer said. "Or is it Mr. Court? Is Court your given name or your family name? It doesn't say here."

"Who are you?"

"Right, of course, yes. I'm Kas Joranko. I'm your appointed counsel."

"What does that mean? Appointed by who?"

"Appointed by whom."

"What?"

"Never mind. I'm your duly appointed advocate for your upcoming arraignments, hearings, negotiations, and payment scheduling. You're an odd case because there are no records of you anywhere. The governor's office assigned me to assist you. Anyway, enough on me. All it says here is Court. Is that your family name?"

"I don't have a family name. It's just Court."

"Like Madonna?"

"Who?"

"Never mind. A really, really old reference and not a very funny joke, if I'm being honest. Anyway, is Court your full legal name then? That's what your mom and dad called you when you were a bouncing little baby boy?"

Court was feeling like a deer dazzled by a spotlight.

"Sorry, you're who again?"

"Kas Joranko. We've already established that. I'm trying to figure out who you are, Mister Court with no last name."

"You're like a lawyer?" Marsh had told Court about lawyers. He hadn't held a very high opinion of them.

"Sort of, I suppose, although no one's used that term in decades."

"Why?"

"Why what?"

"Why don't people use the word lawyer anymore?"

"You mean aside from all the bad lawyer jokes?" Joranko waited for Court to laugh. When he didn't, Joranko continued, "Most of what I do isn't strictly legal work. It's a lot of contract enforcement, policy violations, and debt resolution for the syndicates."

"What do I need an advocate for?"

"I'm going to get to that. I was trying to get your name first. Call me old-fashioned but I like to start with the basics."

This Kas character was the first person to say more than five words to Court. He decided that he needed to play along while he tried to understand his situation.

"My parents named me Harcourt but everyone's called me Court since... since I was young. I'm from an independent village out east."

"Independent meaning off grid, no electricity, cut off from the world?"

"We weren't totally cut off, but—"

"But, yes, that's the type of place?"

"Yes."

"And you met the girl when she escaped with Dr. Clint Donovan from a nearby Aldebaran research facility?"

"We rescued her, after a Qyntarak killed Clint Donovan."

"Allegedly."

"Huh?"

"After a Qyntarak allegedly killed Dr. Donovan."

"No, it did kill him. I saw it."

"That's why it's alleged. There's no evidence other than your claim that you saw it."

"I know what I saw."

"It doesn't matter. And it doesn't matter whether or not I believe you. You need to deal with the situation you're in now. Let me explain how this is going to go down. Your friends will get hit with so many fees and penalties to the syndicates that they will end up in forced work programs for the rest of their lives. Frankly, the same is likely to happen to you unless we can figure out a way to plead your case. Now, tell me what happened. How did you get mixed up in all this? Why are you and the girl working with smugglers?"

"I'm not mixed up in anything. I was helping to deliver a message about Clint Donovan's death."

"If that's how you want to play this, that's fine by me. I get paid regardless. But you're in a heap of trouble and you'll be paying off your newfound debts for the rest of your life. My job is to help negotiate the best possible settlement for your case. I can only do that if you're forthcoming with me."

Court massaged the bridge of his nose between his thumb and index finger. He was in over his head. He had no one he could trust, no one he could turn to, except this advocate.

"Alright, since you're the only person who cares about getting me out of here, what do I need to do? What do you need to know?"

"Everything."

Court sighed then inhaled deeply. He explained life in the village and described the day Elle had arrived, the day Dr. Donovan had died. He talked about the grav flyers swooping in and the murders of everyone he'd known and loved.

Then Court told Joranko about helping Elle make her way to Toronto, meeting Britt, and being taken by the Qyntarak.

"Wait a second," Court said. "I forgot about falling down the stairs. How come I feel totally fine?"

"You did take quite the fall. Brain scans showed that you suffered a concussion. You had numerous contusions and broken bones in your, let me see here, left hand, it says."

"How long was I out?"

"Oh, not that long. Maybe ten or eleven hours."

"How is that possible?"

"Seriously? You must really have lived in the middle of nowhere. According to my records, you had four hours of surgery and therapy with a medical bot. You also received a fairly large dose of nanobots that are doing internal repairs. Your bone was reconstructed by a surgical bot and you were given a high strength tissue growth accelerant to deal with swelling and bruising. These corporate syndicates don't like the appearance of brutality. They're pretty good about making sure that people are healthy and clean before they show up at a hearing."

"What are nanobots?"

"Nanobots? They're—well, I suppose you could call them microscopic robots that get injected into your bloodstream to repair tissue. Think of it as a robotic enhancement to your body's ability to heal."

"They did that without my permission."

"Trust me, kid, in the state you were in when they brought you here, you wanted them to do that. With the bang you took to your head, you may not have been mentally fit to even make a decision about your own healthcare. You're lucky. A lot of people who have a run-in with the syndicates end up bleeding somewhere in a dark alley."

"I feel like I've been violated or something."

"Don't be silly. It's standard practice. I've had nanobot repairs at least a dozen times over the years. It's no big deal."

"So what happens now?"

"Now we'll find out what damages are being claimed by your actions and involvement. The young woman that you were with, according to our data systems, her official designation is L37. Why do you call her Elle?"

"That's what she told us to call her."

"Interesting. Depending on how we need to position your involvement, you may want to refer to her as L37 when you're in front of the juries or hearing committees. It may not be to your advantage for them to think that you have a close relationship with her."

"It sounds like you're thinking you can help me by putting blame on Elle."

"Yes, that is one possibility. I want to keep all of our options on the table until we know what we're dealing with."

"That one's not an option. Elle is my friend whether that's convenient for me or not."

"Well, aren't you just a hopeless romantic? I suspect you would change your mind after a few months of labor on a red ship."

Chapter 47: Britt

BRITT RUBBED HER eyes, trying to convince her brain to sweep away the cobwebs that were clouding her thinking. They'd sedated her, she'd pieced that much together, but she didn't know where she was. The two people who'd checked on her had refused to answer any of her questions.

She had to assume that Elle and Court had been taken as well. She felt some guilt about that. Her plan to negotiate their freedom in exchange for a data vault was flimsy even if they hadn't realized it. It would be worth it, though, if Bear and Wilm could get the real data vault to the *Willow Wisp*. A few lives down here on Earth were a fair trade to save ships full of the sick and dying.

She prayed that Bear and Wilm had made it out with Ainsley, Ursula, and the doctor. If not, her sacrifice would be a waste.

A formal-looking guard in a stark gray uniform opened her cell door.

"Follow me, ma'am."

"Where am I going?"

"Someone posted your bail."

She led Britt down a hallway that smelled vaguely of antiseptic and anxiety. Britt noticed that the walls had signs posted in human languages. Given that Qyntarak had taken them, she had expected a more alien facility.

"Position your eyes in front of the camera, press your hand on that sensor. Now hold out your arm. You will wear this tracking bracelet for the duration of your bail release. We will know where you are at all times. Any attempt to tamper with the bracelet or otherwise circumvent the conditions of your release will result in revocation of your release, forfeiture of the bail payment, and additional fines. In other words, breaking your bail would be expensive and there's nowhere you can go that you can't be found."

"Thanks for the pep talk. Who bailed me out?"

"She's waiting outside."

Britt wondered if it might be Ainsley.

"How are my friends? The ones who were brought in the same time as me?"

"Their status is confidential and not your concern."

"Please, can't you at least tell me if they're being released too?"

"Sorry." The guard shook her head side to side and Britt could see that there was no progress to be made there.

In the next room, Britt found a woman she neither knew nor recognized sitting straight backed on a stool at a simple metal table. The woman's hair, shaved at different lengths on each side and dyed (or genetically engineered) a brilliant blue, was not a style she'd seen in the Toronto area.

"Dr. Barrett, my name is Petra. We shouldn't talk here but I have friends who would like to make your acquaintance."

Why is my old name coming up so much all of a sudden?

"What friends?"

"Come with me and I'll introduce you."

Given her limited options, Britt followed the woman out of the building.

"Where are we?"

"New Boston. Part of the reclaimed land after the Qyntarak restored sea levels."

"New Boston?"

"Yes, the human affairs task force headquarters is here."

A car pulled up in front of them.

"After you," Petra said. "It's not far but we shouldn't linger together in public."

Britt's heart pounded in her chest. Letting a stranger whisk her away after posting her bail felt reckless, but she told herself that forward motion of any kind was better than being trapped in a cell.

Once the car was moving, Petra continued, "The human affairs task force is effectively a human brute squad. A man named Kane runs it. He works for the governor."

"The governor? As in, the Qyntarak governor for the entire planet?"

"That's the one."

"And who do you work for?"

The woman smiled. "To be honest, I'm surprised that you got in the car with me before you had that answer."

"This hasn't been a typical day."

"Indeed. To answer your question, I wear a few hats but I'm here representing a group within the Qyntarak leadership who are dissatisfied with the way Qyntarak operations on Earth are managed. Given everything that has happened and the nature of the data Dr. Donovan smuggled out of his research facility, they want to speak with you. They would like to see if they can help facilitate further transmission of that data."

"You're taking me to see the Qyntarak leadership?"

"Yes, some of them. I can hear the skepticism in your voice. They're the ones who provided Dr. Donovan with his data. They are very invested in seeing the rest of his mission completed."

The car came to a stop outside a bleak concrete and metal building with few windows and none of the regular features of a typical human complex such as a front door or steps.

"There's an unofficial entrance for humans over there. Useful for times like this when people need to enter discreetly."

Britt followed Petra under a canopy that covered the full width of the alley beside the building. In the reduced light, Britt could only make out what looked to be a door with no handle. Petra pounded on it with the palm of her hand.

"Security for this entrance is intentionally low tech. This canopy," she said as she waved at the fabric less than a meter above Britt's head, "acts as a signal blocker. Nobody, in theory, can see or hear anyone who uses this entrance."

"Will that be problematic with my tracker?" Britt waved the arm with the black and silver band clamped on her wrist.

"It would if the signal were blocked for any significant amount of time. Once we're inside, my friends have technology for spoofing your tracker signal. The long-range sensors will think you've taken a leisurely stroll to a nearby restaurant."

"You have the technology to spoof Qyntarak tracking devices?"

"Technically, they're not Qyntarak. Like a lot of stuff built by Aldebaran, it's mostly human engineering. But having some Qyntarak allies helps in situations like this."

With a click and a hiss, the door receded into the wall and cool air rolled out. The room was even darker than the alleyway. As Britt's eyes adjusted to the reduced light, her breath caught at the sight of a Qyntarak wearing a partial suit. The rest of its leathery scale-like skin was exposed, something rarely seen by humans. Britt felt gooseflesh crawl up her arms. She'd seen her fill of Qyntarak the last two days. It would not be easy to trust one.

"Nora Barrett, it is my honor to introduce you to Rex, Assistant to Undersecretary Traxonorn."

"Rex?" Britt whispered, looking at Petra warily.

"A nickname. Its real name is long and very difficult for humans to reproduce. The nickname was its idea."

"Human Nora Barrett, I am honored to partake in an introduction with you. I am full of awareness of the brave labor that you undertake in great service of your people trapped in starships under the threat of serious disease that takes life."

The alien words came through a box attached to what would be a helmet equivalent for Qyntarak anatomy. It looked like a sleeve or sock over the caterpillar-like shape of its upper body. Despite its thin construction, the sleeve concealed most of the Qyntarak's sounds and broadcast human language instead.

Britt bowed, hoping the movement communicated the

appropriate respect without using the demeaning kneel that was often demanded of humans in the presence of Qyntarak officials.

"It is an honor to meet you as well."

"My service was requested by my patron and its colleagues to communicate with you about certain matters. The undersecretary and its colleagues hold large concerns in consideration of the treatment of humans on this planet. They have concluded that the treatment of humans and other native species on your planet is not in resonance with the philosophy and respect for life and home that is most prevalent among the Qyntarak peoples on our other worlds. The undersecretary befriended the human Clint Donovan, a researcher of genetic compatibility between our species. Clint Donovan held many philosophical positions that were in great alignment with the beliefs and philosophies of the undersecretary and its associates. Speaking with you directly would be a reckless step for the undersecretary to embark upon of its own accord. I was instructed to interface with you and to assess what help and assistance and guidance and advice shall be required from the undersecretary and its colleagues in order to guarantee the safe delivery of the data provided to Clint Donovan to the Reclamation leaders on the starship known to humans as *Willow Wisp*."

"Just a moment," Britt said. "Are you telling me that you are part of a group of Qyntarak that want to help humans get rid of the Qyntarak on Earth?"

"If that is what ultimately is required in order to achieve the return of liberty to the human species. Our preference, if the possibility is greater than nothing, is to establish long-term trading relationships that are economically viable and mutually prosperous for both our races. We do not believe such an arrangement is possible with the current Qyntarak representation in this system. The governor, the syndicates, and other influential Qyntarak are concerned solely with profit and the establishment of new markets for human resources on Qyntarak worlds."

"You mean selling humans for food."

"That is accurate."

"Then bring on the help."

"Is the data vault intact?"

"As far as I know, it's still safe in Toronto. If you can help us, there might still be time for us to get it on the next delivery shuttle on which we have people able to deliver it to the *Willow Wisp*."

"Does the achievement of this mission require the release of all of your staff from the holding facility where they are awaiting their penalties?"

"I will need the help of my people, yes, but I don't know which of them were taken or where the others are."

"I have that information," Petra said. "Three of you were taken at the University of Toronto. The one you call Bear was apprehended outside watching when you were loaded into the grav flyers. Dr. Barton returned home, but she's not of any real concern to anyone now. It looks like the security chief at the university went to ground, although I'm sure I could find her in a pinch. The other two are holed up together in a squatter town."

"How do you know all that?"

"It's what I do."

"So Elle, Court, and Bear are in custody. Can you get them out?"

The Qyntarak made a noise that its helmet broadcast rather than translated. Britt wasn't sure what it meant.

"Much difficulty is involved in securing the release of debtors accused of stealing property from an organization such as Aldebaran. The governor has personal interests. There is much difficulty to guarantee that the accused humans are treated fairly. My patron and its colleagues will not have liquid capital sufficient for the payments of the debts to be levied against you and your three colleagues. They would not be able to allocate sufficient assets to pay the fines and debts without raising suspicion. Should this mission not succeed, the undersecretary and its colleagues must remain distant from suspicion so they have the freedom to try again in the future. I have need to further investigate. Intuition instructs that we will only be able to release the three humans temporarily as we have done for you."

"Chances are they won't want to release L37 on bail at all," Petra said. "I'll see what I can do about that. Maybe I can hack into the system and tweak her records to make it possible."

"Then we have come to a beneficial conclusion of action. I will allow the funds for Petra to arrange temporary release of your staff. I look forward to a productive and successful collaboration, human Nora Barrett."

"Please, call me Britt."

Chapter 48: Court

COURT WOKE TO the sound of someone entering. He'd lain down to close his eyes for a few minutes but obviously had fallen asleep. The man who'd killed Marsh stood at the door of the cell. Everything went out of focus except that man and his uniform. The same uniform he'd been wearing that day.

"What do you want?" The hostility in Court's voice was not ambiguous.

"I see the nanobots and accelerants have done their work. You'd never know you'd fallen down a flight of stone stairs."

"I said what do you want?"

"My name is Kane, and you should be more polite to the man who holds your future in the balance."

"That's not what my advocate told me."

"Your advocate? You honestly believe the governor's office would assign you an advocate competent enough to get you out of a mess this big? You've been a massive pain in the ass to a lot of people and they all want to bury you. Between the fines and processing fees plus the accommodation charges you're racking up by the hour in here, you'll be so far under water that you'll never see the light of day again."

Court glared in response. He wanted to lunge across the room and grab this monster by the throat, but he suspected that might get him killed.

"I'm here to help."

Court shouted, "Like you helped Marsh?" The rage was making his body tremble.

"Come on, don't be so naive. I never had anything against the old man personally. Ultimately, Clint Donovan's the one to blame. It was him who mixed up your village in his treason."

"You had the data vault. You had what you wanted. You didn't have to kill him or anyone else. I saw the whole thing."

"Yes, so I've heard. I must admit I'm impressed. And I don't say that often or easily. I was a little embarrassed to learn that two people hid at the edge of the woods without my team noticing.

"Listen, Court, to be completely transparent with you, I'm sorry that we had to do what we did. If there had been another way, I'd have taken it. I'm just one player in this game. The Qyntarak make the rules and the governor calls the shots. This is their planet. We just happen to still live on it."

"Then we have nothing else to talk about."

"No, there is still one more thing. You're going to want to help your friend L37 get out of here, aren't you?"

"How?"

"You do something for me and I do something for you. It's the way the world works, kid. You help me keep my boss happy and I'll do what I can to make sure you and your friend don't spend the rest of your lives in prison. Or worse."

"I'm listening."

"The data vault we recovered from Marsh Lapin was encrypted. With the help of some Qyntarak quantum computing, we cracked it easily enough. But once I heard what it contained, I knew we only had the first piece in a larger puzzle."

Kane scratched at his jaw like it was bothering him. Having just experienced the itchiness of tissue growth accelerant himself, Court wondered if he had suffered injuries of his own recently.

"I believe the reason you and the girl traveled from your little woodland community to Toronto was because you were following instructions in the message that we don't understand. All I need from you is help finding the next piece of the puzzle. In exchange, I'll recommend for you and L37 to have your fines and penalties expunged in recognition of your cooperation. I work directly for Governor Torkanuux, so when I recommend something, it's taken seriously."

Court contemplated his options for a moment but he had so few that it took very little time. He could help Kane or he could take his chances at whatever an arraignment was. Ursula had copied the data vault and hidden the original. If he showed Kane where to find it, there was still the copy. And the data vault contained data obtained from the Qyntarak, so he wouldn't be leading them to information they didn't already have. If he could get Elle freed in the process, there was a chance that she could somehow deliver the data where it was needed.

"Alright. I'll help."

"That's the smartest decision you've made yet, kid. Now, this old friend that Clint Donovan wanted L37 to meet, is it Nora Barrett, the woman you were with? She had a data vault on her, but I know it's a ruse. It was using outdated Reclamation encryption keys and the data on it was old and useless. I believe there's another data vault out there and that Donovan was smuggling secrets, in which case you're mixed up in something way out of your league. It's not your battle. There's no need for you to be a scapegoat. Take me to the real data vault and we can forget all this ever happened."

Court hesitated for a few seconds. Was he actually going to do this? Was he going to trust the man who had murdered his adopted family? Did he have a choice?

"Yes, there is another data vault. It contains information about Qyntarak technology. I don't know the specifics, it was all over my head."

"And where is that data vault now?"

"Still in Toronto. They hid it before you kidnapped us."

"Kidnapped you? We took you into custody."

"Taking someone into custody when they haven't done anything wrong? How's that different from kidnapping?"

"If you think you haven't done anything wrong, you're more naive than I thought, and that is saying something."

"I told you what you wanted to know. Now let us go."

"Oh, you're not done yet, kid. You're coming with me to Toronto to show me where you hid that data vault."

Chapter 49: Court

A GUARD IN the detention facility insisted that Court wear a tracking bracelet when he left with Kane. Once they were outside, Kane produced a T-shaped device from one of his pockets and waved it over the bracelet, which clicked and fell from Court's wrist.

"I don't like people tracking my movements. Remind me to reactivate this thing when we get back."

They boarded a small flyer and Court fought back nausea as it rose and accelerated.

Traveling in the grav flyer made him feel vulnerable. The sound of it dragged his worst memories to the front of his mind no matter how hard he tried to push them away. It was permanently connected to the day he lost his parents and the day he lost his village. He was finding it hard to breathe.

The two of them rode alone in the flyer. Court knew nothing about the way Kane and his team operated but this felt off to him.

"You like music, kid? It's going to be twenty-five or thirty minutes to get to Toronto from here. We can listen to something."

Court didn't have much experience with music. What he knew were the little songs they sometimes sang at the campfire or when working around the village. He hoped Kane didn't expect him to sing.

"It makes no difference to me."

"I find it helps me relax."

Kane tapped a button on his wrist computer and vaguely musical noises filled the air. Court couldn't tell where it was coming from. Kane waved his hands around in time to the music, which helped Court decide that he didn't care for it.

By the time they reached the university building, Kane did seem relaxed, like he and Court were friends out on an excursion. That fleeting thought triggered a memory of Walker. He felt the initial tingle of tears and blinked repeatedly to keep them away.

"Here we are."

As they ascended the steps to the building, Court asked, "Why did you bring me?"

"Don't ask stupid questions, kid. I need you to get the data vault."

"I mean why me instead of someone else?"

Kane scratched at his jaw again. Court felt like he was taking too long to answer.

"The old lady is a pain in the ass. And L37 needs to stay put. Besides, I kind of like you, kid."

Unlike Court's first visit, the university doors were locked. That made sense, given that Ursula was unlikely to be here. The door's lock yielded after a swipe from Kane's wrist computer. Once inside, they found Maud at her desk, the same place where she'd extorted qynars from Elle.

"Kane. What are you doing back here?" She stammered as she struggled to stand from her chair.

"Don't get up on my account. I'd hate to be responsible for you having to do any more work than absolutely necessary."

"Can I help you with something?"

"Have you been down in the basement since we took the prisoners out yesterday?"

"No, the Qyntarak told me not to touch anything in case they had to come back."

"Good, that's good. I'm taking the kid down with me to locate something we missed."

As they went down, Court realized his memories from the day before were a bit fuzzy. He remembered Ursula making a copy of the data vault. Now that he was here, he wasn't confident about where they'd hidden it. The copy, the one with Reclamation encryption, where did she say that would be safe? He couldn't recall. The other one, it was, where?

Think, Court. Come on.

The smell of the basement prompted a partial memory. He did remember.

"Over there, there's a hidden storage room."

Court opened the wall panel the way he'd seen Ursula do it.

"Where's the data vault?"

"There was a box, a green box, and a fake brick in the wall behind it."

"That fake brick?"

Kane pointed at a gap in the wall. On a shelf below it, a hollowed out brick lay without a data vault inside.

"This means there are more people involved. Who else is there?"

"Nobody, I mean, nobody I know about," Court hoped like hell that his lie was convincing.

Kane said a word that Court didn't know—it sounded like axe can—and threw the brick at the wall. He turned his back on Court and swiped at his wrist computer.

The data vault had been Court's only advantage. If it wasn't there, Kane would send him back to his cell. He wouldn't get Elle out.

Court watched the gun bobbing on Kane's belt as he moved. Court panicked and reached for it. The clasp resisted initially and then the gun came free in Court's hand. Kane spun, his eyes narrow, and bared his teeth like a wild animal. Court aimed at Kane and pulled the trigger.

Nothing happened.

Kane brushed the gun aside with one hand and hit Court in the stomach with the other. The punch doubled him over and he stumbled back with a grunt. Before Court realized it was happening, Kane pried the gun from his hand.

"That was stupid, kid."

Kane took the Scorpion from his thigh and jammed it into Court. Pain consumed his entire body. Burning from inside came in waves. For a fraction of a second, in a surreal moment of lucidity, he realized that he was bawling and tears were pouring from his eyes, but he didn't care. He just wanted it to stop.

The pain overwhelmed him again.

He tried to say something, to beg for it to end, but the words sounded like nonsense.

Then the pain seared through him with even more force,

if that was possible, until the mercy of numb blackness replaced it.

Chapter 50: Court

COURT WASN'T FULLY conscious but the cold dampness compelled him to move. He rolled to his side and it ached. All of him hurt.

Where am I?

He opened his eyes but there was nothing to see in the dark. Not just dark but blackness. He couldn't see anything. Were his eyes even working?

"Hello?"

There was no answer. There were no sounds at all. He pushed himself up to his feet, the spot from the Scorpion's shock burning as he did.

He moved across the floor slowly until his fingers brushed something. Probing with his hands, it felt like a shelf. Kane must have left him in the university basement. That meant he could find the door and get out. He groped his way along the shelves and walls until he found the gap under the false wall panel.

The mechanism released but the door wouldn't open. He pushed harder with no success. It was blocked from the outside.

He felt his way to the other false wall and leaned into it with his shoulder. That door didn't budge either.

"Nacking piss bucket."

In his panic, he'd forgotten to pull the latch. He dropped to his knees again and found the metal lever at the base of the wall. He pulled up and heard a satisfying click. The door swung open.

Enough light came from the far end of the tunnel for him to make his way. He kept one hand against the wall as he went. His pants were wet and once he was aware of that, the smell of urine was unmistakable. He didn't know how long he'd been unconscious but the Scorpion had left him exhausted and thirsty.

Where do I find safe water to drink? Or food?

Taking a moment to think, he grasped the precariousness of his situation. He didn't know where to go for anything.

He stopped walking and leaned against the wall. Kane had left him trapped in Toronto. Where did the advocate say they had been before? New Boston? Court had never been keen on geography; he didn't know the distance between Toronto and New Boston.

A shuffling noise startled him. A small animal, possibly a rat, made its way along the edge of the hallway. With his heart pounding, Court decided he needed to keep moving. He needed to get away from the university.

When he reached the doors to the outside, the sun was high in the sky. Either he had been out through the night or not very long at all. He licked his lips. He was thirsty but not completely parched; it was still the same day.

There were no signs of anybody nearby so he burst out into the daylight and walked away as fast as he could, trying not to look suspicious. With urine-soaked pants, he hoped anyone he encountered would give him a wide berth.

He was reasonably sure that he could find his way back to the Rofchild, and there was a place near there that had food. Maybe if he pled his case, someone would help. A little food and time to think were all he needed for now. Then he would figure out how to get to Elle.

Chapter 51: Britt

Petra looked at the notification on her wrist computer.

"Well, this is interesting. My boss made a little trip up to Toronto. And he took your friend with him."

"Which one?" Britt asked.

"Court. He must have taken him to find the data vault. Seems Kane abandoned him at the university. I just picked him up on a video feed walking away from the building where you were captured. He's by himself on foot."

"That doesn't make any sense. Why would Kane let him go?"

"Hold on."

Petra scrolled through a flood of data on her wrist computer, flicking her finger and taking in the information at a rate Britt found unimaginable.

"Kane sent me a message asking for someone to go pick up Court. He left him there unconscious. Something obviously went wrong. Kane isn't the type to trouble himself with dragging an unconscious body when he can send his minions to do that for him. He's on his way back to New Boston, probably to question one of you. He's going to be royally pissed off when he realizes they let me bail you out."

"What will he do when he finds out?"

"He won't find out who did it. I've already hacked the records. And the detention facility had an unexplained technical malfunction with its video archiving today. This is sort of my area of expertise."

Petra gave a smug smile and Britt felt relieved that she was helping instead of hunting them.

"So Kane left Court behind. Now Court's on the move. Where's he going?"

"I'll track him as he pops up in video feeds. From that, we should be able to extrapolate his approximate destination, if he even has one. He doesn't know the city, right? He might be wandering aimlessly. I could send a car to pick him up and patch into its audio system so we can talk to him. It would have to be short and vague. I'm not the only one who monitors audio and video feeds."

"I know a place he can go. You send a car for him. I need to make a call."

Chapter 52: Court

A CAR STOPPED a few feet in front of Court and he heard Britt's voice telling him to get in. He looked inside but the car was empty.

"Where are you?"

"Get in quickly, please, and I'll explain."

Court did as he was told.

"Just listen and don't use any names. I'm with a new friend. There's more going on here than any of us realized. I can't promise you that everything is going to be fine but I think we're going to be able to accomplish what our friend asked us to do. We can't talk long. There's a chance that somebody might overhear this conversation. Your car is taking you someplace safe. When you get there, go inside and look for a man not much older than you with long red hair. Say that you need to talk about a coffee delivery. Tell him as little as possible for his own safety. He'll know what to do. Then you just need to lie low until we can come for you. Do you understand?"

"I understand the instructions but I don't understand what's going on. Who is this guy?"

"I know it's a strange situation but you need to trust me on this."

"What about Elle?"

"I said no names. We need to get off this connection. We've already been talking too long. Remember, you need to talk about a coffee delivery. After that, wait for us. We'll come find you eventually, when it's safe."

"How long will that be?"

No reply came.

The car delivered Court outside a rundown-looking building with a hand painted sign posted on the door that read FOOD AND BEER.

Inside, a man behind a long wooden counter had hair as red as a ripe apple tied back in a high ponytail, exposing the shaved sides and back.

"What can I get you, pal?"

"I need to talk about a coffee delivery."

"Right. Come with me."

He led Court down a flight of stairs into a musty, old cellar.

Great, another basement.

For a second, Court worried that this could be some form of elaborate trap. Maybe the voice in the car wasn't the real Britt. Maybe this wasn't a safe place to talk.

No, that didn't make sense.

"Through here. We've got a soundproof room built inside a Faraday cage in back. Toronto's most private place."

Outside the door, the redheaded man asked, "Is Britt

alright?”

"I was told to tell you as little as possible for your own safety."

"Well, that sounds like her. The others are waiting for you inside."

"Others?"

The redheaded man pulled the door open. Inside, Ainsley waved from a chair and Wilm jumped to his feet to clasp Court in a tight hug.

"Glad to see you're alright, mate. You smell like piss, though, and you look like an inmate. Mac, can you get our friend here some some clean clothes and a plate of food, please?"

"Sure thing, boss."

Chapter 53: Kane

"WHAT DO YOU mean she's not here?" Kane's spit sprayed on the window separating him from the clerk.

"We released her on bail."

"How could you release her?"

"The authorization was in order and someone made payment. It was by the book."

"By the book? Are you kidding me? She's basically a walking state secret. There's no book for that."

"I'm sorry, sir, but—"

"You need to recall her. Revoke her bail and get her back here this instant."

"I can't do that."

Kane read the name badge stuck to the guard's shirt.

"Do you know who I am, Jensen? Do I look like I'm in the mood for bureaucratic horse shit right now?"

"It's not that, sir. I literally can't. I'm not authorized to override a legitimate bail release. The system won't let me.

You have to go a few rungs up the ladder for someone who can."

Kane slammed his fist into the window and Jensen jumped in his chair. By the time Kane finished playing chase the middle manager, L37 could be anywhere doing who knows what. He'd have to go directly to Kantarka-Ta, which he was loath to do.

"Just tell me where she is then."

"I don't have access to that either. I just do the processing."

Kane stormed out and climbed back into his grav flyer. He didn't need people witnessing his humiliation while being ridiculed by the Qyntarak. Even though the detention facility was part of Kantarka-Ta's organization, somehow the alien prick would turn it around on him and make the loss of L37 his fault.

As predicted, they were four sentences into their voice call when the Qyntarak said, "Enormous shame descends on you for this failure to ensure the proper safeguarding of the Aldebaran asset. The governor will be filled with much disappointment."

"Don't think you can blame this on me. It was your people who brought them in and left them in this facility."

Kantarka-Ta made a sound that Kane was sure was accompanied by frustrated body movements. He couldn't help but grin. Despite his own frustration, he'd take any minor victory.

"Tell whoever runs the detention facility to revoke her bail release and give me access to her tracking data. I'll go pick her up before she gets too far."

"Your success in obtaining the human L37 was absent in

previous attempts."

"I'll go personally and take a stun gun. It won't be a problem."

"I will fulfill your request. Do not fail again."

Kantarka-Ta ended the call and Kane collapsed back into the grav flyer seat. It wasn't very comfortable when the flyer wasn't moving, the smart foam having been designed with the primary purpose of absorbing the force from high acceleration.

L37, the one called Bear, and the old woman had all been released on bail. Only mentioning L37 to Kantarka-Ta was a calculated risk. If it knew that three of the humans were loose, it might insist on using its team to clean up the mess. Once Kane had access to the tracking data, he would find them. That would look good for him and, more importantly, look bad for Kantarka-Ta.

Kane's wrist computer beeped and announced an incoming call from the human director for all Earth-based detention facilities.

Within minutes, the director had revoked bail for all three missing prisoners and the tracking data was feeding to Kane's wrist computer. It surprised him that the three fugitives were in different locations scattered around the edges of New Boston. He synced the first location to his grav flyer's navigation system, and the machine jumped to the sky, the smart foam cushioning Kane's body as it moved.

It descended into a green space that contained the rusted remains of a children's play structure and a solitary light pole that was many years out of service. Kane double-checked the tracking data. It pointed him at the light pole.

"What the hell?"

His wrist computer reported L37's position as five meters and forty-seven centimeters off the ground. He set the grav flyer to hover at that height and opened the hatch.

On top of the light pole, splattered with bird shit, was a transparent restin bubble protecting a silver box.

"Those bastards."

Someone was spoofing the tracking signal of L37's bracelet. Kane didn't have the expertise to reverse engineer the device. He'd send someone to collect it.

He synced the next tracker location and set the flyer to move at maximum speed with priority clearance. That would broadcast ahead to clear the flight path so he wouldn't lose time avoiding other transports. It took him several minutes to confirm that the other signals were also spoofed.

He screamed at the control panel of the grav flyer, a primal yell that wasn't helping to solve his problem but felt cathartic.

Once he'd composed himself, he called Petra.

"I need your help."

"What's up?"

"They released three of the people we brought in yesterday on bail because we're surrounded by idiots. Bail has been revoked but they are spoofing their tracking signals. I need you to get someone to collect the devices and figure out where the real bracelets are."

"Will do. Anything else?"

"Has anyone retrieved the kid in Toronto yet?"

"No, not yet."

"Then just leave him. I'm going back there. Maybe he'll know something about where the others might be."

"It's worth a shot. Send me the tracking data for the

spoofed devices and I'll work on that."

Chapter 54: Britt

PETRA DISCONNECTED FROM the call with Kane.

"Well, that's inconvenient. Kane is also on his way to Toronto."

"But he doesn't know where Court is, right?" Elle asked.

"He thinks he's still trapped in the university, but I don't like the idea of him flying around the city while we're there. It's a bit close for comfort."

"We'll just have to be extra cautious," Britt said.

Bear squirmed in his seat. The smart foam of Petra's commandeered grav flyer wasn't designed with someone his size in mind and the seat frame bit into various body parts as he shifted in search of a comfortable position.

Petra noticed. "We're almost there. Another four or five minutes."

Britt cradled a white box that would hold the data vault once they rendezvoused with Wilm. It looked so simple but she knew it was engineered to withstand the brutality of open space—the heat of direct sunlight, the extreme cold in the shadows, and the radiation that would fry the tiny data vault if left unprotected.

Not so long ago, Wilm was the new guy. Now he's guarding Ainsley, Court, and a data vault that can save humanity.

Petra set the grav flyer down in the ruins of an old parking lot.

"Let's review the plan one more time. Britt, you go retrieve the data vault from your people here. Then we fly to the warehouse to meet Bear's contact. I'll hack into their security systems to keep your faces off the networked video feeds. You'll activate the transponder and Bear's friend will give the box to the shuttle pilot. Once that's done, I can get those tracking bracelets off and leave you here with your friends.

"The Qyntarak collaborators will lose the bail money they fronted but they will consider that an acceptable loss if the data vault gets off planet."

"We'll be on the run the rest of our lives," Bear said.

Britt reached over to squeeze his hand. "There's still a chance it will be temporary. If the Reclamation can do some good with the data we're sending, it will all be worth it."

A squeeze back was his answer and she smiled, knowing he believed.

"I'm throwing out interference to local video cameras. I can safely do that for fifteen minutes in an area like this before anyone starts to care."

Britt disembarked and saw frightened stares from the handful of people outside. They attempted to look casual as they walked away from her. She resisted the compulsion to smile.

If they only knew what was really going on here.

Despite the small number of people visible outside in the waning daylight, this was a vibrant and well-populated neighborhood by modern standards. The previous residents had been early targets during the expulsions and squatters had moved in over the years, eventually creating a new community complete with shops and places to eat and drink. Wilm had inherited his modest establishment from his parents after they'd died in a riot a few years earlier. Britt supposed he'd inherited their disdain for the Qyntarak as well.

The redheaded bartender took her to the basement. Inside the secure room, Wilm's grin stretched wide across his face. He wrapped his arms around her, something she never would have allowed from her crew in the past.

"I was so scared that I wouldn't see you again. How are the others? Where's Bear?"

"I'm afraid I can't stay long. Bear's fine."

"What about Elle?" Court asked.

To Britt's surprise, Court looked better now than at any point in the short time she'd known him.

"She's safe, don't worry. We're going to deliver the data vault and then we'll all figure out next steps."

"I want to go with you."

"I don't think that's a good idea. The more people, the more attention we attract."

"The only reason I'm here is to keep Elle safe while she sees this thing through. I can't stay holed up in here."

"We have a plan that needs four people and we already have four."

"We both know that there's something different about Elle. They don't just want the data vault. They want her. I'm nobody. If there's any risk of getting caught, you need to send me instead. Please, Britt."

She knew he was right. Elle was unique for reasons she didn't understand. There was nothing remarkable about Court other than his naive bravery and kind heart.

"You understand that you'll be putting yourself at risk? If something goes wrong, we may not be able to do anything to help you. You could end up in a forced work program or even sent off planet to a red ship."

"I know the risk."

"With respect, I doubt that you do. You have a good soul, Court, but you've lived a sheltered life, and you've only gotten a glimpse of the suffering that happens elsewhere."

"Those nacking monsters killed my parents, they destroyed my village, they murdered Marsh and everyone else in front of me. Don't tell me I don't know about suffering. Elle is where I draw the line. They can't have her."

Britt recognized the look of a person who'd made up their mind. She'd seen it in Bear's eyes the day she proposed their first job. She'd seen it in Ainsley's eyes and in Wilm's. And she'd seen it in the mirror.

"Very well. Now, Ainsley, I'm sorry about this, but we're going to need to get that data vault."

"It'll be fine. The doc gave me anesthetic and antibiotics."

She removed the wrapping from around her knee and Wilm pressed a needle into the flesh next to her wound. He counted down from thirty and when Ainsley signaled that she was ready, he peeled back a flap of skin and removed the data vault with tweezers.

Wilm dropped it into Britt's hand. She tried not to grimace.

"Things won't be the same after this, Wilm. Keep your head down, keep pouring that shit beer upstairs, and keep yourself safe, alright? If the chance comes to do more, I'll reach out to you."

He pulled her into another hug. She felt a wet tear fall on her neck. Part of her wanted to hold on and cry herself. That would have to come later. They had a job to finish.

Chapter 55: Elle

PETRA OPENED THE flyer's hatch and motioned for them to hurry. Elle's heart leaped when she saw Court walking back with Britt. The flyer was designed to seat four people, but Court was able to squeeze in between the seats with only Bear's knee pressing into his ribcage.

He surprised her by taking hold of her hand. She started to bristle but changed her mind. She was relieved to see him safe and his touch was comforting.

It only took a few minutes for them to reach the warehouse. Petra handed out earpieces before they disembarked.

"These are emergency communication devices. I'm programming them to run on an encrypted, off-network, peer-to-peer protocol. That means they'll only work if you're within a few hundred meters of each other or the flyer. Just stick it in your ear. Hold your finger against it to talk. Tap three times to lock the mic on. Three times again to turn it off. It's a shared audio channel so everyone will hear what everyone else says. Got that?"

Everyone nodded and put in their earpiece.

"Good. Give me a minute to hack into the security feeds and then you're good to go."

She tapped and swiped on her wrist computer and the flyer's control panel.

"You're all set. Good luck, everyone. I'll be waiting for you when the package is delivered."

Bear climbed out first and the rest followed. Court stuck close to Elle.

"You don't seem too worse for wear," she said.

"They patched me up after my fall down the stairs. Do you know anything about nanobots? They can't control me or make me sick or anything, right?"

Elle laughed and Britt flashed her a stern look over her shoulder.

"Control you? What, like a nanobot zombie?"

"I don't know. We don't have nanobots in the village. I mean, we didn't."

The crack in his demeanor was brief but she saw it. He was still struggling to deal with the pain of losing his people. Everything had happened so suddenly. He still needed to finish grieving. She had at least had the handful of days in the village after that beast had taken Dr. Donovan from her.

"Don't worry about the nanobots. Your body flushes them out in six or seven days."

"Good. That's good."

He looked relieved, and she was reminded of how different their experiences were. Once again, she wondered when he would get to return to his home. Now that they were fugitives, it might never be safe for him to go back there.

The warehouse in front of them was enormous, more like a geographical feature than a building. Bear led them to a door that was a speck on the massive wall.

"We've been running shipments through here for several years. I used to work with some of these folks. This isn't exactly an authorized entrance. Don't talk to anybody unless I introduce you. Don't even look at anyone. Understood?"

He punched a code into a keypad and the door opened with a gentle buzz. Inside, the warehouse was organized into collections of containers. A handful of humans and robots roamed the space, moving crates or examining tablets. Bear stopped at a makeshift office of crates stacked around a desk.

"Why's it smell so much like robot lube over here?"

"Bear, you son of a bitch, how you doing?"

The man at the desk was heavyset with dark circles under his eyes. He came out from behind the desk and Bear clasped him by the shoulders.

"It's good to see you, Kamil."

"You brought a whole entourage with you."

"Look who's been learning big words. These are some friends of mine. We need to get a package to the *Willow Wisp*. It's important."

"No can do, compadre. Since your last shipment got snagged, management's been making a bunch of changes. I'm getting rotated out. I'll be working logistics in Arizona end of next week. By the time that shuttle goes up, there's going to be all new ground and shuttle crew here. We won't be able to drop anything off for the *Wisp* on that run."

"Well, shit."

"Unless the shipping schedules change, the *Wisp* won't be

back in range for months," Britt said. "That's too long to wait. What other options are there?"

"None. You've got to have a human up there who can override the airlock and toss the packages out into space. The people we trust aren't going on the next shuttle run now, and the people who will be going I don't know if we can trust yet. All the other upcoming shipments are smaller payloads going up in automated pods."

"Please, this is unbelievably important. More important than anything you've helped us deliver before."

"I'm sorry but without a human component, it just doesn't work."

"What if a person went?" Elle asked.

"I just told you, we don't have anyone on the next staffed trip."

"Not on the shuttle. What if someone was in the automated pod? Could they open an airlock?"

"Those pods are glorified shipping containers. They don't even have airlocks. In theory, someone could travel in a suit inside a pod and open the door, but that's a suicide mission. It'd be a one-way trip."

"When does the next pod shipment go up?"

"No," Britt said. "We'll find another way. I won't ask someone to make that sacrifice."

"You don't have to ask. I'm volunteering."

Elle didn't have to see Court to know his reaction. She could sense it, and it was unmistakable in his voice. "Britt's right, Elle, we'll find another way."

"You don't know that. This could be our only chance. My options are to spend the rest of my life running or to go back to a prison to be a science experiment. Or I can do this thing and help the people who can literally save humanity. When's the next pod launch?"

Kamil looked at Bear nervously before he answered. "Tonight. In roughly ninety minutes."

"Can you put me in a suit and get me on it?"

"Like I said, in theory, but—"

"No buts. Too many people have already lost their lives over this. Better to lose one more than for all the others to be for nothing. Besides, there's a chance the *Willow Wisp* would pick me up in time, right?"

"A slim chance. A very slim chance." Kamil looked to Bear again, his concern evident. "This is a lot different from sending some supplies up on the sly."

"I agree with Britt and Court," Bear said. "This isn't a good plan."

"Yes, it is. It just doesn't make anyone feel good. The Qyntarak literally want to send starships full of humans to their planet to eat. How will we live with ourselves when that happens knowing that we stood here at this moment and didn't try to stop it?"

"They want to eat humans?" The horrified expression on Kamil's face told Elle everything she needed to know. The others might not like it but she could get him to help, she was confident of that.

"Yes, and we know how to stop them. We have to tell the Reclamation leaders on the *Willow Wisp*."

"No," Court said, "this is insane. We are not having this discussion."

"There's no discussion to be had. I'm doing it. It's my choice. They've been telling me what to do my whole life but not anymore. This is how I finish the job that Dr. Donovan started."

Bear, then Kamil, and then Court looked to Britt. Elle saw a shimmer of moisture in her left eye before she blinked it away. Britt handed the little white box to Elle.

"It's not how I want to see this through, but you're right. We all want our autonomy and it would be hypocritical of me to say that you can't decide this for yourself."

"There's not much time," Kamil said. "We must hurry to make the launch."

He took them to a storage area and hauled a blue and silver suit from a storage crate.

"This is a long duration EVA suit for use in microgravity. I'm going to have to do some creative accounting to explain this thing going missing. We'll need to carry it to the pod. They're one-size-fits-most and it's pretty easy to get suited up, but once you're in, you can hardly move in full gravity.

"It has self-contained atmospheric and biological management, meaning it can keep recycling oxygen into the air and convert your piss into water to keep you hydrated. It's almost a closed system but relies on some chemicals and batteries. Sunlight will keep your batteries topped up but the chemicals are a fixed quantity. When those run out, the clock starts ticking."

"How long will she have?" Court asked.

"It's designed to let maintenance crews work in vacuum for up to thirty-six hours. If you don't exert yourself and you take a few hits from the sedatives to slow your system down, I'd guess you could stretch it to forty-eight hours."

"Sedatives?" Elle said.

"Yeah, when you get in, the suit pops a needle into you. That's how it manages your hydration level. There are a few things it can pump into you. Some emergency calories, painkillers, sedatives, and stimulants. Just enough to buy you a few extra hours on an EVA in case of emergency."

"So I've got forty-eight hours for the *Willow Wisp* to chase down the transponder and pick me up."

Elle said it for Court's benefit because she could sense his anxiety about her decision. She was pretty sure everyone else knew there was no chance of the Reclamation ship finding her in time. She was going to die from carbon dioxide poisoning inside this suit in order to get the data out there.

Kamil gave her a thorough tutorial on how to operate the suit while Court hovered over their shoulders, his anxious energy nearly palpable.

"It's time to go," Kamil said. "Bear and Court, help me carry the suit. Elle, you bring the package. Britt, I suggest you stay in here. It's a bit of a jaunt."

Tears flowed freely down Britt's cheeks as she took Elle's hands in her own.

"Thank you for what you're doing. For all of us. Humanity will remember you, I promise."

Elle smiled at the older woman and broke eye contact, worried that if she thought about any of it for too long, she would lose her nerve.

Petra's voice interrupted their final goodbye. "Hey, folks, we've got a situation here. I need to move. Kane's grav flyer is heading our way. ETA four minutes."

Chapter 56: Elle

"You need to get moving. Now."

Britt's command was fierce, almost harsh, but the sentiment was clear. Bear carried the legs of the EVA suit, one under each of his arms, while Court and Kamil hustled to keep pace holding on to the arms and sagging torso section. The path from the warehouse to the launch pad in the distance was at least a kilometer by Elle's estimate, and it was slow going with the heavy suit. It would be impossible to get there before Kane arrived if he was heading their way.

A whirring sound from behind grew louder. She turned to see a man driving after them in a six-wheeled open vehicle.

"Kamil," the man shouted. "Why are you carrying that thing? Want a lift?"

"So much for going unnoticed," Kamil said softly. "Hold up, everyone."

They set the suit on the ground and Kamil waved to the arriving driver.

"Last minute addition to the payload. I didn't want to bother you with it since you're already busy getting the pod ready to go."

"It is no problem. Everything is loaded. You can borrow the cart. I am due for my break anyway."

"Thanks, Valentin."

"Are these new trainees or what?"

"Nah, just private sponsors sending an EVA suit upstairs. They've got family on a ship."

"Trying to buy favors. I get it." Valentin winked at them. "Good luck." He unwrapped a ration bar, the only food Elle had known until she met Court, then walked toward the warehouse.

"That was fast thinking," Bear said. "Can't believe he bought it."

"Valentin's always been as witless as you are ugly. You know that. Doesn't even recognize you."

"That concussion he took on my last day might have something to do with it."

"True enough. Let's put the suit on the cart. Its limiter won't let it go very fast but it'll beat walking."

The cart moved at the speed of a casual jog. If Kane had figured out they were here, he might find them before Elle was stowed away. She chewed on the inside of her cheek and forced her breathing to slow.

Kamil brought the cart to a sudden stop.

"They already pulled back the loading ramp. We'll have to carry it up the rest of the way."

They slid the suit from the back of the cart and Kamil stared at its left forearm, which was empty except for a series of shiny gold contact points.

"Oh, shit. The op con isn't here. I can't believe I missed that."

"What's the op con?" Bear demanded.

"The operator's console. We need it to activate the suit. It must still be in the crate."

Bear tripled tapped his earpiece. "Britt, you there? We need you to check the crate from the suit. We're missing a piece."

"It's white, looks like a rugged wrist computer," Kamil said.

"Yes, I see it."

"She sees it."

"I'm such an idiot. We need to go back for it."

"I'll go," Elle said. "You guys get the suit on the pod. It'll be faster if I run."

She didn't wait for a discussion; she turned and sprinted. Over her earpiece, she heard Bear say, "Elle's on her way for it."

"Elle, I'll meet you on the path."

Her legs burned as Elle pushed herself to maintain maximum speed. She didn't even speak when she reached Britt, just grabbed the op con and sprinted back.

Over the comm, Britt said, "Oh no."

In front of her, Elle saw not one but two grav flyers land on the road between her and the pod. Through one hatch, she saw Kane. Behind the other was Petra.

"Petra, what's going on?" Britt said over the comm. Petra didn't answer, but she was pounding on the transparent enclosure. "Bear, you there? We've got company."

Bear said, "Kamil, you stay here and get the suit ready." Then Elle saw Bear and Court running back down the road.

The hatch of Kane's flyer opened and he slid out.

"Looks like everyone's been a bit naughty." He tilted his head toward Petra, who appeared to be locked in her grav flyer. "Good thing I tracked this one down before you all managed to do something really stupid."

Bear whispered over the comm, "Elle, stay out of sight. He doesn't know you're there."

Bear didn't waver as he walked toward Kane. Court followed on his heels.

"You got a lot of nerve selling out your own species."

"Oh, please, spare me the melodramatics. We're all just doing our best in difficult times. We're all the same."

"We're not the same," Court retorted.

Britt said, "Elle, move to the other side of the flyers. My left. I'm heading your way. I'll help draw his attention. Run when he's distracted and get suited up."

Elle moved to the side, ducking under one of the fin-like stabilizers of Petra's flyer. Petra looked expectantly and Elle wondered if she could hear what was happening. Kane was talking but Elle could no longer make out the words.

She heard Bear's reply clearly over the comm. "That's a load of crap and you know it."

Britt said, "This is a long walk. Bear, tell him I'm coming, let's see if we can get him to come my way. Elle, be ready to run if I say so."

"People up there are dying. We're trying to help to them. Do you even know what we do? We send medicine to the sick. How dare you stand there and say that we're the same?"

"That old bat turned you into a zealot." Bear or Court must have moved close enough for their comm to pick up Kane.

"She saved me."

"Not for long, I daresay. After I'm done with you two, I'll find her and L37, and this will all be over."

"You won't have to find her. She found you."

There was a pause in the conversation and then Bear said, "Whoa whoa whoa. Alright, alright. Just hold on."

"What's going on?" Elle whispered.

"Kane drew a gun. He's moving Bear and Court so they're between him and me. He's facing away from the pod. You're clear, Elle. Go."

Elle took off, being careful to run with delicate footfalls until she was far enough away to break into a full sprint. Tunnel vision set in and all she saw was the ramp ahead of her. Kane and Britt were beginning a debate about something but the words floated past Elle's mind as unimportant sounds.

She went up the stairs and around a corner, nearly slamming into Kamil. Elle slapped the op con device into his hand.

"Made it," she said.

"Hey, folks, nobody react," Petra said, "but I got the emergency manual release opened on this flyer. Kane's an idiot thinking he can trap me with a remote override. I have a stun gun. I'm going to come around behind him and put him down, just keep him talking."

Britt started into a speech on human moral imperatives and Elle was surprised that Kane let her ramble. Maybe he was actually listening to what she said.

Then a crack rang out through the air and over the comm simultaneously.

Britt screamed, "Petra."

"She'd have been up on treason charges anyway. This is a better death."

There was a long silence and then a series of unidentifiable sounds. Elle took a cautious look around the pod and saw Bear on the ground wrestling with Kane. It was too far to see who had the upper hand.

Court moved abruptly and then she heard him over the comm. "That's enough. Don't move or I shoot."

The two men stopped struggling. Bear backed away. If he said anything, the comm devices didn't pick it up.

"You're a nacking pot of goat piss, Kane. After what you did to my people, I should put a hole in your head."

"You don't have the stomach for it, kid. Besides, my gun is paired to my ID. It won't work for you. You people never learn."

"This one's not," Britt said, holding up Petra's stun gun.

Kane steadied himself on his knees and raised his hands, palms out, to shoulder height. And then most of Britt's upper body vanished, replaced by a cloud of gray dust. The sudden hum of another grav flyer over head provided the explanation—a Qyntarak black hole weapon. The third flyer descended to the ground at an alarming speed and a Qyntarak in full body armor leaped from it before it had even settled into a stable hover.

"Kamil, there's a Qyntarak out there. I need to go help."

"The suit's almost ready."

"I won't let my friends die. They don't stand a chance."

"And what, you're going to fight off a Qyntarak?"

"It won't be the first time."

She ran, anger and terror pressing her forward even faster than before. It was time to find out if Master Zheng was right about her. As she closed the distance, the Qyntarak knocked Court to the ground, using a pincer like a boxing glove on his gut. With its other pincer, it lifted Bear by his neck. The big man was struggling to keep some of his weight on his feet so he didn't suffocate. Kane was getting back up and brushing off his pants.

Faster.

She wished she had a weapon. Her biggest risk was Kane seeing her too soon. She adjusted her course a foot to the right so the Qyntarak's body hid her from Kane. She could still see one of Bear's legs flailing.

Faster, faster, faster.

From Master Zheng's unofficial training classes, Elle knew that Qyntarak armor was weakest around the long tentacle-like appendages because it had to be flexible. It was strongest over the sensitive feeding slit. The leg armor was plated around the joints to allow for movement. If she hit the lower joint on a back leg, it would have to steady itself with its tentacles. It held Bear in its left pincer. If she went for the rear right leg, there was less chance of the alien's bulk landing on top of him. Bear would be in a weakened state from lack of oxygen so his reactions might be slow if the alien dropped him.

Yes, back right leg, bottom joint, that's the target.

She saw the alien twitch at the last moment, perhaps hearing her, but she had already launched herself legs-first through the air, one foot extended toward the joint. She heard a welcome crunch as it absorbed her momentum and buckled. The Qyntarak emitted a bone-chilling sound and stumbled backward. Elle scrambled to avoid being trampled under its other legs as the alien tried to get its balance.

Bear hit the ground with a thud. Elle rolled to her knees and glanced at him. He wasn't moving.

The Qyntarak hit Elle and knocked her over. She rolled with the direction of movement to get clear of the other swinging tentacles. As she pushed herself back up to her feet, she saw Court kick the stun gun from Britt's orphaned hand as Kane was reaching for it. Court jumped back as Kane took a wild swing at him.

Elle narrowly avoided an incoming swing from a stabbing tentacle. She hit it with her elbow, which hurt her but didn't seem to bother the alien. Then its other stabbing tentacle and both of its pincer tentacles came looking for her. She scurried underneath its body and drove her shoulder into the leg she'd already hit. The alien bellowed again and used its tentacles to steady itself.

She caught a glimpse of Court stepping away to dodge another swing from Kane. Court would be in trouble once Kane got his footing.

"Bear," she shouted. "Bear, we need help."

No response.

The Qyntarak spun itself around so it was facing her. It was unbelievably fast. The alien lunged at her, long stabbing tentacles swinging out so they could stab her from behind while the pincers came at her from the front. It was a classic Qyntarak attack, one that Master Zheng had taught her to counter until the movements were second nature, requiring no conscious effort. She grasped the pincer arm on her left and hoisted herself over it, her body weight throwing off the symmetry of the attack. The most common outcome was that you moved yourself to safety. If you got lucky, a sharp stabbing tentacle would hit the Qyntarak's own pincer and do a bit of damage.

She got a little lucky, the Qyntarak poking itself but not enough to do any serious harm through the body armor. She dove at its injured back leg and landed a blow with the palm of her hand. A few more good hits and the leg would be unusable, dramatically limiting the alien's mobility.

Reducing its attack options wasn't much of a bar for success but one step at a time. She'd taken down a Qyntarak before, once, in a training gym. Never mind that she spent two hours with a surgery bot afterward—she beat it and she intended to beat this one. Somehow.

Court grunted and she looked to see Kane's fists pummeling his torso; Court's arms were up to protect his face. She was distracted for too long because the Qyntarak had time to spin in place again, and the sides of two tentacles hit her like a pair of swinging tree trunks. The impact sent her to the ground several feet away and knocked the wind out of her.

A stabbing tentacle came at her and she rolled to avoid it. The other stabber followed and caught the edge of her shirt, tearing open the fabric. She didn't have time to look, but it didn't feel like it punctured the skin.

She came to a stop on her stomach and saw Petra's stun gun. Elle pawed at the ground with her hands and feet to build up momentum as she lunged for the weapon.

It looked like a Morris M14. As the name implied, its standard capacity was fourteen stun rounds. At maximum setting, each one could knock out a human. They weren't designed for Qyntarak physiology and even if they were, they wouldn't puncture the body armor. But a hit close to the protective covering over the alien's thermal-optical organ would be like shining a spotlight in a human's eyes, temporarily blinding and disorienting it.

Elle sucked in a deep breath while her fingers grabbed the gun. She rolled and landed on her back. Giving herself a fraction of a second to center her focus, she pushed the air out of her lungs and pulled the trigger. Then she pulled it again.

And again.

Again.

Again.

The alien veered sideways, staggering and thrashing.

Elle chanced a worried look at Court and was relieved to see Bear with one arm around Kane's neck and the other hammering on his side. Kane's hands were scratching at Bear's head but the big man wasn't yielding.

Remarkably, Court still had Kane's gun in his hand.

Elle tried to shout at him to help Bear but all that came from her mouth was a scream. Unthinkable pain surged through her body, and she looked to where the alien's sharp tentacle had sunk deep into her upper leg.

"You are an irritation, human L37."

"Court," she shouted. "Court, you need to go. You need to get on the pod. I can't, not now."

The alien leaned forward, pressing more of its weight into her leg and she screamed as the stabber slid through to the ground beneath her.

"Please, Court. Go."

"She's right," Bear said. He released Kane's twitching body and took the gun from Court. "Hurry."

Elle fired several more stun rounds into the body armor, causing the alien to thrash and wail.

"Go!"

Court stared at her for what felt like much too long and then he ran, moving at an angle away from the Qyntarak. She fired another stun round before the other stabber sunk into her upper chest. She heard something snap.

Collarbone? Maybe a rib?

The pain didn't seem to register. She felt surprisingly clear-headed.

The alien turned, dragging her body along the ground as it did. It was searching for Court. She tried to raise the stun gun but her arm was no longer working.

The alien turned its thermal-optical organ in her direction. The protective covering of its body armor was scuffed where the stun rounds had landed.

"Such irritation. I look forward to eating you, human."

Chapter 57: Kane

Kane sucked in air in short gasps as the world came back into focus. Kantarka-Ta had L37 pinned to the ground. The kid was running away. Next to him, his gun hung from the big man's hand.

Kantarka-Ta said that it looked forward to eating L37.

No. No, it wouldn't...

He forced his head off the ground and saw Kantarka-Ta removing the body armor from around its feeding slit.

Out in the open like this?

The air on Earth was uncomfortable for Qyntarak, which is why they stayed in the controlled atmosphere of their bunkers and ships. It was why Kane had spent so many hours of his life trapped in a suit to protect him from the air mixture native to their home world. For a Qyntarak to expose its sensitive feeding slit this way was unprecedented in Kane's experience.

"Give me the gun."

Kane's voice was almost nonexistent after his near strangulation and Bear didn't react. He pushed himself to his knees and pulled the gun from Bear's hand. That snapped the big man out of his terrified stupor. Kane had the gun pointed at him before he could react.

"Back up."

Bear raised his hands and took several steps back. Kane moved toward the alien.

Kantarka-Ta's mandibles had stretched its feeding slit wide and it swayed over L37, who was clawing pointlessly at the tentacle embedded in her chest.

Kane fired three shots into Kantarka-Ta's feeding slit, top, middle, and bottom. The alien made a painfully loud screeching sound. Its mandibles snapped shut and it yanked its stabbing tentacles from L37. Kane saw the damaged plating on its back leg and fired at it. The first shot was a couple inches high and bounced off the body armor. His second shot went straight in and Kantarka-Ta's back end collapsed to the ground.

Bear jumped forward and dragged L37 away. The alien swung a wild tentacle at them but missed.

Kane aimed at the spot where the covering over a tentacle met the plating of the central body armor and fired. The Qyntarak screeched again.

Seven shots fired. Three left.

The Qyntarak only let humans use projectile weapons, saving the powerful and versatile gravity-based weapons for themselves. Modern bullets couldn't pierce Qyntarak body armor, let alone the exterior of their facilities and ships, and the aliens had minimal concern for how much humans shot each other as long as it wasn't cutting into their profits.

The rules might change after this.

Kane charged at the writhing alien, dodging its tentacles, and threw all of his weight against it, sending the much larger creature tumbling back because it couldn't brace itself with its damaged leg.

Kane slid his hand into the outer opening of the feeding slit and grabbed a mandible. Its tiny teeth-like ridges tore at his hand as he pulled. Several surrounding mandibles opened partway sympathetically and Kane shoved his gun into the opening. He fired toward the end where the Qyntarak's internal organs connected to its emotive antennae. The bullet would bounce off the inside of the body armor, magnifying the damage.

Kantarka-Ta spasmed and its tentacles collapsed into limp piles.

His arm still covered in Qyntarak digestive fluids, Kane unfastened the body armor and slid off the covering to expose the thermal-optical organ and antennae fronds.

"You were always such a son of a bitch."

He pressed the gun against the thermal-optical organ and the Qyntarak twitched, a single tentacle flying into the air and straight through Kane's stomach. Kane made a gagging noise and felt the world around him start to spin.

He pulled the trigger and dropped the gun. He wrapped both hands around the tentacle and tried to push it out but his hands slipped on the blood that was coating the outside.

His blood.

He closed his eyes, it was too hard to keep them open, and let himself slide to the ground beside his impaler.

Chapter 58: Court

THE INSIDE OF the pod went dark as the door closed. The only challenge to the blackness was the faint light from the heads-up display of the EVA suit. As his eyes adjusted, he saw the outlines of cargo boxes.

The heads-up display announced, "Establishing intravenous connection."

He felt pressure and then the sting of the needle.

The status box in the helmet display showed LAUNCH -0:05.

Court tightened his grip on the little white box. The transponder's green light flashed momentarily, reminding him that it was on and ready to respond to the *Willow Wisp*'s locator signal.

LAUNCH -0:03.

Deep breath, Court.

LAUNCH -0:01.

He didn't feel anything and then without warning it felt

like the weight of the world was pressing down on him. The outlines of the cargo boxes grew blurry and everything went black.

Epilogue: Elle

Elle watched the water ripple in her glass in response to Bear's bouncing leg. Their advocate seemed indifferent to their distress as he read on his tablet.

He looked up when someone knocked on the door. A woman stuck her head in and asked if she could have a minute with his clients.

"Of course." He left them alone in the room with the woman without asking for their opinion on the matter.

"How are you two holding up?"

"Do we know you?" Bear asked.

"That's right, you haven't seen me since my alterations. It's Ursula."

Elle leaned forward and studied the woman. Her hair color was different, the nose and cheekbones were wrong, and contact lenses obscured her eyes. Her voice sounded familiar but not right. Elle didn't believe she would misremember Ursula that much even though it had been weeks since they'd seen her.

"You don't look like Ursula," Bear said.

"Reclamation leadership sponsored a physical identity redesign for me. Facial reconstruction and vocal cord alterations to change my voice. I'm like a whole new person. No facial recognition or voice analysis system will trigger on me now."

"I don't mean to be rude, but you'll have to excuse me for being skeptical."

"Then ask me something that only I'll know."

"Tell me about when we met," Elle said.

"You came in with Court. He looked sick."

"What did you give him?"

"Water, in a chipped glass. And then you let Maud swindle you out of sixty qynars."

"I've never told that story. It has to be her."

"Do you know how Ainsley and Wilm are?" Bear asked.

"I do. I wish it was all good news. Both have new clean identities with no debt records, same as you. Ainsley has full use of her leg now. Unfortunately, Wilm got himself into some trouble trying to restart Britt's antiviral smuggling operation. We're doing what we can but chances are he'll be spending some time in a forced work program."

"That kid is more heart than head."

"So it would seem. The whole lot of you don't quite appreciate how expensive and time-consuming it is to acquire new identities."

"What about Court?" Elle asked.

"Still nothing. No word from the *Willow Wisp*, but that doesn't mean he wasn't successful. They might have reasons for keeping quiet."

"You didn't come here to see us in person because there was no news," Bear said. "What's going on?"

"The reason the leadership had me change my appearance is because I was raided. One of the agents you tangled with, a man named Wilkes, was out for revenge. They took everything, including the original data vault and all the copies I'd made of the data. I'd only gotten a fraction of the information distributed to other parts of the Reclamation. They're funding a few research projects based on the bits we've been able to piece together, but it will be a long road. I wanted to let you know so you'd be cautious... We don't believe the ruling will go in your favor today. We think they're going to sentence you to an off planet forced work program."

"A red ship?" Bear said and wrapped his big hands around the back of his neck.

They sat in extended silence until the advocate came back into the room. "The committee is ready for us."

"Good luck," Ursula said.

She didn't follow them into the hearing room where three women and two men sat on a platform several inches higher than the rest of the room. A handful of onlookers were in flimsy chairs at the back. Elle didn't recognize any of them.

"Eleanor Blake and Quinton Basque, the two of you were caught attempting to remove wards of the state from an officially sanctioned Aldebaran research facility. You misrepresented your identity to Aldebaran staff. You bribed or attempted to bribe numerous employees. You were in possession of stolen Aldebaran property, including uniforms and ID bands. The research facility in question is a high security installation. The seriousness of your actions cannot be overstated. After hearing from the affected parties, calculating restitution, evaluating your lifetime earning potential, and factoring in the specific circumstances, the conclusion of this committee is to assign you to involuntary labor aboard high orbit service ships. Because of the collaborative nature of your actions, you will be assigned to different ships in order to prevent future collusion. The next launch is in nine days. You will remain in custody until that time. Thank you to the committee members for their thoughtful deliberation on this matter. This hearing is concluded and you are dismissed."

THE END

If you enjoyed this book, please consider writing a review.

Keep reading for an excerpt from book 3 of the Reclamation series. Coming in 2021.

Rook Winters IS a tea-fueled writer with a weakness for dad jokes. He lives in New Brunswick, Canada with his family and is definitely a dog person.

Learn more at **rookwinters.com**, follow **@rookwinters on Twitter**, or search for **Rook Winters Author on Facebook**.

AUTHOR'S NOTE

The seed of the idea for this book came from a satirical sci-fi short story I wrote in 2017 about alien bureaucrats expropriating Earth to use as a nursery for the larval development stage of their offspring. Since the larvae are non-sentient omnivores with voracious appetites, the aliens are evicting humans for their own safety. The story is structured as a series of letters and memos over a 200 year period.

At some point, I will edit that story and release it. You can sign up for my newsletter at rookwinters.com to make sure you get a copy when I do.

When it came time to write this novel, I didn't want to do a comedic story, but I was intrigued by the notion of a gradual, non-military invasion. On the recommendation of sci-fi author Cary Caffrey, I read *The New Confessions of an Economic Hit Man* while conceiving the plot of this book. It was a good reminder not to underestimate the terrifying potential of economic influence combined with targeted violence. Big military actions aren't the only way to devastate a people group.

In the Reclamation series, we don't see the first contact event or the early decades when the aliens are peacefully building up their economic and political clout because a lot of that time period would have seemed like utopia. Instead, we start in the dystopian aftermath in which humans are second-class citizens and the colonizers are taking away even more rights. Writing it made me wrestle with some tough realities. I hope reading it does the same for you.

GIVING BACK

I HAVE PLEDGED a minimum of ten percent of my proceeds from my books to global relief and development aid. Please join me in supporting the work of organizations that tackle poverty and injustice. If you aren't sure where to give, I recommend **World Vision Canada** for its financial accountability and the integrity of its leadership team.

- Rook

EXCERPT FROM RECLAMATION BOOK 3

THE MONSTER RIPPED its tentacles from her body at the sound of gunshots then everything swirled. The gunshots morphed into the banging of a gavel. Bear stood beside her in front of a committee of bored middle-aged humans.

"The seriousness of your actions cannot be overstated... involuntary labor aboard high orbit service ships... launch is in nine days... you are dismissed."

More banging and Elle was jolted awake.

Not banging, clanging. Metal on metal.

Her seat shifted underneath her and she bumped against the person in the next seat. Without warning, she felt inexplicably light—her body wanting to float away and only her harness preventing it.

"Folks, this is your shuttle pilot. We're docking with the *Arkaxon* now. You probably noticed that we just cut our artificial gravity. The *Arkaxon*'s gravity will kick in once we finish the docking procedure. Your chairs just injected you with a stimulant to brush off the cobwebs from the sedatives. You've also received an anti-nausea cocktail to help keep your tummies settled while you adjust to your new home."

More clanging and a hiss came from everywhere and nowhere at once. Her arm tingled as the needle retracted. She felt a tug on her insides as gravity returned.

A no-nonsense woman stood to address the fifteen involuntary workers strapped to benches. "Alright, everyone, listen up. We have to pass through the *Arkaxon* to get to the service ship where you will eat, sleep, and shit. The Qyntarak prefer a lower room temperature than you're probably used to and humans can't breathe their air for long without side effects. So take a deep breath and follow the person in front of you. Ninety seconds of exposure is totally fine. Don't do anything to delay us unless you want your last memory to be gagging in the cold, toxic air of a Qyntarak spaceship. Any questions in the life-and-death category?"

The woman's tone made it clear that she did not want questions and the shuttle passengers obliged her.

With a click, Elle's multi-point harness and arm restraints popped open and she was free to stand. The artificial gravity had a unique quality to it. It felt stronger than Earth but manageable. Her mind jumped to Dr. Donovan, the man who'd raised her, and she wondered how well someone in their seventies would cope with the burden of instantly feeling heavier. No one on her shuttle looked that old. Forty was probably the oldest, which was twice her age, but still decades younger than many of the scientists in the research center where she'd grown up.

It all felt so long ago, but it had only been a matter of months. Months since they'd fled the research center. Months since Dr. Donovan was murdered. Months since they'd tried to save the world. And she had no idea if they'd succeeded.

Now she might never know. Condemned to a life of indentured service on a spaceship, she couldn't expect much news from the world below.

The air in the *Arkaxon* was cool, maybe eleven or twelve degrees Celsius. As promised by the stern woman, their trip through the main spaceship was brief, and the air was appreciably warmer when they crossed the docking link to the other ship. Elle followed the group in a daze, her mind lost in a muddle of thoughts and fears.

"Eleanor Blake. Eleanor Blake?" The woman tapped Elle on the shoulder. "You are Eleanor, correct?"

Eleanor... right, I'm Eleanor Blake now...

"Yes, that's me."

Elle was the only one left. The others had been left at rooms along the way and she had barely noticed.

"This is your room."

Elle started to say thank you but stopped herself. None of this was a situation to be thankful for. She was a prisoner in space. She wasn't going to thank her captors for giving her a room.

"You're lucky. You got a double room. I guess the quads are full. Your roommate is scheduled to be back from her shift soon. She'll show you around, teach you the ropes. Report to muster point E at 0800 hours for orientation."

The woman left Elle alone at the open door without a farewell.

The room was stark and uninviting. 'Room' was a generous choice of word to describe the tiny space. She stepped in and dreaded the thought of sharing such tight quarters with a complete stranger.

She supposed they wouldn't be strangers for long.

There were two matching pieces of furniture in different configurations. One was flat like a narrow bed and the other was upright and curved like a crude approximation of a chair. Elle guessed they were convertible and that the one in chair mode would be hers.

She lowered herself onto the chair and closed her eyes. Until the last few months, Elle had rarely cried. These days, though, the tears came often, more often than she cared to admit even to herself. She didn't try to hold them back.

Better to get them out now while she had some solitude.

She sat like that until the door buzzed, snapped, and slid open.

***

Coming in 2021

Subscribe to the email newsletter at rookwinters.com to learn about all new releases